Silver M

HAVE
OF 76

OF
EROTIC DOMINATION

If you like one you will probably like the rest

A NEW TITLE EVERY MONTH

Silver Moon Readers Service
109 A Roundhay Road
Leeds
LS8 5AJ
United Kingdom

http://www.electronicbookshops.com

If you like one of our books you will probably like them all!

Write for our free 20 page booklet of extracts from early books
- surely the most erotic feebie yet - and, if you wish to be on
our confidential mailing list, from forthcoming monthly titles
as they are published:-

Silver Moon Reader Services

109A Roundhay Road

Leeds

LS8 5AJ

United Kingdom

http://www.electronicbookshops.com

or leave details on our 24hr UK answerphone
08700 10 90 60
International acces code then +44 08700 10 90 60

<u>New authors welcome</u>
Please send submissions to
Silver Moon Books Ltd.
PO Box 5663
Nottingham
NG3 6PJ
or
editor@electronicbookshops.com

Eve in Eden
by
Stephen Rawlimgs

This is fiction - In real life always practise safe sex!

PROLOGUE TO EVE IN EDEN
"This other Eden, demi-paradise,
This fortress built by Nature for herself,
Against infection and the hand of war,
This happy breed of men, this little world,
This precious stone set in the silver sea,
Which serves it in the office of a wall
Against the envy of less happier lands."
(Richard II Act II)

CHAPTER 1 ARRIVAL

The lean Scot, hesitated as if unwilling to leave a woman alone in this place, then relaxed.

"Well,"he said,"if Mrs Borenson is coming to meet you, you'll be alright. Gordon keeps a strict rod, and has her well in hand."

Before Eve could recover from the insultingly patronising tone of his remark, he had made his farewells and walked off to his waiting car, as she sat and seethed.

When they'd roomed together at college, Daphne had made no secret of the customs of the island, and women's position there; how every woman, whatever her age, must have a male protector and how all, whatever their station, were subject to hot rods on bare bottoms, and other physical forms of discipline, but somehow it seemed remote and unreal. Anyway, it was different hearing it from a woman. She resented this man's oblique allusions to it, just as she resented his 'old world charm', his careful solicitude for her comfort, his attention to manners, stepping ahead of her to open doors, taking possession of her carry-on bag. She found it wholly patronising. She wondered in fact if his anxiety over leaving her alone in the tiny airport arrivals lounge was not so much a matter of caring for her security as a dislike of leaving a female visitor, a loose cannon, at large without some firm male hand in control. She was glad to see him go.

His presence had been a burden to her since they had first come across each other on the mainland, when he had appointed himself her guardian for the flight to L'Ile de Paradis. As a liberated woman of twenty-eight, with a successful career and two husbands behind her, she particularly resented his patronisingly 'protective' attitude. At any minute she expected to be addressed as 'little woman', or 'my dear young lady'. In fact he proceeded to address her as 'gurll' in his pronounced Scottish brogue. She tried to tell him that it was 'inappropriate' but he swept her protests to one side and pressed on in his male arrogance. In her present mental state it was too much hassle to try and reform such an antediluvian MCP; after all she was here to get over the trauma of a second failed marriage, and they were only committed to a few hours of flight together.

Looking back, she could see that she should have anticipated a meeting with a male of this variety, given the reputation Eden had been given by her room-mate at college. She was in fact here at Daphne's invitation, persuaded by the sympathetic and understanding letter she had received, in reply to her own, with its news of yet another failed relationship. Actually she was surprised that Daphne was not there to meet her, but an immigration officer soon explained the absence.

"If you would just wait here a minute," the official said, after consulting her papers, and the letter from Daphne's husband sponsoring her while she visited the island, "Mrs Borenson has some business to conclude in the traffic section. It should not take long."

She already knew the island's reputation for strict immigration controls, and that she was only permitted to land by the sponsorship of Daphne's husband, Gordon, and must stay at all times under his protection, or that of his representative, in this case Daphne. Ordinarily she would not have put up

6

with such blatant discrimination against women, men were not subject to anything like the same restrictions, but she was here to mentally convalesce, and was prepared to over-look such out-dated attitudes for a while.

As the hum of the departing Scot's car faded, total quiet fell over the deserted arrival hall, save for the faint cries of birds in the trees on the far hillside. The quiet was pricked, though hardly broken, by a small sharp sound as of a folder slapped down on a desk, or a sticky drawer thrust home. It seemed to come from one of the anonymous offices a yard or two to her left. There it was again, that small crisp snapping sound. And again, It seemed to have a slow rhythm of its own, a ten second clock beat, that caught her attention and had her straining her ears to detect the next. Four came and with it a small animal sound. Five ticked by in step with four, a faint punctuation mark in the otherwise still hall, then six, and with it the animal sound again, though louder this time, and followed by what she took to be a female voice, though she could not make out any words. The silence drew out, and she thought whatever had caused the snail slow metronome beat was over when a seventh sharp cusp of sound came to her. This time the animal mewl was higher and louder, something in pain, and it was followed by two female voices, one making some sort of statement, the other merely acknowledging, then more silence, or did she detect a shuffling sound.

Suddenly Daphne was there, straining blindly in the doorway, oblivious for a moment of her guest, her body rigid, her head arched back, her face twisted in a grimace of pain, her hands bunched into fists by her sides as if she fought some desperate urge to bring them behind her.

"Daphne." Eve called, conscious that her friend had not seen her, even though she was seated barely five yards away.

"Hello, Darling," Daphne called, seeming to suddenly come back from some distant place. "Sorry to keep you waiting, but I'm afraid I had a parking offence to clear. Ouch!" she groaned, clutching her behind, "That stings."

She screwed up her face in concentration.

"Damn, it's always worst just after. And Gordon thought I needed livening up this morning, eight stingers as soon as my feet touched the floor it should have been six, but he claimed I moved. And I'm walking a pair today. Double threaded too. God, I'll be like steak Tartar down there before I can get back into decent underwear."

Eve looked at her in bewilderment. She knew about the corporal punishment of course, Daphne had warned her what to expect, although, as a temporary visitor, she would be immune during her stay, but it was one thing to hear about it in theory, quite another to encounter her friend, red-faced, clutching her behind as if it was being attacked by a horde of bees, and talking of liveners and strange references to underwear.

"Eh, what do you mean, 'walking a pair'," she began, "and what's all this about liveners?"

"Tell you later," Daphne promised, still rubbing her well developed rump. "Just now I'm in a limited parking zone and the state my bottom's in, I think a further 'fine' might be a tad uncomfortable."

Sensing her friend's urgency, Eve didn't delay her further and followed her out to the car. Daphne opened the passenger's door for her to slide in, then went round to the other side to let herself into the driver's position. Looking across, Eve noticed the driver's seat carried a small grid of triangular section wooden slats, on top of the usual upholstery. As Daphne lowered herself onto this uncomfortable looking 'cushion' she hiked up her skirt behind, so that it did not come between her and the ridges of the slatted frame. Eve's eyes widened even further than at the strangeness of the wooden mat, and Daphne's partial barring of herself, when she saw the nature of her present underwear. Her ample, but shapely bottom, in contrast to the stylish sophistication of her designer suit and accessories, was adorned by a drab grey pair of antique pattern 'Directoire' knickers, that came almost to her knees, where elastic gripped her ivory flesh tightly below the unbecoming loose cotton 'bloomers'. Before the humiliatingly clad rump touched the sharp slats of the grid, she could see that there were two scarlet threads sewn across the full width of their widest part. She could see also that, on the right flank, a small smudge of red had stained the thin cotton fabric.

But there was more. Before she actually lowered her buttocks onto the slats, Daphne deftly hooked her thumbs under the waist of the unlovely garment and pulled the rear part down until her shapely rump was exposed. Eve drew in her breath at the sight of the angry red stripes that covered it. Her mind went back to the strict girls' boarding school she had attended and conspiratorial sessions in the changing rooms after discipline hour, when girls had stripped and proudly displayed just such spoor.

A pained grunt marked Daphne's first engagement of her bared striated flesh with the hard ridges of the slats, and she wriggled as if trying to find the least uncomfortable position.

"What on earth are you sitting on?" Eve couldn't help asking. "Is that some sort of exercise thing?"

"An exercise in humility, Darling," Daphne told her, "I have to put this on my seat every time Gordon disciplines me. Helps to drive the lesson home while I drive, he says. Certainly doesn't let one forget one's been caned."

"But he didn't know you were going to be caned again so soon," Eve protested. "Couldn't you just not use them, seeing that you've been so badly beaten?"

"Well," Daphne replied, "Gordon might excuse me or he might take the view that I'd brought it on myself by careless parking. In any case I'd always obey his orders until he gave permission to do, otherwise."

"But can't you ring him at the office and ask?"

"No way. That would be a real no-no. One does not ring a man at his office about something so trivial as domestic discipline, and a sore bottom."

Eve gave up the struggle and tried another tack.

"And what on earth are you wearing? You used to tell me a girl could never be really smart, even in a designer dress, if she wore cheap undies. It had to go all the way to the skin, you used to say, not just surface."

Daphne sighed.

"I see I'm going to have to confess all," she said, starting the car, "I'd hoped to break it to you gently, a bit at a time, but that beastly Parking Offence Officer wouldn't let me commute it to another time, so you got to see me in the heat of the moment as it were. Best I explain, before you get too overcome with curiosity, I suppose."

"Yes please, Dee. I'm bound to find out sooner or later, so I'd rather you prepared me for what goes on around here. Then I won't make a fool of myself," she added, "by letting my jaw drop every time some drawers drop, as it were."

"I expect you're right. I'm probably not thinking too straight. Gordon always does maintain we women keep our brains in our bottoms, and just now mine's sure feeling battered."

She concentrated a minute on getting the car out of the park, and onto what passed as a main road on the delightfully under-developed island. Eve noticed a little tightening of her lips from time to time as the car's movement caused her weight to shift on her seat. When they were clear and bowling sedately along the highway, Daphne took up the tale again.

"It's like this," she said, "as you know all we women have to have a male sponsor, father, husband, brother, son, who is responsible for our discipline, and that is by very physical means. By that I mean, usually, the cane, though some favour the strap, the crop, or even a rope's end. Floggings are not entirely unknown either but, thankfully, rare."

Eve shuddered but held her tongue, as Daphane continued.

"We get punished for every sin of commission or omission but, sometimes, just to make sure we feel our position

10

appropriately, for nothing in particular, just a general livener. This morning Gordon thought I'd been getting a little lazy recently; not enough exercise, a drink too many here, a few cream cakes stuffed down there. Getting a bit of a roll on my belly he said, though he'd seemed to enjoy rolling on it himself last night. Anyway, by dawn's early light I have to slide out of the warmth of our bed and bend in the chill morning air and touch my toes, while he limbered up for the day by delivering six nice tight ones to my tender bottom."

"You said eight before," Eve corrected her.

"Don't remind me, "Daphne pleaded, rolling her eyes, "Normally I can take a sixer without too much fuss, but I was cold and sleepy, and Gordon was hitting really hard, to warm himself up, and I did wriggle a bit, I guess. Didn't get up of course. Not a good idea to do that round these parts, but I waggled my arse and he added a couple to remind me to keep still another time."

"Oh wow! First thing in the morning!" Eve exclaimed, "I'm never at my best then. At the coll we got them in the evening usually, although I did once get a whacking before breakfast, when we used to get up early in the summer to do exercises. I remember it seemed to sting a lot more."

"It does," her friend confirmed, emphatically.

"And then you got it again?"

"Yes, my own stupid fault," Daphne admitted, "I didn't look at the notices properly. Actually, they've altered the layout since I was last here, and the short stay spaces are at the other end. I had my mind on other things, principally the sting in my tail, and the sore seat I was sitting on, and the thought of meeting you again soon, and just didn't spot the change. Drove blithely into the Airport Manager's personal slot. Might have got away with just a warning if it had been any one else, though remission is a word almost unknown round these parts, but the Airport Manager! Next thing to God round here and I had to bend and bare for six crackers. Gordon can hurt, but he usually contents himself with a school type cane, except for serious offences. Here all offences are serious and it's a penal rod every time."

She screwed up her face at the memory.

"Nasty vindictive bitch that Parking Officer, and a local tennis champ as well. My bare bottom against her penal rod; definitely no contest."

"Always on the bare?"

"Always," Daphne confirmed, "knickers down and bottom up. At least they give you a desk to bend over in there; it helps, but even so she claimed I moved and gave me another for luck."

"Thinking of knickers," Eve said, this talk of seemingly endless cuts on bare female bottoms beginning to raise ambiguous feelings in her belly and her feminist soul, best diverted into some other topic, "what on earth are those monstrosities you're wearing? I used to look up to you as the dictator of taste, from your shoes to your smile. Besides," Eve added with a giggle, "we always used to quote the old adage about what would happen if you had an accident while out or, better still, were surprised by the neighbourhood rapist."

"I was rather hoping you wouldn't remind me of those," Daphne sighed, "I'm not too happy about them myself. Apart from the humiliation of wearing such gross objects, I do still take a pride in my undies. Even so, I can assure you, I'm not looking forward to handing them back. I was sent them this morning by the Bridge Club Committee, and have to return them at the meeting tomorrow evening."

"Oh, that's not too bad them," Eve said, with relief. "Beastly for you to have to wear such horrid pants, but only until tomorrow. Is that what you meant by 'walking a pair'?"

"Got it in one, girl," Daphne replied, "but there's more to it than just wearing them. It goes like this. If you do something that offends one of the women's groups, the tennis club, the swimming club or, in my case, the bridge club, the committee may decide to "send you a pair', and have you 'walk' them until the next committee meeting, or whenever. These arrived this morning, with a Bridge Committee card attached '7.30 tomorrow' written on it."

"So?"

"So, tomorrow I have to report to the Bridge Club committee and lower these disgusting drawers and take another thrashing on my poor sore bottom. Not funny since there will already be fourteen welts on it. That is if Gordon doesn't decide on a few more liveners before then, or decides I've offended in some way," she added glumly, "He's not above punishing me himself for getting into this scrape, but I'm hoping he'll be kind and not insist this once. After all, he did give me my 'liveners' on the basis that I didn't seem to be likely to get anything else in the near future. Bad forecast that."

"You poor thing, "Eve sympathised then, overcome with feminine curiosity, "how many?"

"That's the worst of it," her friend answered with a bitter laugh, "I expect you saw those scarlet threads. One thread, six strokes; two, a dozen. That makes twenty eight in two days, always assuming I don't collect any more along the way, and that I manage to stay down at the club. Not easy with Angela on the end of the rod, and she's bound to be. She'd never turn up a chance to whip my arse. Mind you," she added, "I'd do the same for her."

"Are you such sworn enemies then?" Eve said, surprised.

"Enemies! Oh no, we're the best of friends. I can see you've a lot to learn about our way of life during your stay."

"It would seem so," Eve replied dryly, "it all seems over the top, and more like torture than discipline, to me."

"You poor thing, "Daphne replied, "you did rather walk into it at the deep end didn't you. Me with my sorry arse cut to ribbons, and more promised for tomorrow. Don't worry. It's not all like that. You just caught me on a bad day, I'm afraid. Usually I reckon on going at least a fortnight, and sometimes three weeks or even a month without getting myself welted to this degree. Well, not counting Gordon's liveners, of course; he'd never neglect me for that long, but they are by way of love strokes really and, if I'm really raw down there, he has been known to keep them down to two or three at a time. He doesn't say anything, but he's just an old softy underneath."

"A softy!" Eve almost squeaked in her indignation. "When he gives you even a couple on a bottom like you've got now?"

"Well, you must admit I'm no child; I've a fine broad bottom and there's plenty of room for a few. He'd never do anything to harm me, and I'd have to be pretty bad or foolish to earn a beating that would put me out of action for any time. Normally I can take his canings and come up smiling the day after, especially, "she grinned evilly, "if he gives me another kind of seeing to after he's dealt with my sins. Actually I can usually rely on it, as my naked arse reddening under the rod seems to get his rod equally red, and twice as stiff as that whippy cane. On the whole," she added pensively, "I think the afters are worth the entree. Sore but satisfied might cover it I think."

"You mean you actually enjoy it?"

Eve's outrage was beginning to surface despite her best efforts to avoid commenting on the customs of the country.

"Well not exactly enjoy it," Daphne cautioned, "but there are compensating factors. Being beaten by the women is the worst. They seem to be able to whip your soul as well as your butt. Ugh. Get right to you where it hurts your pride. They can humiliate you until you squirm and want to sink through the floor. And no real erotic compensation afterwards."

"I thought you liked girls? I seem to remember some pretty hot nights at coll.," Eve reminded her, blushing herself at the memory.

"Oh, I do," Daphne assured her, "But not in the same way as men. Can't seem to get the same cure for a burning bottom from a girl. Of course the men encourage these inter-women discipline sessions. They know they hurt physically as deep as their own thrashings, and that the effect on the soul goes even deeper. Also, greedy beasts that they are, they can take advantage of our need for a little erotic therapy when we get back."

Although Daphne delivered this last in tones of hurt indignation Eve more than suspected that her real feelings on the matter were very different, and more close to the cunt wetting type than any sense of injustice about the matter. All this time they had been driving steadily along a narrow, though well maintained highway, first through a level plain, with cultivated areas that seemed to Eve's casual glance to be mainly fruits of all sorts flourishing in the semi-tropical climate, then the foothills, where the road became more winding, with the views becoming more spectacular with every metre of height gained. A temporary notice warned of road works ahead, and Daphne slowed then came to a halt as a uniformed woman stepped into the road.

"Sorry to delay you, Madame," the official said, through Daphne's opened window, "but we've had a slight spillage ahead, and it'll take a few minutes to clear."

Eve could only gape. The spillage was little enough, just a wagon that had sunk into a ditch and tipped its load of ballast across the tarmac, it was the gang that was busy frantically shifting it with shovels and barrows. They were all women, and they were all stark naked, apart from straw hats to protect them from the sun. But that was all, unless one counted the steel bands on their ankles, and the gleaming chains that connected each woman to her neighbour on a classic chain gang.

"It's barbaric!" she exclaimed. "You can't treat women like this."

Daphne sighed.

"Just our luck to run into a road gang your first day. I was hoping to introduce you to our little ways in easier steps."

"But why are they here? Are they criminals?"

"In a way. Actually I suppose some of them might be serving time for offences you'd recognise as crimes back home;

15

embezzlement, fraud, drunken driving, but many of them will be here for crimes against womanhood."

"You mean they attacked other women?"

"Only in principle. No one is likely to have hit another woman over the head with her stiletto, though it has happened. Crimes against womanhood are those offences where the woman's behaviour has not been up to the standards required of women here and, hence have let all the other women down. Actually," she said, looking carefully at the line of sweating women, "I know one of these."

"Which one? What's she here for?"

"Hey slow down a minute," Daphne warned, "one question at a time. You see the well-built woman third from the right? That's Marjorie Pemberton. One of the bridge club, and plays tennis too. She and Bob come over to have dinner quite often. I did hear she was serving a term."

"What on earth for?" Eve wanted to know,"it must have been something pretty terrible to have her stripped and put to forced labour."

The expression was not unjustified. The guards, for now it was clear that that was the status of the uniformed officer who had stopped them, carried short plaited whips at their belts and were now using them to encourage the women to even greater activity. The guards seemed to take it as a personal insult that they were responsible for a road hold-up, and leather cracked on the bare back or buttocks of any woman not obviously busting a gut to shift the offending gravel.

Daphne regarded the straining crew with a jaundiced expression.

"I wish those lazy cows would get a move on," she complained, "These bloody slats are killing me. I don't appreciate having to sit here with a bottom as raw as meat, while they play sand castles."

Having seen the havoc in Dee's hinds, Eve could understand her impatience to get home, but thought her comments a little unfair on the naked crew shovelling the heavy ballast off the roadway. She could see the muscles rippling in their thighs and backs as they strained, the breasts of the older women, pendulous and heavy as they hung on their bent chests, flopping up to almost hit their chins as they threw great shovels full of grit into the side, the sweat making dark runnels in the thick coating of grim that covered their labouring bodies. As she watched, the strenuous whip-induced motion threw one woman's wide straw hat off her head to hang by a cord between her shoulder blades. She gasped in horror. The woman was bald, her head a smooth shaven dome bobbing on her shoulders as she continued to dig as if the hounds of hell were after her, not daring to stop for even a second to replace her head covering.

"Why is that one bald?" she gasped.

"Oh they all are," Daphne replied evenly, "they all have their body hair, top and bottom, removed when they join the gang and are shaved again from time to time depending on their sentence."

"You haven't told me what your friend did that was so terrible."

"Oh, Marjorie you mean," Daphne replied, "Actually she's one of those that's been sent here without actually committing a crime as such. It's very much a matter between husband and wife but from what she's let drop from time to time, I gather that, when they were first going together, before they were married, they came across one of these gangs, just like we have today. Bob was fascinated by the situation and said he was going to make sure she went on a gang, once they were married. She made this bargain with him. If he didn't have her put away in the early days of their marriage, as he quite well could if he pulled a few strings, she would not try to contest a sentence if he applied for an order on their seventh wedding anniversary."

"And now they've been married seven years I take it. The man must be a bastard. How long has she got?"

"Oh Bob's no worse than any other normal man round

here. He treats her very well usually, just has this thing about wanting to see her working her guts out on a stinking chain gang, and he did keep his bargain, even though he would have loved to have seen her sweat earlier. She was going to have to do a month but at the last moment he told her he wanted to take a friend's wife to Europe for a month and he didn't want to be short changed, so she'd have to do another as well. He promised they'd come and see her before they set out, and he'd come and see her at work every day, once he got back. Actually it was Mary, his mistress, who drove Marjorie down to hand in her papers and join the gang."

"The bitch. That was really cruel," Eve protested.

"Oh that sort of thing happens all the time. Just a little finishing touch. You learn to accept it. What worries me more is that the other men might take up the idea. A sort of seven year stretch. I don't fancy the idea of sweating on a gang one little bit. I gather Bob was so keen on the idea he and Mary went to see her, her first day out, on the refuse collection in the city. Of course, it wasn't the same, she was wearing a clout, it being in town, so he'll be hot to come out as soon as he's back and catch her quite bare-arsed. Not that a clout hides much."

"What on earth is that, then?"

"Just a strip of cloth, a sort of modesty rag. You have a cord tied round your waist and this long narrow strip of cloth is threaded under the cord in front, down and through your legs, then back up your crack and under the cord again in back. Covers your pussy, but not much else. Still it saves frightening the horses."

It was on the tip of Eve's tongue to express her disgust at the whole set-up and the supine way that women allowed men to trample on them when the guard who had stopped them blew a whistle and waved to Daphne to proceed. She engaged gear and rolled slowly past the line of panting perspiring women, their naked skins clotted with dirt, their bare feet scratched and calloused. They stood stock still, with military

18

precision, their eyes set rigidly ahead of them, wearing their stripes like campaign ribbons. Eve sucked in her breath. Seen close to the welts were vicious. Most were on their backs, and away from her, but enough had curled round to leave savage bites on tender tit and belly to make it clear these were no love taps. The women varied in age from about twenty to somewhere about the forty mark. She could make a guess at their time on the line from the state of their sunburn on unprotected bodies and the state of their musculature, especially on bellies and forearms. Even the oldest displayed well-defined abs, and straight firm shoulders. No wonder she thought, gazing absently at the line of sweat encrusted shaven vulvas steaming in the sun.

As they passed the one she had pointed out as a dinner guest, Daphne rolled down the driver's window, letting in a fetid smell of hot unwashed woman flesh, and smiled at her. The woman stared straight ahead, forbidden to acknowledge civilians, tied tightly by the discipline of the line and the fear of the overseers' whips.

Her eyes drawn unaccountably to the woman's groin, Eve saw that she bore the number 387 in inch high numerals across her plump shaven mons. A quick glance showed that all the women sported a number, though the dust and sweat partially obscured them. As they drew away from the scene of feminine servitude she commented on them to Daphne who dismissed them airily.

"Just their prison numbers, "she explained, "they all get a number when they go on the line."

"Oh well," Eve said, "I believe tattoos can be fairly easily erased now. They can get them removed when they come out or, perhaps, tattooed over with some more suitable design."

"Who's talking about tattoos? Those are put on with a hot iron. Brands. They're more or less permanent. We don't do things by halves in Eden. Besides, it's part of the ethos. A woman has too much pride to try and remove her marks, just as nobody here would seriously try to mitigate any ordeal or punishment"

"But they're disfigured for life!" Eve exclaimed, horrified.

"Oh I wouldn't say disfigured, some people find it quite attractive. Besides, they've been branded on their shaved mounds. When they've done their time they can let their muffs grow again. The fur will soon cover the marks and no one will see but their lovers. Even then, he or she would have to be a fan of cunnilingus."

Eve would have liked to ask a million more questions; a gang of naked women labouring on a chin gang is not your normal tourist attraction, but Daphne seemed to have become exhausted by the enforced delay.

"Actually darling I would like to concentrate on the road. I really can't afford another traffic violation. It's not just the state of my arse; that will heal, but if you accumulate too many debits it might be decided that you should spend a month or two on the hook to rehabilitate you, and I really wouldn't like that. Besides, I wouldn't be here to take you round and satisfy that 'satiable curiosity of yours."

By now though they had reached the long driveway that led to Daphne's home and Eve's mind was taken up by the beauty of the scene. The island had been everywhere pleasing as they had crossed it and climbed into the hills where the Borenson estate lay, but Eve's delight in it had been blunted by the distraction of Daphne's revelations, literally so in the case of her bottom, of the real nature of women's position here, but the actual sight of the house, set against a backcloth of trees and looking out over the plain to the sparkling edge of the sea, quite took her breath away. Eden indeed. Daphne seemed grateful to get off the subject of her martyred backside and, having seen Eve's bags carried to her room, the two of them explored the house and grounds happily until Gordon's car swept up the drive as evening fell.

He greeted Eve affectionately, telling her he'd heard much

about her from Daphne and looked forward to getting to know her better, a sentiment that sent a strange electric sensation into her groin and knees, then kissed Daphne passionately, a passion that was fully returned. Eve could not help but wonder at their apparent love for each other given what she knew of his attentions to her in more brutal ways. Did she not resent his beatings for no purpose other than to 'liven her up'? It appeared not. She didn't even appear to object to his hand patting her roasted rump, though its continued soreness was reflected in a quickly suppressed tightening of her brow.

At dinner though she gave a pronounced wince as she sat down, having forgotten her bruised state for a moment in the animated conversation between the three of them. Gordon evidently spotted it for he laughed and remarked that he must have been on good form that morning if she was still feeling it.

"You were," Daphne replied with feeling. "But that's not all I've got down there," and she proceeded to give a blow by blow account of the afternoons events.

Gordon grinned.

"I'm sure it did you a power of good," he remarked, "let's have a look at the damage."

"Oh, men!" she complained to Eve. "They're all the same in these parts. Always want to get a peek at your bottom, especially if it's got roasted with a cane," but she didn't appear to her friend to be particularly unhappy about the fact.

As she lifted her skirt, and was about to pull down the hated drawers she was 'walking' Gordon checked her.

"What's this?" he queried, pointing to the shapeless grey pants.

"Got sent them by the Bridge Club," his wife informed him, "to be returned tomorrow."

"And double-threaded too, I see, "Gordon observed, "what have you been up to?"

Daphne looked a little ashamed for the first time since she had begun her strip.

21

"Eh. I guess I might have started a few too many post-mortems. Only trying to help other people's game, you know, but it seems they didn't appreciate it."

Gordon laughed.

"Seems not. Better keep your mouth shut after rubbers in future I suggest. My aren't we going to be one sore girlie tomorrow night. I'll have to think of some way of soothing it."

"You know damn well what I need," Daphne said, "I can see it tenting your trousers right now, and I shan't give you any peace until I get it."

It turned out to be a much more relaxed and enjoyable meal than Eve had expected but she took herself of to her own room soon after. It wasn't entirely because she was tired from the journey. Her host and hostess clearly had business of their own to attend to.

She slept like a log and awoke to the sound of unfamiliar birds and the sun streaming through the gap in the curtains. As she showered she thought of the previous day's revelations, snorting at the abuses that women seemed subject to out here. For some strange reason her hand kept soaping the same part of her anatomy and she suddenly realised she had been sliding her palm over one rounded buttock for a minute or more, contemplating it dreamily as if envisaging it striped and wealed like her friends. She snapped herself out of the alien mood and went down to breakfast.

She was joined in minutes by a tousle headed Daphne in a negligee that did little to hide her exuberant charms, her eyes smudged and bruised looking, her lips a little puffy, but her mood totally cheerful.

"Sorry I'm such a sight, Darling, "she exclaimed, "but I couldn't wait. Sex gives me such an appetite, I could eat a horse," and she proceeded to demonstrate the truth of the claim, demolishing a mound of toast, and a platter of eggs and bacon that would have satisfied a coal-heaver.

Eve gathered that Gordon had done his duty by her, and

that the bruised eyes and lips were battle scars in the war of love, not the result of her previous day's ordeal, and relaxed, as Daphne chatted happily and made plans for the day. They would explore the house and grounds, swim in the pool, laze in the sun, enjoy this Eden.

As they lay idly by the poolside Daphne asked her about her journey over the previous day.

"I should have asked you earlier," she apologised, "but I had other things on my mind."

"Like a dozen welts and a pair of drawers," Eve filled in mischievously, "nothing much to report really. Oh there was this really patronising MCP on the flight. Local man, has an estate on the other side of the island. Long, lanky Scot. I think his name was Angus but I didn't really take it in, I was too busy trying to tell him I was an independent woman and didn't need a man's protection."

Daphne grinned

"That'll be Angus McKensie. Must have loved your attitude," Daphne said, "he comes from the Highlands."

"Of Scotland?"

"Well that's where he was born, I think, but I meant the Highlands here."

"I thought this was the Highlands," Eve replied, looking out over the land below their hilltop eyrie, to the distant sparkle of the sea.

"Oh the real Highlands are on the other side of the island, behind our backs. Mountains almost. Your Angus lives on a big estate right up in the hills."

"He's not my Angus," Eve replied with feeling, "I wouldn't mind if I never saw him again. A totally disagreeable MCP."

"You mustn't be too hard on him," Daphne replied. "Underneath that rugged exterior there's quite a man. Strict I grant you. I knew his niece who was brought up by him. She says she was never beaten so hard as at home, but she still loves him dearly and is totally grateful to him for the way he raised her."

"I can't see me ever submitting to a man like that," Eve retorted with feeling. "It degrades women to have men like that around."

She was saved from further recollections of the disagreeable Scot by the arrival of a visitor. A figure on a bay horse emerged from the spinney below them and climbed the path to where they lounged beside the pool. The pretty brunette that sat the horse called out a greeting as she approached and Daphne rose to return it.

"Lovely to see you, Joyce. Stick that nag in the stable, Josh will look after it, and come and join us by the pool. There are some of my spare cossies in the changing room."

Joyce seemed to hesitate a moment.

"I think I'll just come as I am," she said.

"Nonsense, " Daphne said firmly, "You can't possible sit by the pool in those hot sweaty jodhpurs. Wouldn't be the right thing at all," and Joyce bowed to the inevitable and took her self off to change.

"That's Joyce Besant," Daphne explained, while the newcomer was away, "she comes from a neighbouring estate, best part of an hour's ride across the hill, where she lives with her aunt and uncle and various cousins. Nice people, but her Uncle George gives his wife responsibility for female discipline in the household and I gather she makes it very hot for all the girls.

"Always nice to see her," Daphne continued, "we're very good friends, even though she's a few years younger and unmarried, but I've a sneaking suspicion that there's more to it than just a social call. Did you notice how stiffly she sat in her saddle?"

"Can't say I did," Eve replied. "To tell the truth I'd had my mind on other things. Is that significant?"

"I think so. Let's wait and see how she looks when she's in a bikini."

She looked stunning, tall slim, with good breasts and a

24

delicate waist. Her long legs were topped by a delicious pair of tight buttocks, only nominally encased by the miniscule bikini bottom that she had no choice but to wear, since Daphne did not believe in hiding her own delights and all her costumes were of the briefest tanga type.

This left their visitor sporting two swelling globes crossed by the unmistakable spoor of the disciplinary rod, seven or eight thick purple tracks, well raised and, doubtless, hot and throbbing from their confinement in tight britches and the pressure of the saddle. The effect was noticeable in her gait.

"Trifle saddle-sore, Darling?" Daphne enquired innocently.

"Don't mention it," Joyce replied with feeling. "Seven sizzlers from Aunty June after breakfast, then told to take some exercise on a horse, to thump the lesson home. At least I had the thought of you to comfort me on the way, but it didn't entirely compensate. Who's your friend?"

Daphne made the introductions, and the three women all exchanged friendly kisses, something more than air pecks, more light pressure of lips on lips.

As they settled Joyce winced at the contact of the wooden slats with her bruised bottom cheeks.

"Wow. June really laid them on," she gasped.

Eve could contain herself no longer.

"Is everybody on this antediluvian island walking around with bruises on their behinds?" she enquired. "It's positively barbaric."

"Well fifty percent aren't, that's for sure," Daphne laughed. "The men don't go in for that sort of thing, and as to the other half of the population; well you've certainly had a rude introduction. First my raw meat yesterday, then Joyce's ripe cuts today. It isn't usually quite as bad. I dare say if you went down to the capital, right now, and could look into the panties of all the women, half of them would have significant marks, but you have to remember that a good beating lasts for weeks, so that probably means that they aren't beaten much over once a month, or put another way, we all get a good hiding every other month. A woman can't expect to stay healthy on much less."

"I can't believe I'm hearing this at the end of the twentieth century," Eve protested. "How can you talk so calmly about this gross oppression of women?"

Joyce's delicate plucked eyebrows lifted a fraction, and she looked across a trifle uncomfortably towards Daphne.

"You'll have to excuse my friend," Daphne said, "she only arrived yesterday, and hasn't had time to find her feet yet. Once she knows us better I'm sure she'll see things differently."

"Never!" Eve declared with feeling. "Of course, I'll always respect your rights as women to do your own thing, but you'll never see me accepting such gross injustice and lack of respect for females."

"But darling, we're not abused and as for respect, you won't find any women on this island complaining that their men don't respect and love them. Isn't that so, Joyce?"

Joyce nodded in agreement and Daphne continued.

"The whole point is that both sides recognise the universal truth that your feminist friends persist in denying, that we women are creatures of wonder and fancy who will run amok and disrupt all around us, to our own unhappiness, if were not carefully guided by strict discipline. You wait until you have met a few of us, and compare our lives here with what you left behind."

It seemed pointless to argue, Eve thought, these women seemed inexplicably to have taken leave of their senses. If it wasn't that she'd seen livid evidence on both their bottoms, she'd have believed they were conducting some elaborate hoax at her expense. She let the matter drop and asked Joyce about her Uncle's estate.

It appeared it was even larger and, Joyce claimed, more beautifully sited then the Borenson homestead, and Joyce insisted she had to see it for herself.

"Of course you must," Daphne agreed, "It's only a short ride away and you would love it there. Besides it would be good for you to meet some other people rather than be cooped up with me all day."

"OK, OK, you win," Eve laughed, "I can see you won't give me any peace until I promise. I'd love to come Joyce, just give me a few days to settle in and I'll be right over. I'm dying to ride one of Daphne's lovely horses and it would be just the opportunity."

"Thinking of which," Joyce said, "time I was back in the saddle, though I don't think I'm looking forward to the ride quite as much as you. Ugh. It's hard on a girl's bottom when she's got to put stripes to saddle. Aunt June hits hard and put them just where the saddle fits. Thanks for the drink and the chat, Dee, but I've got to get back before I'm posted AWOL. No way I'm going to risk any more for a day or two."

CHAPTER 2 THE PRICE OF A PAIR

Every slap of the girl's shapely bottom on the hard hot leather of the saddle, had Eve wincing as she imagined the thick sore welts taking fresh punishment with every touch.

"Hell!" cried Daphne looking at her watch as Joyce disappeared into the trees again, "Is that the time? I'd better get going. Got to walk these pants tonight, damn it."

Eve had forgotten the looming session in the excitement of meeting a new friend but now all her old doubts came flooding back. She found herself torn between a feminist distaste for the whole proceedings, a need to respect Daphne's privacy and not add to her humiliation by being present, and loyalty to an old room-mate. Just possibly a dash of feminine curiosity perhaps in the background as well, although she did not admit it to herself at the time. Finally loyalty, aided and abetted by that traitor curiosity, won out and she announced that she would accompany Daphne to the bridge club to give moral support. At first Daphne demurred, saying she'd be quite alright and she wouldn't dream of letting Eve in for yet another example of the island's strict way with women.

"It's out of the question," Eve darling. "A discipline night is no place for a girl like you. Just hearing about our beatings afterwards upsets you. No, I'm a big girl now, and I'll look after myself."

"Even big girls need a friend in trouble," Eve declared firmly, "No, I don't approve of women being whipped, but yes, I can take it, and I'm definitely coming along."

It was the irresistible against the immovable, but finally Daphne gave way.

"OK I know when I'm beaten. Oh God that's not what I meant to say. You can see it's getting to me, and I think perhaps I do need a minder. We'd better get going. I'm not anxious to earn any more than I'm going to get anyway."

Eve seemed to drift quite naturally into Daphne's room to watch her dress for the evening. First a shower, then a rueful contemplation of the already ravaged bottom.

"You poor thing," Daphne murmured, stroking her hand over the raised ridges of her underhang and addressing her bum, "I'm sorry to say I'm going to have to take you and put you out again for the rod. You're going to be even more sorry for yourself in a few hours."

"How can you joke at a time like this?" Eve asked. "Aren't you worried?"

"Aren't I just, I'm feeling quite weak at the knees if you must know, not to say a bit sick in my belly, but one's trained to put a good face on things here in Eden."

She dropped her nervous caressing of her own buttocks and set about getting dressed. Not a very elaborate costume; a black bra that hugged and cradled her splendid breasts, smokey dark 'stay-up' stockings, black suede pumps.

"Yuck, now for those horrid underpants. They're revolting enough at the best of times, but I particularly hate wearing knickers for two days in a row. I get so juicy down there and there's nothing more disgusting than having to put on a sticky crotch."

Encased from knee to waist in the hated underwear she slipped a straight jersey dress over her head and smoothed it down.

"How do I look?" she asked.

"Delicious. I could eat you," Eve replied, and was suddenly hotly conscious that, though she'd started out just to say something facetious, to comfort her friend, she actually meant the words. She covered her confusion hurriedly.

"Don't you think we should get going? It's nearly seven already and I don't suppose you'd like to be late, even if it's not an event you're looking forward to."

"Too right, darling. Best be off, or those poor sitters of mine will be even worse roasted and neither they nor I want any part of that."

The big car sped smoothly down the road, the conversation nervous and disjointed. Each was acutely aware of where they were going and the disciplinary circumstances awaiting them. Eve found it difficult to think of any topic that did not seem to lead back directly to the caning of female bottoms, while Daphne tried her best to point out the beauties of the island along the way, but was distracted by similar thoughts. They were each almost relieved to reach the venue for the evening's events, the Ladies' bridge club.

Relaxing after a strenuous afternoon of bids and tricks, doubled and redoubled, points won and lost, contracts made and hands played, a score of smartly dressed women were sitting about in the well appointed room, sipping cocktails, and exchanging gossip. One or two actually indulging in the very crime that had brought Daphne the pair of degrading grey underpants she had now arrived to redeem. A long languid blonde waved a slim bare arm and called to them to join her.

"Hi Dee. Who's your friend?"

Daphne introduced Eve.

"This is Isobel Hakes, one of the regulars. Bel, I've got business with the committee. Could you take Eve under your wing while I do my stuff?"

"Business?" a plucked arched eyebrow rose an interrogatory fraction of an inch.

"Eh, um, that is I'm 'walking'," Daphne replied a little more nervously than Eve remembered her doing any time in the past.

Isobel grinned like a cat.

"I did wonder," she said, "word had got around. Nothing definite you understand but well, you can see that rather more members than usual stayed on for an extra drink tonight. You'll have to put on a good show for us."

"I'll do what I can but I'm double-threaded. I can't promise to entertain you."

"Oh but you will. You have a lovely bum and there's a lot of women in the room creaming at the thought of it being put up, up there."

"You amongst them, I can tell. Well I don't care if you wet your knickers, so long as you take care of Eve for me. Wish me luck."

They did and Daphne disappeared in the direction of the committee room at the end of the hall.

Beside it was a raised stage. At present it was bare, save for a single hard backed chair, set in its centre. After five minutes or so an older but still handsome woman, with neatly shaped dark hair and a full but shapely figure, climbed the short stair to the platform and rapped on the chair with the stiff cane she carried to gain attention. She got it. It was a sound to strike echoes, if not actual fear, into any female heart present and, besides, they were here to have their senses thrilled by the display about to take place on the stage and were not inclined to delay their anticipated pleasure by chattering on. All fell quiet instantly, though not before Isobel had leaned across and whispered," That's Julia, the Hon, Sec. Now the fun's about to begin. Poor Dee."

"Ladies, may I have your attention. Before you go to-night, we shall witness a disciplinary proceeding. There is a pair to be walked."

There was a subdued murmur as the rumour was confirmed, quieted as Julia held up her hand for silence.

"Will Mrs Borenson stand forward please."

All eyes turned to the corner of the stage, where Daphne appeared from the wings. She had shucked off the jersey dress and stood clad only in her bra, hose, heels, and the dire drab drawers.

"Daphne has been found wanting by the committee, who have received many complaints about the nature and, particularly, the frequency of the 'post mortems' she has been wont to conduct after rubbers. Unfortunately this is not the first time that the committee have been forced to reprimand Mrs Borenson and it became inevitable that she should be sent a pair."

She turned to the waiting Daphne and invited her to walk.

Half naked, Daphne did just that. She was obviously familiar with the drill and walked with studied steps the full width of the stage to the left hand side, turned her back to the audience and, with a lissom bend, doubled over, stretching the unlovely pants over her generous haunches. The audience gasped as they saw clearly for the first time, the two scarlet threads that crossed the spreading seat.

The shameful promenade continued. Eve realised that 'walking a pair' had a definite meaning, apart from the obvious wearing of them for twenty-four hours beforehand. There was a specific pattern to the display as Daphne rose, walked with equal formality to the right-hand side of the platform and again, turned away from the audience, bending to grasp her ankles and parade the spectacle of her broad buttocks and the coded announcement of her sentence. Finally she rose and went to stand at the back of the chair, facing away from the audience again, her hands stiffly by her sides.

The secretary was now joined by another woman, slightly younger, athletically built, a brunette with her hair in a tight plait which set off her rather aquiline features. Isobel whispered the information that this was the club President.

"You may remove the drawers," the secretary announced and Daphne's hands went to her waist and her thumbs hooked into the elastic and drew the hated pair off her hips and down her legs. Eve had no doubt though that she was less eager to be rid of the loathsome objects, now that their removal would expose her cringing flesh to the rod that Julia was testing on the air, where it sang with a lugubrious and sullen sound.

Daphne completed the baring of her buttock flesh and hung the drawers on the chair behind which she stood, displaying the delights and decorations of her bountifully beaten bottom to the salivating women below. Eve had become used to seeing its ripely welted expanses, reminiscent of bruised fruit, but Isobel at her side sucked in her breath through clenched teeth.

"Oh wow!" she breathed, "Poor Dee. I thought she was taking this a bit more seriously then expected, but I can see why now. No-one would look forward to paying for a pair with a bottom like that, and she's drawn a double stripe too."

It relieved Eve's mind a little that the apparent insensitive cruelty of these watching women could be touched. They were not totally. heartless after all. Still all around her she could hear low voices, thickened with lust, detailing to each other the state of the exposed flesh, the thickness of the welts, the depth of the bruising, how that tender field, so ploughed and harrowed must feel already, and what might be the effects of a 'butchers' laid into it with the lethal stick that the secretary was exercising on the stage.

If the parlous state of Daphne's bottom had touched at least one of the audience, it made no difference to those charged with the execution of the sentence. With only the briefest glance at the welted withers, Julia announced, "First thread, six strokes. Bend to the chair."

Well experienced in these matters, Daphne bent over the chair back, her hands reaching down to grasp the seat on either side. The buttock slabs lifted until the bruises sheltering under the jut of the rounded hinds were stretched and exposed, placed where the rod could do its work at their expense. Partly to steady herself, partly because it was expected of her, Daphne shuffled her feet a little further apart, until her thighs had opened and her fat fig could pouch back in the public gaze. The smokey black of the taut nylons cut off the whiteness of the thighs near their tops, leaving the pale rounds of the buttocks blatantly displayed, crossed by the purple spoor of the rod's earlier tracks, the setting punctuated by the fat plum coloured mound of the vulva, where it pouted through the gap at the crotch. It came over Eve in a rush that it was a picture of pure femaleness, which sent an electric rush of heat through her belly. She could almost feel the erotic emanations of the women all around her, as each drank in the carnal scene.

And not just the swelling straining buttock, with its sexual centre, but the woman's straining features as well for, at the back of the shallow stage, directly in front of the bending woman, was set a large plain mirror. In what was obviously a ritual pose, Daphne was bent over the chairback, her hands grasping the edges of the seat, but her head was lifted, so that she stared straight ahead. In this position she could see the rod's descent behind her as it flew to cut her in her tenderest flesh. As importantly the audience could watch every expression on her face, from fearful anticipation, to intense shock, as the cane cut in, to a twisted agony of struggle as the after-pain blossomed in her hinds for seconds after each stroke.

Ruthless rattan, toughened by the struggle for survival in the primeval rainforest met tender woman hide; it was no contest. The limber stick rebounded with nothing more than a little extra warmth from the scorched buttocks, the feminine integument blossomed in hot throbbing welt, a searing line of contused flesh, ravaged nerves protesting the crushed capillaries and bruised fat and muscle. Daphne groaned. If this was how it would begin, how could she endure until it ended? With bitten lip she set herself to take the next. One cut at a time, that was the only way to do it. Try to envisage the whole doleful progression, and she would be lost. Fear and despair would undo her and see her try to rise and flee. No she must bite off this rising tide of agony the fresh cut on old bruises had brought and fight it down, before the next could strike.

Watching from the floor, Eve felt heat suffusing her loins as the buttocks leapt under the stroke, and she was already wet before Daphne's face had finished screwing up in the effort to resist the flowing tide of anguish that continued to mount so desperately long afterwards.

With a frightening and implacable steadiness, the secretary laid on each stroke, the score slowly mounting, each delivered with strength and precision. A woman reared on this island not only received much discipline, and learnt to endure it, but often had responsibility delegated to her for servants and growing girls, not to speak of such social discipline as that being delivered tonight, and a mature woman like Julia could wield a rod with fearful efficiency. Daphne writhed and groaned at every cut, her face betraying her struggle to retain control. Gradually the count rose and she dropped her head momentarily as Julia announced, "Six strokes given. First thread complete."

There was a universal letting out of breath held too long in the intoxicating excitement of the flogging. A buzz of excited conversation swept the hall as women relaxed their clenched thighs, closed gaping mouths that had dropped open in their abandon or even guiltily withdrew hands from rubbed crotches. For two minutes there was a suppressed murmur of comment and analysis of Daphne's performance by women who could all claim some expertise at this sport themselves, then the secretary was calling for order again.

"Second thread, seven strokes. Prepare yourself."

This latter was addressed to Daphne who pulled her

34

drooping frame together, lifting her head again, while the rod passed from Julia to the President. Once more the ordeal was repeated, but this time there was evidence that some damage was being done. Julia had laid all her strokes on the previously thrashed strip at the base of the lacerated buttocks and the already bruised flesh had become swollen and sullen, darkly purple with even darker blotches on the right. For these thick pulsing blisters the new assault proved too much. Daphne might set herself to endure, but her hide could not. At first there was a mere extrusion of tiny bright droplets where the ravaged capillaries discharged through the skin's pores but, as the suffering woman flinched and moaned under the rod's next bite, the skin of one blister parted and a red trickle welled up to run weakly down the back of the right thigh. With the last three strokes came more scarlet droplets, the rod striking raw flesh now in parts. Daphne mewled through clenched teeth, her lips drawn back in an agonised rictus, the audience gazing in wonder at the transfigured face, distorted out of recognition by her pain and effort.

"Discipline complete," the secretary announced, as the President stepped back, leaving Daphne slumped over the chair, her thighs still parted, the fig of her vulva now gaping as a result of her contortions and the engorgement that seemed to follow on the violent stimulus of the surrounding blood supply. For ten minutes she remained in this position while the audience took their leave of each other, each in turn pausing on her way out to contemplate the ruined buttock from close to. When all that wished, and not many declined the opportunity, had had their fill of the naked bruised flesh, Daphne was allowed to straighten painfully and limped off stage to recover her clothes.

"Here she comes," and Eve looked up from the table where she had been sharing a drink with Isobel to see Daphne coming across the hall from the committee room.

Thighs stiff, legs moving with more a waddle than any fluent gait, she approached painfully. Eve got up and drew out a seat.

"Are you joking?" Daphne protested. "Not a chance, But thank you all the same. Perhaps I can manage to kneel, while you get me a drink. A double and don't worry about the tonic Bel. I'll take it just as it comes."

It was on the tip of Eve's tongue to enquire if this was in the true Eden spirit, or did alcohol contravene the ordinance about doing nothing to mitigate the effects of a beating, but decided it was not the proper time. A couple of drinks later and Isobel made her farewells.

"John's collecting me," she explained. "In fact he's waiting outside now. I think I've stretched his tolerance as far as is safe; I don't want to get a seat like yours when I get back. Besides," she confided, and had the grace to blush,"you were delightful, Dee darling. I've soaked my pants and I can't wait to get them off and have John perform his proper manly duty. There's rape on the menu tonight, and I'm going to be the one doing it." She delivered a more than socially conventional kiss to Daphne's bruised and swollen lips and was gone.

"There's gratitude," Daphne groaned in mock hurt, but Eve sensed that she was actually a little flattered at the effect she had induced in Isobel and the rest of the roomful of women.

"Come along," she said, coming round the table, and offering Daphne a shoulder to lean on, as she got down from the chair she was kneeling on, "it's time we got you home."

But it was not so easy as that. When they had got to the car, sitting all alone in a deserted car-park, Daphne groaned and said.

"I can't do it. I just couldn't sit on this mess for the best part of an hour and, if I did, I don't think I'd be safe to operate the controls."

"You're right," Eve agreed, "Besides, you've had three very large doubles to my knowledge in the space of twenty minutes, and that after a pretty traumatic experience. There's only one thing for it. I'll drive, you kneel on the back seat."

"Out of the question," Daphne replied, "You haven't registered as a driver yet; you have to take your British licence to the Traffic Department. If you're caught driving without it's a mandatory ten with a penal."

"I'll risk it," Eve declared, "We don't have a choice. Everyone else has left, and I don't fancy sleeping rough. You said yourself there was rain forecast for tonight and we've got about enough clothing between us to cover a good sized mouse."

Blazing bottom won out over prudence. Too hurt to argue any further Daphne allowed herself to be helped into the back, where she got onto all fours across the rear seats, her bum in the air, the jersey dress pulled up so as not to catch on the ruined backside. Eve winced when she saw the state of it, bare of the benefit of underpants, now that the hated drab directoires had been so expensively disposed of. Hot throbbing welts, swollen bruises and a big patch of sticking plaster on the right where someone had provided first aid for the open splits in the skin on her flank.

Even more convinced of the rightness of her decision, the doleful sight of the wounded haunches confirming Daphne's unfitness to take the wheel, Eve slipped into the driver's seat and pulled out of the parking lot. It was not a relaxed journey for either of them; Daphne trying to hold steady against the movement of the car, which set off new waves of fire in her tortured bum with every bump, Eve's attention divided between concern for her friend's dishonourable wounds and the need to keep an eye out for traffic police. Though she had made her offer in the heat of the moment, when she'd have accepted the mandatory ten on the spot, if that was the only way to help Daphne home, more sober consideration left her with a slight sinking feeling in her stomach, and an acute consciousness of her own trim buttocks, pressed without the sanction of authority into the driver's seat. At every turn she expected to see the menacing outline of a cruiser, to hear a siren calling on her to stop and show her papers.

God! Ten with the penal! She hadn't been beaten for ten years now, since she'd left the beloved but rigorous boarding school she'd gone to. That was all long behind her now and she'd almost forgotten how the bite of cane on flesh felt. Almost but not quite. She remembered enough to produce a slight shaking of the knees, an empty feeling in the pit of her stomach, each time they met the lights of other cars. Twice a uniform patrol car passed, once meeting them head-on and passing without pausing, the second time pulling in behind for nearly a mile, before pulling out and sweeping past without a backward glance. Eve let out a breath she had been holding far too long, and tried to still the butterflies that danced in her belly, then suddenly became aware of a wetness between her thighs. I'm sweating, she thought, and didn't stop to consider why it was not beneath her arms or below her breasts.

It only took a little under an hour to reach the Borenson estate but Eve felt she had driven half way round the world with a dozen police forces chasing her with waving canes. With relief she pulled up in front of the big house and helped Daphne out onto the drive.

"Thank you darling, I could never have managed. Now all I want is my bed and a nice stiff fuck to help me sleep. See you in the morning," and she departed, leaving a quick hot kiss pressed to Eve's parted lips.

Back in her own room, Eve felt she could relax for the first time since she had taken control of the situation at the club and put her buttocks on the line. She stripped, throwing her sweaty shirt into the bin, then pulled her panties out of her crease, where they had crept and flushed at the soaked gusset, flooded from her reaction to the scene at the club and reinfused by that strange wetness on the road, when the police car had sat on their tail for what had seemed an age. She threw it after the shirt and climbed naked into bed.

The sun was streaming through the curtains again when Eve woke, and the breakfast room deserted. The maid informed her that Gordon had left early for work as usual. Ten minutes later Daphne wandered in, distrait and still limping, but otherwise little the worse for the previous evening's tanning.

"You don't look the wreck I expected," Eve commented.

"A good hard fuck and a solid night's sleep does wonders for a girl," Daphne replied. "You should try it sometime."

"Almost forgotten the feeling; besides I haven't a man at the moment," Eve countered.

"Mmm, that's true. Perhaps I should lend you mine," her friend suggested, "though I'd want him back after he'd serviced you."

Eve covered a blush by suggesting she was a bit free with her man.

"You may be right," Daphne agreed, "in fact I'd probably be earning myself yet another correction for presumption if there was a man present, but this is just girl talk, and that doesn't count."

They spent the day by the pool again, nursing Daphnes wounds, though she seemed to have recovered her spirits well enough, even if it cost her a groan or two from time to time as she tried to settle herself comfortably.

"It's best to lie on your tum at times like these," she remarked, "but its hard on the elbows after a while."

With the evening came Gordon and cocktails by the pool, warm kisses for both women and a fond pat on the tender rump for Daphne, who squealed, but didn't seem particularly distressed by the show of affection.

Eve was first to dress, and found Gordon walking on the terrace above the pool, drink in hand. He equipped her with similar sustenance then fixed her with a very direct look, that found her belly contracting beneath the thin cotton of her dress.

"Daphne has told me how you drove her home last night," he opened without preamble. "You haven't registered your British licence yet, I understand."

"No, not yet. I plan to do it as soon as possible though and Daphne wouldn't have been safe driving. She was quite badly hurt last night you know."

"I do know. I found she needed more than usual attention when she came to bed. Nearly made me late to the office this morning as it appeared a repeat injection was necessary to complete the cure. Still her sexual needs are not the point. You could have caused serious trouble if you'd been stopped."

"I was fully aware of that but I was prepared to risk a beating to get Dee back in one piece to her bed and your attentions as you call them."

"Well actually you weren't risking anything, as you would simply have claimed immunity as a visitor, though you would have been asked to leave at once, with no chance of returning. Daphne though would have been punished for allowing it to happen; she is at least nominally, my representative. By the same token I would have been fined for not keeping you women under control."

"I'm sorry. I didn't realise. Anyway I would have paid the money back."

"Again, you miss the point. The money is nothing. It's the damage to my reputation that would hurt. Not able to control his women they'd say. And how about Daphne? Did you really think she should risk her bottom yet again in the state she was in?"

"Of course not," Eve replied indignantly, "what sort of friend do you think I am. Besides," she burst out, carried away by her emotions, "I wouldn't have run away. I'd have stayed and faced the music, even if it did mean taking a caning."

"Would you just," Gordon mused, looking directly at her again, "Have you ever been caned, young lady?"

Eve's indignation boiled over; young lady indeed!

"If you must know, I have. I attended a very strict school, where the rod was well used, and I know just what it is like. We could take our licks there I can tell you."

"Could you still, I wonder? Still the question's academic; you'd never be called upon to prove the point. Just please think in future before you let someone who has to live by the rules here, risk getting into trouble with the law."

Thankfully Eve spotted Daphne coming to join them and was able to avoid any need to reply, and the subject was dropped. After dinner, which Daphne took, by special favour, kneeling on a padded stool, Gordon took himself off to his study, saying he had some papers he wanted to look at, and the two women settled with the latest magazines he had brought out from the capital that evening. Eve found her attention wandering from the fashion page she had started, reverting time and again to Gordon's 'carpeting' before dinner, and his accusation that she had risked nothing for herself, only for her friends. She laid down the glossy pages and excused herself.

Gordon's study door was in the old style, heavy dark oak, all a man's study should be. It echoed dully to her knock and its thickness barely allowed her to hear his 'come in'. Closing it behind her, she leaned back against it and faced him across his desk.

"I've been thinking about what you said before dinner," she said, after clearing the lump that seemed to be constricting her throat, "I wouldn't have taken the easy way out, if we'd been caught. I'd have stayed and taken my punishment. You don't believe me, I can see, but I'm here to prove it."

"And how are you going to do that?" he asked, one eyebrow raised in scepticism.

Like a swimmer about to dive into dark cold water, she took a deep breath.

"I expect you keep a cane in here," she said.

"You mean?"

"I mean I'll take a caning from you to show you I meant it. Also, perhaps it might just be deserved," she added dropping her eyes from his.

"And how many did you have in mind?"

That threw her. She hadn't thought that far when making her precipitous decision.

"Er, um," she stumbled. "We generally got six of the best at school."

"It would have been ten with a penal, if you'd got caught," Gordon reminded her, "will you settle for eight?"

She nodded dumbly, not trusting herself to speak.

"It'll have to be on the bare," he said.

For reply she reached under the dress, pulling the flimsy nylon of her panties down past her knees and balanced on each leg in turn while she slipped them off and stood there holding them out as if offering them to him.

He laughed grimly.

"I don't think I need those just now, " he said, "just put them on the desk and come and stand over here."

'Here' was a mat in front of a wall cupboard from which he was extracting a menacing length of yellow rattan that had her buttocks clenching before she had even bared them.

Her heart was pounding as she stood on the spot prescribed and then bent at his command to grasp her ankles where the straps of her evening sandals wrapped around their slimness. The short cotton dress rode up to her thighs and was assisted on its way by the cane tip, which lifted it over her hips onto the small of her back, the swelling fullness of her firm bottom cheeks ensuring that it lay there without falling back.

The air was cool on her skin, emphasising her nudity and her exposure, reminding her of moments of equal fear and anticipation in Miss Fletcher's study. There was something else this time, though, a man's gaze. She was suddenly acutely aware of her plumpness between her thighs, the fatty lips so cool and moist. Oh no. She flushed an even deeper red. What was happening to her? She was flooding there, thinking of Gordon's eyes upon her. She was sure he must be able to see the wetness as dewdrops glistening on the curling strands that fringed her fig.

Then all thoughts of modesty and shame disappeared in a sheet of flame, blasted from her mind as the rod bit deep into the stretched integument of her lower buttock. She had been determined to take her punishment in dignified silence but the shock forced a strangled squeal from her open mouth. She clamped it shut, determined nothing more would escape her, and tried to deal with the fire in her bottom. It wasn't easy. It was years since she'd indulged in this sport and she was woefully out of practice. Besides, that brute of a rod looked twice as heavy as the school canes she'd known before. Her grip tightened until her ankles went white as she set herself for the next.

Again the rod sang on its path to her bent bum, but this time she was ready, or as ready as a girl can be for such stroke play. It flamed as hotly in her hinds as the first, but she only gasped, then hissed through clenched teeth as the real pain flowed in a second later. Gordon let her savour the full flavour of the stroke, watching the writhing cheeks to gauge her progress before cutting in again.

He was working her low, as all good beatings should be, three strokes placed a finger's width apart until they defined a band no more than two inches wide just above where the stretched skin still just defined a crease to separate thigh from bottom proper, the optimum 'sitzplas' of the classic caning, a spot that would respond for days to the pressure of the wearer's body when she sat, reminding her of her sins and, as importantly, of her redemption.

But that was still to come, as were a fistful more of these searching corrections. Four followed in regular sequence, Eve puffing and blowing in her concentration, her face beet red, her knees trembling, but after five she heard Gordon's voice growl behind her.

"You're clenching," he accused. "I don't intend to continue until you relax those cheeks. The cane does its best work on a loose seat and I won't have you trying to get out of it."

He'd watched the well fleshed rear lifting to the rod, the welts springing up, thickening darkening, but she was tightening. Sometimes even the fat fig could scarcely appear, so tightly was she clenching her thighs. It was generally held that a woman felt it more if her flesh was slack. Besides, it

43

encouraged self control if she was made to resist the urge to tense her muscles, and was made to leave them loose for the rod

Eve groaned, but would not be defeated. Gordon watched in admiration as the tight cheeks relaxed and the exquisite purple fig of her vulva sprang into full view again, an exposure not lost on the bending woman whose body was now a frenzy of feeling, shame, pain and, oh God! a hotness in her belly that joined to a flooding warmth in her womb. She set her jaw as tightly as, previously, she had been clenching her buttocks and prayed for it to be over. Gordon whipped the rod twice more directly into the hot raised band of plum coloured bruise that lay accurately and level across the quivering seat then paused again.

"I'm not going to count that stroke," he said. "You're not holding straight."

Indeed she wasn't. Up on her left toe tip, her right knee a little bent, she had dropped her right hip to turn the thick pulsing contusions on her flank away from the rod. She whimpered but forced her unwilling buttocks to straighten and braced back her knees, to take the rod with straight legs and level buttocks, the right flank exposed again for the humming rod tip to wrap around and burrow deep. Gordon watched in admiration. He had intended to use this opportunity to see if the girl was made of the right stuff and was fully satisfied she was a real woman. If not yet ready for the Eden life, certainly trainable. Calmly he lashed the rod into the offered hinds, wrapping it round the aching flank. Whining, Eve held her position, though the legs quivered, the knees fretting together in distress. He let her absorb the cut and struck for the last time, once more aiming for the low set band of bruise, then stepped back. He waited for a count of five, watching the ripples in her thigh muscles as she fought to hold still, then ordered,"Get up."

She rose stiffly, her hands seeming to have difficulty releasing her ankles, then turned to face him, as the dress fell back over her beaten hinds.

"Thank you," she whispered hoarsely, and stumbled towards the door.

"Haven't you forgotten something?" he asked, using the rod like a lecturer's pointer to indicate the discarded knickers lying on his desk, "I don't think Daphne would like me keeping your pants as a souvenir."

She grabbed the scrap of feminine underwear and fled.

Daphne was lying on her left side in a nest of heaped soft cushions to favour her own wounded right flank. She looked up to see Eve coming towards her from the far end of the long library. She was walking like a woman does when she has been caned; the back a little stiff, the legs very straight, swinging in small outward arcs from the hip, without bending the knee, the buttocks clenching as if to try and squeeze out the fiery bite still smarting in them. Later she will still walk in the same style, but clenching to remind herself, deliciously, of the extraordinary level of living she had experienced under the rod, and the quiet glow of satisfaction that would fill her; a sense of being 100 per cent woman.

The irony was, Daphne thought, that she would be the last one to know it. Any woman on the island would recognise the walk, and the feelings behind it, even without the forgotten knickers still grasped in her unconscious hand. Ah well, she'd come to understand eventually. She was sure she had not underestimated her friend's needs and potential.

"Are those a present for me, Darling?" she asked, looking directly at the scrunched panties. "Or just a souvenir of something?"

Eve looked down at the scrap of fabric in her hand as if she had seen it for the first time.

"Oh!" she blurted, "Jeeze! I'd forgotten I'd got them."

"Do I gather you've been indulging in some post prandial exercise with my husband? I hope you haven't tired him too much. I'll be needing him myself soon."

"You needn't worry, it's only his strong right arm. I'm

sure he can give you adequate attention without it."

"You mean to say he gave you a licking and then didn't follow up with some consolation. How mean of him. How many incidentally and why?"

Eve explained. "I settled for eight but it became nine. He said I was twisting away from the rod."

"Very proper; it should always be worse than you think. Still nine with any of Gordon's rods can't have been a picnic. Let's have a look!"

With her panties already in her hand it didn't take much to bare the seat of learning. Daphne whistled as the hot throbbing welts came into view. Ten minutes into their ripening they had matured in height and in the depth of their hue, blue purple ropes that merged in places to a single hot raised mass while there was a thin sprinkling of red specklets on the thumb-sized swellings left by the rod's tip on her flank.

"My he did make it a good one," Daphne commented, her eyes open in wonder, "I can see he meant to find out what your limits were."

"It certainly seemed like it from my end," Eve admitted ruefully, "and I think he succeeded. I couldn't have gone even one more, whatever the cost."

"So you say darling, but you've yet to learn what we women can take out here. Wait until you've been to a GOD whipping, or seen how they treat offenders in the courts or the prison camp."

"GOD whippings! What on earth are they?"

"The Society for Good Order and Discipline. Naturally discipline of women is meant and, equally naturally, it's an all male committee. You'll find out soon enough I think. Gordon has just been appointed to it and I believe they've something planned soon. Anyway there are more urgent things to consider, such as how are we going to treat those bruises on your bottom and the tension I can see in you face. A little TLC is called for, I think. I recommend some balm for the bruises and as for the tension, well let's see if I can think of something once you're lying on my bed."

CHAPTER 3   GOOD NEIGHBOURS

Languid and lazy, Daphne seemed to have been softened by her thrashings, not exactly cowed, but not raising her eyes to Gordon and never challenging anything he said. A hint dropped here and there gave Eve the impression she was needing, and receiving, copious sexual attention from her lord and master. Something she could have done with herself, she caught herself thinking, and blushed at the thought, and that of the regular intimacies the two women now shared which gave the expression 'licking one's wounds' a whole new meaning.

What was happening to her? What mental derangement had led her, a modern liberated feminist, to accept a beating, and from the hand of a man at that! Had it been pique, perversity or some hidden flaw in her nature? It had not been coercion, she was honest enough to admit that. It, like much else she had already learnt in her short stay on this strange island, was most unsettling. It was all very confusing and she tried to put it to one side and relax. Daphne had taken to spending her time mainly by the pool, lying on her stomach or settling in a nest of soft cushions. Eve, with a posterior nearly as sore did not complain of neglect. They were far from lonely. Word seemed to have got about of Daphne's 'walk', and her monumentally bruised buttocks, and there were visitors aplenty, come to gossip, sympathise and sneak a peek at the multicoloured 'sitzplas'. It wasn't long before word of her own introduction to the rod got out, and there were polite but insistent requests to view the damage. A visitor who waived her privileges to accept the kind of discipline the indigenous females were subject to was a curiosity indeed. Before long both women simply went without any covering to their rainbow-hued buttocks and left them on permanent display for all comers.

Eden seemed to have a frankness of its own in such matters and it seemed quite natural after a while for Eve to lie naked on her belly and be admired. Besides, it was a lot more comfortable not to have even the lightest bikini bottoms chafing her welts. The two 'stars' lay and chatted to a handful of women visitors, their chairs strategically disposed to watch the show, drinks in hand and tongues at the ready.

"I must say, I don't think I've seen such a well-beaten pair, since poor Sally got herself a double dozen two weeks running that summer there was all that trouble over the smoking ban," a tall blonde who had been introduced as Angela from the tennis club, remarked thoughtfully, "I wouldn't care to be in your pants right now."

While one of the women sniggered at some private interpretation of the idea, Eve felt almost relief at the acknowledgement of the exceptional nature of Daphne's thrashing. She had been beginning to wonder if the lash of the cane on bare buttocks wasn't going to be the constant background to her stay. She'd come to find peace, or at least some diversion from her failed relationship, but that would have been a diversion too far.

"Oh, there are worse things," Daphne replied, "A good beating's not the end of the world."

"Mmm," one of the other voyeurs agreed, "at least a beating's over and done with. It's the things that go on and on that get me."

"Go on and on?" Eve couldn't help asking.

Daphne turned her head to face her, but left her bottom comfortably in the air.

"Sometimes we get to endure some pretty uncomfortable adornments, and don't get to take them off for hours or even days. Not usually as painful as cane strokes to start with, but they grow on you with time."

Eve looked as mystified as ever.

"Nipple clips for one," Angela offered, "I know I haven't got the largest boobs on the island, but what I lack in cup size I make up in the teat department, at least that husband of mine seems to think so."

Since like most of their other visitors, Angela had stripped off her top to sunbathe by the pool, the truth of her assertion was plain for all to see. Two small but nicely formed breasts, given maximum prominence by the well-developed pectorals of the serious tennis player, crowned by fat brown teats as large as a baby's toe,

"Dennis takes advantage of their tenderness to clamp me when I need disciplining, rather than get it over with quickly with a swift six to the backside. Nasty crocodile clips with teeth. Tits like mine are very tender and after a while I feel like howling. It's hell at the time, and I sometimes have to keep them on half a day, but the worst thing is knowing what happens when they come off. Sheer bloody murder for at least a minute while the blood comes back. The devil makes me stand with my hands at my sides until he's satisfied it's all over. In fact I'm not allowed to touch them for half an hour at least."

"That's terrible," Eve blurted out, forgetting her resolve not to question her hostess's way of life, "It's inhuman to treat a woman like that."

"Nipple clamps are bad," the woman who had complained of things that 'go on' contributed, "but I'd rather an hour or two of that than the crotch strap."

"You know what, Penny darling," Angela said thoughtfully, "You said that with such feeling you make me think you might just be suffering from a cunt cutter right now."

"You know damn well, I am," Penny replied without bitterness, "since you watched me waddle across the lawn earlier. A girl can't easily disguise it. That's part of what makes it so humiliating."

Once more Eve had looked baffled but politely held her tongue. Daphne took pity on her curiosity.

"Come on Penny, the cat's out of the bag now, even if the chain's in your pussy. Showtime for crotches. Let my friend see what gives."

Penny pouted but didn't protest. She rose stiffly to her

49

feet and unwrapped the sarong-like garment that was all she wore. Eve gasped. Around the woman's waist a tight leather belt bit in deep, indicating it was cinched tight. From the front of it a short strap engaged a curious buckle level with her belly, from which, in turn, a shining metal chain ran down between the lips of the freshly shaven pussy. It was apparent that this chain was under considerable tension and, when Penny obligingly made a mannequin's pirouette to display her back and buttocks, Eve saw that it was pressed so hard between her bottom cheeks that it did not emerge until almost the top of her 'crack'. She did not care to think where and how that tension was pressing on the tender tissues of the feminine parts it crossed, or the vulnerable wrinkle of the anus. It only dawned on her at the last moment that the curious look of the chain was due to the fact that its links were square, the outer corners unradiused. The tension caused the links to interlock at their inner corners presenting, in effect, a series of right angle teeth to the crushed flesh beneath them. She gave an involuntary shudder at the thought.

"How long have you been wearing that?"

"Since first thing this morning," Penny responded with a grimace of distaste, "Damn sore already, and it doesn't come off until tomorrow breakfast. It's a twenty pounder and don't I know it."

"A twenty-pounder?" Eve's curiosity won out over manners. no contest!

Daphne explained.

"You see that buckle thing on the front, just above Penny's pussy, well that's got a built in indicator. You have to pull up on the strap until the coloured flap in the middle flips over, then you're up to tension. Hard luck if you've only just passed a hole in the strap. You have to go on to the next and that may be an even heavier loading."

"It must hurt horribly," Eve protested, "how can you let it happen to you?"

"It doesn't just hurt," Penny said ruefully, "It damn well

humiliated a woman. Have you any idea what it's like when you want to pee, with those horrible links pressing into your urethra? And when you need a shit!! Ugh. I can't bear to think about it."

"My man made me wear one for three weeks without a break," contributed a sophisticated looking brunette, the epitome of English aristocratic good looks, "I was nearly in constant tears by the end. It hurt like hell. A caning you can cope with, after you've slept on it. just a twinge or two when you sit and a little humiliating when you wear a bikini or shorts, and he's cut you a bit low, but everyone here wears welts as a matter of course and thinks nothing about it. But a Crotch strap! It just gets worse all the time. It cuts you more and more, until you could shriek at the soreness but the worst thing is the humiliation. As Penny said, peeing's bad enough, but when you crap...."

She shuddered delicately and the other women made sympathetic gestures.

"You feel you're never quite clean and that everyone can smell you, however hard you try to wash yourself. There's no point in trying to hide it from the other women. For a start, after a few hours, there's no way you can walk properly, if it's been put on tight. You waddle like a duck, and everyone knows what's going on under there. That you've got a chain cutting your cunt, and savaging your bumhole. Ughh!

"I imagine you just have to take it easy and stay out of sight," Eve said sympathetically.

"If only it were that easy," Penny sighed. "You're expected to continue as if nothing had happened, social, sport, business the lot. I guess Frank made you do the same, Caroline."

"Yes, he made me go through my diary and show him how often I went walking, visited friends, rode horses or played tennis and made sure I kept up the schedule. And a bikini for the pool or beach. You can conceal nothing there; everyone can see the belt round your waist, and the chain running down

51

your belly and up your bum, and be well aware of where it's been in between."

"You must have been in some trouble for Frank to give you such a hard time?" Angela suggested.

"The usual thing. Been getting a bit lippy, tried to get my own way too often. Even suggested that he didn't deserve me. Now I'm quite cured thank-you. There's nothing like three weeks with a chain in your cunt to break a woman's pride."

"There are worse things than crotch straps though," Daphne remarked darkly.

"Such as?"

"Well there's infantilism for a start."

"Oh God. That!" Caroline moaned, as if the very thought upset her. None of the others looked any happier, and a gloom seemed to descend on them all.

"Yeah that."

"What IS it?"

Once again Eve could not contain herself. Daphne explained.

"You won't want to know, but I'll tell you all the same. You should know the worst. You get fitted with a tube right up your anus, so your sphincter can't do its job. There's a flap to keep out infections and such, but you've no control whatever over your bowels. Then you get a catheter in your peehole, with the same result, besides being a trifle painful. You just can't help soiling yourself all the time. If you're lucky," she added gloomily, "you get to wear nappies and a monstrous pair of plastic pants, like a baby, hence the name. You change as often as you can, but you always believe you smell and everyone can smell you. Sometimes, just to make it extra humiliating, you have to ask a maid to change you."

"It's pure punishment," Angela confirmed. "There isn't a woman here who doesn't cringe at the thought of it. We'd all choose a beating, every time. Whippings are painful, and one howls and wishes it would end at the time but after - usually one can rely on one's man servicing you comprehensively and it's twice as satisfactory. Some women even enjoy the whipping itself, but no-one wants to be put in diapers. Utmost humiliation and discomfort with not a scrap of sexual charge to compensate. Even the crotch strap has a sensual element to it, connects directly to the cunt in a way, even if not particularly comfortable, but nappies. Ugh!"

The subject seemed to have dampened spirits all round and Eve sought to turn the topic away from the humiliation of infantilism by enquiring after the males' motives in disciplinary matters.

"Do they only beat you for specific offences?" she asked, "I get the impression that, cruel beasts that they are, they sometimes do it for no reason at all, other than that they enjoy it."

"Oh, they're not as bad as all that," Caroline protested. "They only beat us because they love us, even if they do get turned on by it. Sometimes I wonder if it doesn't hurt them almost as much as us, when you see how tight their pricks have got in their pants. They look about to burst."

"I wouldn't go as far as that," Penny chimed in, "But I think its very rare for them to just do it for pleasure. Sometimes though there's only the general statement that it is for our own good, or to liven us up. Sometimes I guess the punishment is undeserved, but no woman worth her salt would dishonour her man by complaining to him, let alone any one else, despite there being some ultimate legal safeguards. After all it would be very strange if there wasn't SOMETHING that had gone unobserved, seeing what sort of creatures we women are. Nothing of course is ever let go unpunished but they can't be everywhere and, although we make a point of confessing our sins, we do sometimes forget. No, there's bound to be some good justification for a beating, even if it isn't the one stated."

"Don't they ever relent?" Eve asked, "what if a woman has been beaten several times recently? Your bottom's like raw meat what with you having to walk a pair after your liveners from Gordon, and the parking fine at the airport.

Surely he wouldn't beat you again, just now, even if you did deserve it?"

"You don't have to spell it out," Daphne said with a mock shudder, "Christ am I ever sore. Still, it wouldn't make any difference if Gordon found me out in some other offence. Actually it's regarded as a sort of automatic regulation. If you have been beaten already it hurts more, and you deserve to be hurt more because you have been guilty of multiple offences. In fact it tends to work the other way. If you've already got a sore bottom, and you still go astray, it's obvious the first dose isn't working, and you need an even more severe lesson than if you'd kept your nose clean recently, and you're quite likely to get some extra strokes on that account. For which reason, "she added with some feeling, "I would not at this moment say boo to a goose, and I treat my lord and master with one hundred and fifty percent of the respect I owe him. These," patting her livid buttocks very gingerly, "are staying out of trouble for a few weeks yet, if not months."

Her semi-comic gesture seemed to break the ice, and soon after the visitors departed, still admiring Daphne's awe-inspiring rump, and congratulating Eve on her own colourful introduction to the delights of Eden's discipline.

"It's still a month to Lady Day," Caroline said, on parting, "so you'll be fit for that, if you keep your butts out of trouble in the meantime."

Daphne stated very firmly that she had every intention of doing just that.

"I'm not courting a single whack I can avoid just now. A really good little girl, that's me. My Sunday school teacher would be proud of me."

"Remarkable what a few slices to a girl's bottom will do to her behaviour," Angela observed. "Just goes to show where we keep our higher senses."

As the last of the cars disappeared into the trees, Eve enquired about Lady Day.

"At home it was March 25th, but it seems to be summer

here."

"Hmm, Lady Day when that poor little teenage virgin found she was up the spout. Hadn't let a man lay a finger on her and there's this great big shiny person, with wings, comes and tells her she's got a babe in her belly. The poor girl must have wet her pants, except that they didn't wear them then. Well March 25 is a lady day here, but so are all the other ancient quarter days, Midsummer, Micklemas and Christmas. Big social occasions. All the girls dress up to the nines and congregate to pick holes in each other's outfits. You'll see, if you haven't decided you can't take it here and haul your ass back to Limeyland."

"What do you mean, can't take it," Eve retorted hotly, "I took Gordon's cuts didn't I? I'll be there."

It had been a good beating and sore for several days afterwards but, within twenty four hours Eve had started to feel that sense of pride that a woman feels for a beating taken well, and a well-marked bottom. Later still, shopping with an also recovering Daphne, she had an almost irresistible desire to run up to strangers in the street and spill out all the details of her caning, or lift her skirt and drop her drawers to display her colourful bum to the assistants in the stores they entered. Then shame would overcome her for her depraved desires and she would blush at the bizarre thoughts that kept flooding her brain. Daphne noted the flushes and correctly guessed what was happening, but let her get on with it at her own pace. Like all the other women on the island she'd find herself in time.

A few days of rest had done wonders for both, though each still favoured multiple soft cushions for sitting, and as often as not took their meals in buffet style, eating off a hand-held plate while standing. What had started as torture, with a bottom too tender to sit upon was rapidly becoming something to be tested and savoured, clenching her buttocks to provoke the throbbing ache, deliberately reminding herself of the pain of the caning, though she was not entirely conscious of what she was doing. After the fifth day this unconscious bravado led her to declare that it was time to take up Joyce's invitation to visit her on the estate where she lived.

"I thought I'd ride over. Joyce said the path was easy to follow and the views magnificent," she said to Daphne, as they lay by the pool, naked as usual.

Daphne looked across at the healing wounds on Eve's pert buttocks. She let her hand drop gently on the top of one shapely bare thigh.

"Hmm. You're coming along nicely, but you seem to be in a hurry to bounce that pretty painted butt on a saddle."

The fingers slipped as if unconsciously into the shadowy grotto. Eve squirmed slightly, and they disappeared from view.

"I've too much respect for my own ass at the moment to want to pound leather with it. I'll take a rain cheque on this one. Besides, it's Friday tomorrow. I have the health club. Good thing it is on a Friday" she mused, the hidden fingers playing absently with secret femininity, "I wouldn't have fancied it earlier in the week."

After the first wriggle of acceptance, Eve had not moved, but her breath had started to quicken.

"Don't tell me you're going all the way into town for a workout in your state?" she said in amazement. "Surely you could miss once in a while?"

"I can see you're due for another lecture on the terrors of life in Eden," Daphne replied, her knowing fingers still steadily working the engorging clitoris she had discovered sheltering between the folded labia, suddenly laved in female juices. "It's a compulsory thing here. All women, regardless of the high degree of sports we enjoy, must spend a half day per week doing a vigorous workout under supervision. These same establishments also run 'penal' sessions, with much harder regimes, for women who let themselves go and are referred by their husbands, sons etc., or even by an unconnected male. If a man finds a woman's appearance offensive, and it's something she can improve, like her figure, he can make a complaint to a magistrate who will in turn issue an order. Such things are of course very rare, but have been known to be used to wake up a too complaisant husband or guardian who's not being paying attention to his charges. In really bad cases the magistrate can order the chain gang. As you saw, it does wonders for the physique, but it's a bit hard on the complexion, so it's a last resort for really intractable cases."

"And I suppose I can take it there's no similar provision for the men?" Eve retorted bitterly, but the force of her protest was a little marred by her red flushed face and her panting breath. Those fingers were clever and she'd had no male service in months. Her body was desperate, even though her mind tried to deny it.

"Well, it's not nearly so necessary," Daphne answered, smiling to herself as she watched her friend sliding slowly but inevitably toward capitulation to the digital stimulation. "Let's face it; we women are just not put together to experience civilised living without taking a great deal of care."

"What do you mean?" Eve was still resentful at what she saw as discrimination against her sex, but there was something else against her sex, Daphne's clever fingers, and the words came out thick with lust. Daphne grinned and continued with both her projects.

"It's a matter of evolutionary adaptation, darling. During tens of thousands of generations the human female adapted to be able to eat almost unlimited amounts of food when it was plentiful and store it up round her hips and thighs, to say nothing of her belly, for a rainy day. After all, even in quite temperate climates there would be several months of near starvation before the new harvest was gathered. And it was kept in balance by being pregnant practically all the time, plus having a little sucker drawing off the fat through your teats. Any surplus energy went into constant hard labour in the fields and in the home."

"Well that's certainly changed thank Goodness. Oh, don't stop," she breathed, as Daphne tested her resolve by letting her fingers fall still between the warm spread thighs, "I'm listening really I am."

The fingers moved again. Eve sighed and settled to hear the rest.

"Yes, things have changed, but women still eat everything they can get, when there's never any shortage all year round, and nobody drops a pup each spring, like they used to do. Even if they do, they seldom suckle it for long enough to make any difference. As to hard labour, we don't know we're born. Most of us have ever done enough to raise a sweat in all our lives."

"I grant you it's an easy life, here in Eden," Eve agreed, her hips bucking slightly now with the rhythm of her pleasuring.

"And in all the developed world. Oh, I grant you a lot of women have a lot to cope with, but it's boring or tedious or irritating, but not hard physically. Women in the developed world all need to eat less, exercise more, to compensate for those missing annual belly swellings and teat tonguings, and back-breaking field work they are spared."

She paused and smiled at the heaving buttocks, with their still livid stripes. She was well aware of Eve's need, and unashamedly capitalising on her vulnerability to get over a message that might, under less distracting circumstances, have evoked feminist protests from this liberated western female, now writhing and bucking with as much raw sexual need as any fertile female in the world.

"As I was saying, attendance is compulsory at one's scheduled weekly session. Lateness or absence is punished in the usual manner, as I imagine you have already guessed. There's a sliding scale from two strokes for mere lateness with written excuse from your husband or guardian to a full eight stingers for absence with no 'chit'."

"That's terrible," Eve exclaimed, though her protest was a little slurred. "You mean you get punished, even if you are excused."

"Exactly. Cuts out all the frivolous excuses. The attendance record is exemplary. Only rivalled by that of the Girl's High School, and for much the same reason."

"Sounds all very regimented. Do you have a uniform?" Eve asked between gasps, her responses now becoming marked in their fervour.

"You might call it that," Daphne replied, recognising the telltale signs and stepping up the tempo of her frotting, "all exercise, normal or punitive is taken nude, although minimal knickers are allowed when menstruating. It helps to make the women more aware of their bodies."

"Oh. I'm aware of mine," Eve gasped. "Oh, more, more, darling. Ooooh, yes, yes, that's it. Ooooh, don't stop. Oooooh, Oooooh, Oooooooohhhhhhhhaarrrrrgh."

Daphne withdrew a tiring hand now soaked from wrist to fingertips in aromatic woman sap.

On the phone Joyce was delighted to hear from her and that she planned on visiting the next day.

"Lovely," she said, then added. "We always have family dinner on Fridays, so tell Daphne not to wait up. We'll send you back in the morning."

Eve wondered what the significance, if any, of Friday dinner was, but didn't bother to probe. She'd find out soon enough any way.

The ride over to Joyce's home, Ladyswood, was all she had promised it would be. Eve found the trail clear and even, though it sometimes did wild and wonderful things among the rocks and trees as it climbed the ridge and crossed over into the next valley, where Joyce's family had their estate. True her bottom was still sore in the saddle, but a bearable soreness; in fact one that gave her a sense of perverse satisfaction and pride. She'd looked at herself in the mirror that morning as she'd dressed, and caressed her own flesh, gazing with pride at the nine dark spoor that crossed her lower buttocks true and parallel, mute if burning testimony to Gordon's skill with the rod. Although they touched in places, there was no room for nine such welts to be packed in anything but close on the taut and tender tush, each could be tracked and their count verified. For a moment she felt a twinge of revulsion, as well as soreness as she remembered, they had been applied by a man as part of the discriminatory female discipline that she so abhorred, but then she rationalised the event into a victory for feminism, a challenge accepted and met, a vindication of her independence and strength. Her ideology assuaged, she could continue to admire them for a minute before donning breeches and boots for the journey. Far from it being a purgatory, she found herself deliberately squeezing her buttocks as she lifted in the saddle as if to remind herself that her stripes were still there and still active.

"Lovely to see you," Joyce called from the terrace above the drive and came swiftly down to walk beside her to the stables.

"Mmm, nice cut," she murmured, admiring the fit of Daphne's borrowed breeches over Eve's pert round rump.

"They are indeed," Eve agreed, "and not just the Jodhpurs. You should see what's underneath."

"I already have, remember?" Joyce laughed, "Bet you were hot in the fork riding over."

Eve blushed at the memory of her un-feminist musings on the way over. Joyce took it for confirmation of her suspicions.

"It's just about perfect this far on, don't you think. All warm and yummy down there. Not quite the same for me the day we met, I'm afraid. Jane made me change into riding gear before she caned me. Afterwards I had to pull up my pants smartish, before the sting had reached its peak even, and get on that bally horse. Wow, was I ever sore. Anyway, time enough for that sort of talk later. Come and meet everybody."

Sir William Boothings estate was even larger and more spectacularly situated than the Borensons'. It looked out over a similar view of mountain, forest and plain, to the sparkle of salt water, perched on a ledge in the mountains where paddocks and plantations surrounded it on three sides. Sir William himself was away on some plantation business, and not expected until dinner, but his sister, and his rather younger wife, Lady Jane who had so unfeelingly scorched Joyce's seat and set her to pound it on an equally unfeeling saddle, were sitting together in an airy day room.

Lady Jane was younger and prettier than Eve had visualised, she had been expecting a middle-aged English aristocrat with horsey features and a loud voice. Jane was aristocratic through and through, her breeding showing in the fine bones of her face and her elegant figure, but she was little more than her own age, perhaps just thirty, in the prime of her considerable beauty, and spoke softly, though with the confidence of command. Eve was very conscious of a brief but all encompassing inspection from the blue chip eyes as she entered. Why did she feel they lingered a little longer on her tightly enclosed rump than some other parts of her body?

"Very nice to have you with us," she said in welcome. "Any friend of Daphne's is more than welcome here and it's nice that you could come for family dinner. I'm sure you'll find plenty of local colour to divert you during your stay."

Was that a fleeting smile that crossed Joyce's face at Lady Jane's remark? Her hostess introduced her sister-in-law, the Hon. Mrs Pamela Harringer, a large handsome lady, who must have been a beauty in her own right when younger and now, at nearly fifty, still retained a fine complexion and a shapely figure of Junoesque proportions.

The tour, like the introductions, proved extensive. The magnificent conservatory, that served as an orchid house for Sir William's prize collection, yielded a lady in the prime of life, who Joyce introduced as Mrs Trevelyan, a widow who lived with her son, recently come of age, on a neighbouring estate, and had come over especially for Friday dinner. Though polite she seemed a little preoccupied and they moved quickly on.

The great library, with its long shelves of leather bound volumes, and comfortable leather chairs, proved to be a male preserve at this time of day. Sir William's brother-in-law, Percy Harringer, a large florid man, who looked as if he might be 'something in the city' was discussing horse-flesh with another man, introduced as Paul Bolton, another neighbour, and Roger Bellamy, a youth of seventeen. Eve found his manner a trifle uncouth, and his gaze at her figure and her blouse, which the heat had encouraged her to unbutton rather lower than modesty usually permitted, irksome. She was glad when Joyce led her away, although not before he had remarked that he would look forward to seeing more of her after dinner.

"Not if I can help it," Eve murmured to her new friend as they made their escape.

In the long high-ceilinged hallway leading to the front door, they ran into a military looking gentleman, with a younger woman on his arm.

"Afternoon, Major," Joyce greeted him. "Meet my friend Eve. She's come over for dinner. Eve, this is Major and Mrs Nicholls, Dolly to her friends."

"Which I hope you will be," the rather languid blonde said with a warmer smile than her seemingly blase appearance might suggest.

"Damn fine filly," the Major harrumphed, Eve could almost feel the heat of his eyes boring through the fabric of her Jodhpurs; the males of this island, and those of the Ladyswood estate in particular, seemed to be almost exclusively aficionados of the female rump rather than their ebonpoint. "Nice haunches too. Respond well if hard ridden I'd say. Look forward to seeing her put through her paces."

"Now now Major," Joyce rebuked him, "You mustn't use such language in front of my friend. Eve is a guest here, and a visitor to the island. She's come over to collect some local colour."

The Major guffawed and smacked his wife smartly on the seat.

"Well she's come to the right place," he exclaimed, as Dolly clung affectionately to his arm with both hands. "There'll be plenty of local colour round here. Sent in a ticket for Dolly. Recommended a public. Thought it might boost her self-confidence a touch; show what she was made of you know. Sporting girl my Dolly."

The blonde winced at his touch and a hot blush spread up her neck, but otherwise seemed unfazed by his remarks, seemingly taking whatever he had planned for her in her stride and wishing Eve well in her explorations.

Having exhausted the main rooms of the house they went out onto the terrace that overlooked the pool. This was where the younger element seemed to have congregated or, at least, the female part of it. Some half a dozen bikini-clad young women were lying in the sun displaying their not inconsiderable charms. From where she stood, Eve was aware that the standards of female face and figure in this Eden seemed uniformly high.

"Do they all live here?" she asked in astonishment.

"Oh no. Couldn't stand that amount of competition everyday," Joyce laughed, "the tall girl in the yellow bikini is my sister Bettina, and the blonde with green spots is my cousin Fleur; you met her brother Roger in the library, but the others all live on estates in the neighbourhood. They've been sent over for the Friday dinner."

"Sent over? Who by?"

"Oh their men, of course," Joyce said, a little surprised. "You know about that I'm sure. We all have a father, husband, brother, who is in charge."

"I still don't understand. What do you mean 'sent over'? What for?"

Joyce looked disconcerted for a moment.

"You mean to say Daphne didn't explain about Friday dinners here?"

Eve shook her head.

"Oh!" Joyce hesitated a moment, then seemed to come

to a decision.

"I just sort of assumed she'd tell you all about it," she said. "Seeing as you're here to see something of our ways."

"Actually I came to get over a divorce," Eve corrected her.

"It may well amount to the same thing," Joyce countered delphically. "This island does have certain effects on women like yourself. Anyway, Friday dinner is a great tradition here. First Friday in every month all the female residents have to account for their behaviour over the previous month and receive appropriate recompense."

"I think I can guess the currency in which it's paid, and the ledger where its written," Eve replied darkly, "Everywhere I look a cane is landing on a female bum."

"Partly right, the tariff almost certainly includes the pounding of the posterior but there are some interesting additional forfeits that you may find add to your understanding of our way of life."

"Perhaps. But what about all these other girls who aren't residents?"

"Well you can imagine that a tradition like this is well known in the neighbourhood, and some of the houses in the district have taken to sending their wives, daughters, even mothers, to be corrected at the session, especially since Sir William gave up correcting the women himself, and delegated the job to Lady Jane. She is a natural hitter with the rod, as you saw on my poor rump the other day."

"You said mothers," Eve reminded her.

"Oh yes. We've got one tonight, Mary Trevelyan. You met her in the Orchid house, looking a bit pensive, and I don't blame her," Joyce said sympathetically. "Her son turned eighteen last year, and has seen to her correction ever since, but this is the first time he's sent her here. He must have denounced her for something pretty serious and she'll be well aware that Aunt Jane will deal out justice in proportion. I shouldn't like to be in her knickers tonight, and it almost certainly won't end with just a beating."

"That's dreadful. Only nineteen and able to have his mother punished."

"It's the norm here, for widows. All the women are used to seeing it going on around them and accept it if the cards fall that way. Mary married very young, she's still well under forty, and she had the comfort of an older experienced man to rule her, but she must have known there was a real risk she'd be passed to her son's care."

She hesitated a moment, then continued.

"We've another young man about to come into his inheritance. Fleur is twenty-two, and nominally in Sir William's charge, though Aunt Jane does the actual sentencing and execution, but Roger is seventeen, eighteen in three months, and will become responsible for her discipline from then on, as her nearest male relative. Of course, he may decide to leave it to Lady Jane, but I suspect she'll have to bare and bend for him from time to time as well."

"That's disgusting," Eve protested, her feminist hackles roused from their apparent slumber by the thought of that uncouth youth lashing the pretty hinds of the composed and beautiful young Fleur.

"Perhaps," Joyce said gently, "but look at it this way. Fleur has everything, money, intelligence, looks, and the awesome power of just being a woman. Such a dangerous combination needs to have checks; I'd almost say cries out for and is unhappy without them. And what about Roger? His rude nature is partly inspired by an equal awareness of the feminine power, especially in younger women. If he can get it out of his system, and realise what a responsibility he has, and there are plenty of older people, who will in various degrees of forcefulness advise him if he abuses his position too much, he might just turn out a man yet. He has the physique for it," she added with almost a giggle, and had the grace to blush. Eve could not help wondering if Joyce had already taken a hand at his transformation into manhood.

"Let's join the girls by the pool," Joyce suggested, "plenty of time before dinner and you can get to meet the younger set."

"Lovely," Eve replied, "but what about these?"

She stroked her hands down the tight cavalry twill breeches that fitted like a second skin, "hardly beach wear."

"Of course not silly. We'll go and change in my room. I've lots of nice tangas and things you can wear to show off your stripes."

Eve wasn't sure she saw it quite that way but raised no complaint as they headed back into the house. Joyce's well filled closets yielded a stunning collection of beach wear for Eve to select from. She was picking up a rather conservatively cut bikini with a deep bottom half that would have covered most of her rump when Joyce stopped her.

"Oh come on," she said, "Don't let me down by wearing those frumpy old things. You're my guest, and they will expect you to turn out real cool. Besides you've got a lovely set on your seat. Don't deny them the chance to ogle a well-whipped visitor's posterior. How about these?"

'These' were two postage stamps' worth of glistening fabric that might just about cover her nipples, if adjusted carefully, and a tanga type bottom, with a triangle of matching fabric, barely sufficient to conceal her lush labia which seemed to be almost permanently engorged these days she noticed, before disappearing into her arse crack for most of its length.

"Er, I'm not sure about the top," she said doubtfully, "my nipples are quite large and I doubt if those scraps will cover the circles round them."

"Well, it won't matter much," Joyce reassured her. "You probably noticed everybody had got their tops off by the pool anyway. These are just for protection from the likes of the Galloping Major, if we meet him on the way down."

"Some protection," Eve muttered, but gave in to Joyce's urgings. It was easier than arguing the toss about what was obviously considered quite unexceptional round these parts.

While they had been talking Joyce had stripped totally and was selecting her own swimwear.

"Come on," she urged, "get those hot things off and let's see you."

Eve blushed at her directness but was soon as bare as her new friend. Joyce stopped, one foot through the leg hole of a minuscule bikini.

"Oh my! You're delicious," she breathed, "and you're right about your nips. Lovely. Can I chew a little?" and without giving Eve time to reply, her hot lips were on the rapidly engorging stubs, pearly teeth nipping gently at the sensitive points.

"Yum yum!" she sighed as she disengaged from a panting Eve, "and the rest is lovely too," she declared stroking a hand over Eve's taut tiger-striped hinds, and letting it wander innocently round her hip to follow the crease of her delta into the thicket of tight curls, "I'll have a better look later. Right now we ought to get down the the pool while the sun's still up."

Eve relaxed the thighs she had instinctively clenched and drew in a rather ragged breath. The atmosphere on this island seemed to make her very easily aroused she thought, as she fastened the tanga, 'good thing there's adequate padding in the gusset, but I hope Joyce doesn't inspect it before it goes in the wash. I'm oozing already.'

The poolside encounter was a further step in Eve's educational process. Though all these girls were here to attend the monthly disciplinary session, none seemed terribly anxious. True there was an intermittent exchange of banter about their forthcoming ordeals, in the course of which there were some bitten lips and quivering backsides, but nothing of the traumatic or cowed behaviour, while the appearance of the newcomers was the occasion for a comparison of stripes, a process made all the easier by the fact that none of them wore more than a titular cunt covering which left their buttocks quite bare. Eve was interested to note that several wore fading spoor from past inflictions, some just possibly the marks of the last Friday dinner, but none so vivid and fresh as those she and Joyce displayed

The gluteal inspections were mutual. Eve was conscious of hot and interested gazes fixed on those well warmed cheeks, as she was welcomed into the bevy of nubile sinners, including Joyce's sister, Bettina, and Fleur, the twenty-two year old sister of the spotty Roger they had met in the library.

"Have you come to be disciplined too?" one asked nonchalantly

"Eh no. Not today," Eve replied. "Perhaps another time."

What on earth had possessed her to say that she thought in confusion, a blush spreading hotly on her neck. She was saved from further folly by Joyce's timely intervention.

"Eve's a guest. She's a visitor to the island, staying with the Borensons."

"Mmm, been doing a little more than sightseeing, I see," contributed another condemned near-naked nymph. She looked pointedly at Eve's rainbow hued hinds.

"Now then Bett," Joyce admonished her, "try to remember our island courtesy. You're in enough trouble tonight already, without adding rudeness to guests to your tally."

"Oh come on, Joy. You wouldn't shop your own sister, would you?" Bettina protested.

"Just you try me," Joyce threatened, but her eyes were laughing rather than menacing and the whole group soon relaxed into their usual good humour.

CHAPTER 4   DINNER AT LADYSWOOD

The sun sank quickly and early in the near-tropical latitude, the sudden cool around the pool sending the bare skinned
belles in doors to dress for the fabled Friday dinner. Joyce had
promised to pick something suitable from her own extensive
wardrobe for Eve to wear and the visitor soon knocked on her
door and entered to find her new friend, nude as a slug from
her shower, contemplating the long lines of dresses in a walk-
in closet that looked as long as a railroad car.

"Now what shall we put you in?" Joyce mused. "Something elegant, but not too dull. A little gold on black might
suit you very well. How about this one. Not disgustingly low
in front, but the men will be assured your boobs are your own,
and the bias-cut crepe will show off your lovely bottom just
right."

"I thought that pinafores were the dress of the day," Eve
said, "I passed at least three women wearing them as I came
down the corridor. Shouldn't we all be wearing them?"

Joyce laughed.

"Not unless you're desperate to have those tiger stripes
added to," she said. "That's the delinquent's uniform. Anyone
you saw wearing one is due for execution at Aunt Jane's knowing hand tonight."

"But one of them was Mrs Harringer!"

"So? You don't think she escapes having her meaty
mounds roasted just because she's Sir William's sister do you?
Actually I believe she may have quite a tight time tonight.
There's a rumour going round that she has been getting above
herself and that neither her husband or Uncle William are too
pleased. I suspect Aunty Pam may not be sitting comfortably
for a while"

"Anyway," she continued, "No pinafore for you, darling,
unless you're about to confess some terrible sins, and you
haven't been here long enough to have committed any that I

know of. Now get that robe off, and let's have a look at you."

The request in London would have had her protesting indignantly; here in Eden it seemed totally natural and she slipped off the bathrobe she'd donned on leaving the shower to stand quietly under the younger girl's inspection.

"Lovely," Joyce exclaimed in frank admiration of the slim nude before her, "but get those knickers off. You can't wear them with crepe, they'd show a panty line for sure."

Eve slipped off the offending underwear without protest, then donned the garter belt and stockings that Joyce laid out for her.

"You won't need a bra either," she was assured," Quite apart from the fact that you've got nice firm tits, the dress has a boned bodice which will hold you nicely, and leave a generous cleavage on view."

Joyce finished off the outfit with a pair of highheeled pumps, a touch higher than Eve was used to. By the time they'd helped each other with their make-up and hair the gong sounded for dinner.

"Come along," Joyce urged. "This is one meal just everyone is on time for. The men can't wait to gloat over us, knowing most are going to get hot arses, that they can take advantage of later, and the women - well you can guess why they are not anxious to be late."

As Joyce had predicted, the entire house party arrived at once in the dining room. As the men ran their eyes unashamedly over the newcomer's delightful figure, only partly covered by the minimal clothing Joyce had chosen for her, Eve was suddenly conscious of how little protected her from their hot gazes. In particular she was very aware of her lack of panties, brought home to her each time she moved by the cool air circulating around her exposed sex, a sensation enhanced by the sudden rush of moist arousal that flooded her loins at their attention. She was glad when their host and hostess arrived and all were seated, although she then faced the new threat that her gushing sex, unguarded by panty gusset, might result in an embarrassing wet patch on the seat of her dress. Ah well, time enough to worry about that when the time came to get up from table, for the moment she was protected below the waist by polished mahogany, even if the eyes still continued to feast on her well displayed cleavage. Somehow it didn't seem to be so difficult to bear out here. In fact her embarrassment had been replaced by pride in her womanhood and her power to attract the attention of these males, who were by no stretch of the imagination, starved of female attractions to gaze upon.

Dinner was surprisingly lively, considering what lay before these nubile young, and not so young, women. There might have been a touch of reserve, a certain introspection, at first, as many of them considered that they were another step nearer to that painful end that inevitably awaited them but, being female, their tongues could not long remain still and, once the ice was broken, the chatter became general, even the doomed Pamela managing to keep up. If there was one more reserved than most it was Mrs Trevelyan, the handsome widow whose son had sent her for correction. She seemed to be brooding on something too deep to be cast aside, even for conversation.

After the dessert Lady Jane rose from her seat.

"The ladies will take coffee in the drawing-room," she announced, "Perhaps you gentlemen will care to join us after a suitable interval," she suggested.

There were a number of enthusiastic affirmatives, and Roger put out his hand to pat the pert taffeta covered rump of his sister Fleur as she passed his chair.

"Getting butterflies sis?" he suggested. "Looking forward to a hot arse? Just you wait until I'm eighteen next year. I'll deal with you myself."

Fleur pouted but did not reply except to toss her head disdainfully, but Eve could see she did not relish the idea of having to bare her bottom before her younger brother, and take his cuts.

In the drawing room the promised coffee only postponed justice by a few minutes, then Lady Jane rapped on a chair back to gain their attention. She got it, at once, not least, Eve supposed, because she had rapped for silence with a wicked length of thick springy yellow rattan; the dreaded 'penal'. Suddenly the atmosphere changed. The gallows humour could not survive the execution's presence. Even though she was in no danger herself, Eve could feel the tightening of her belly, the tensing of the muscles in her bottom, feeling even more vulnerable and unclad in its knickerless condition.

"Time we got started or the gentlemen will be joining us before we've completed our business. They're never shy of watching a bare bottom whipped, and they're eager to make our acquaintance again tonight, so let's have no time wasting. We've a few sins to confess and penance to do before they come. Bettina, you're first."

Joyce's elder sister moved smartly to the front and stood to attention before the mistress of the house, who turned to consult a large black ledger on the stand beside her, although Eve was pretty certain she knew exactly what the score was for each and every one of the half dozen pinafored penitents now standing in an uncomfortable line at one side of the room. Only Joyce and herself were seemingly immune and free to sit together on one of the sumptuous sofas. No doubt this soft deep sensuous upholstery would be much in demand in the not too distant future when anything but the gentlest of seats would be unbearable to whipped sitters.

"Bettina Boothing," Lady Jane read out, "Late for meals, repeated offences despite warnings. Also rooms in a disgraceful state in the morning. How do you plead?"

Eyes fixed straight ahead, voice controlled, Bettina admitted her offence.

"Guilty as charged, Ma'am,"

"Anything to say for yourself?"

"Eh. Well. That is, my room was still a mess because I was late down for breakfast and didn't tidy up before I left."

"Which only compounds the offence," Lady Jane observed, "You may remember I saw it for myself. A sweaty bed, clothes all over the place, and last night's knickers left on the floor where you'd dropped them. By the way, I forgot to ask you. Whose sticky matter was it on the gusset? I've seldom seen a riper pair or a more generous libation. You must have dripped for hours to get your underwear in that disgusting condition."

Bettina blushed and gagged on her reply.

"Come on girl. Out with it. What stallion pumped you so full you soaked your pants?"

"Eh, well, you see.... Well it wasn't just one."

"How many, slut?"

Bettina blushed even deeper, and held up three fingers.

Lady Jane burst into laughter.

"You girls! I might have known you'd get multiple lays. Well that's your privilege, but I won't accept it as an excuse for late rising or septic knickers left lying around. It may be the maid's job to do the cleaning, but she shouldn't have to be party to your sexual secretions. Eight stingers for you, and try and remember to put your dirty underwear away next time, to say noting of getting up in time to tidy your room and come down to breakfast at a civilised hour. As an aid to memory, and to keep your greedy twat empty for a while, you can also wear a ten pounder for a week."

"What's that?" Eve asked in a whisper.

"Crotch strap," Joyce explained. "Tell you later," and returned her avid attention to her lissom sister.

"Frame please," Lady Jane ordered, gesturing with her rod towards the fireplace.

Bettina moved over to the great, carved stone mantelpiece. Eve followed every move with her eyes, as the girl undid snap fasteners at the hem of her calf length pinafore revealing that it was slit up both sides almost to the hip. With the poppers popped it could be drawn up behind and refastened to leave her buttocks quite bare. Eve realised that with the possible exception of Joyce and Lady Jane, she was in good company with her pantiless hinds.

At the fireplace she stopped with her feet against the fender. Suddenly it occurred to Eve that this was no ordinary fireguard, if it served that purpose at all. At the base were two parallel brass rails, which were not out of the ordinary but the further two rails, set vertically above each other, one about a foot, the other more like two and a half, above the floor, were unusual to say the least. A towel rail, Eve thought, but what was a towel rail doing in a lady's drawingroom?

If Eve was puzzled by the odd bars, Bettina seemed well acquainted with the burnished brass rails and their purpose. She stepped between the two lower bars, placing her feet outside the two ornate ferrules that bridged them, making her legs open a little, then bent over and grasped the further of the two lower bars on the far side. Immediately her knees were braced back by the first of the upper bars, while the top bar ensured that, so long as she grasped the lower bar, she could move neither backwards nor forwards, her buttocks bent and stretched, the under-sides lifted, and perfectly presented for the cane to place the coming welts directly in that area of the female anatomy known colloquially as the 'sit-upon', for the wearer's better remembrance later, when she came to sit upon it. As Eve gazed mesmerised at the lovely heart shaped hinds so blatantly displayed, even the plump shaved fig clearly seen where it pouted through the gap at the top of the slightly parted thighs, she could see the faint discolorations of Bettina's last visit to this seat of learning and correction. From their faintness it would seem she had managed to steer clear of trouble until this moment. A pity for her that she'd let unregulated lust carry her away to the point of exhaustion with subsequent lateness and lack of hygiene.

Though she must have been familiar with this particular set of female glutei Lady Jane observed the full protocol of testing their resilience and thickness by palpation of the lower folds and a gently prodding with the stick. Tradition satisfied, she withdrew a pace and kicked off her heels, to stand in stockinged feet. A moment's contemplation of the bent buttock, waiting patiently for chastisement, letting her eye select the spot for the first ringing slice and then she was stepping forward onto her left foot, her right arm and wrist sending the cane thrumming into the bent hinds right in the sucual fold. Eve gasped almost as much as the bent girl. It would have been a formidable stroke half way through a beating. For an opener it was devastatingly hard and accurate.

Bettina for one seemed to find it so. She let out a short strangled "yow!" and her buttocks leapt as much as her posture would allow. As the inevitable and educationally efficient after-agony flooded through her hinds, and the thick welt made its first appearance, she groaned at the realisation of Lady Jane's fine cut. She was obviously on form tonight, a point not lost on the remaining defaulters who variously tensed, paled or bit their lips as the mood took them.

Still, their pain was yet to come; Bettina's was immediate and incisive. With due delay to let her savour the full bite of the first, Lady Jane measured the target with an unerring eye and took a half step forward to unleash the next. It fell a finger's breadth below the first and seemed to occasion Bettina as much trouble in containing it as the first. She gasped and squirmed for a second before she could regain her composure and set herself for the next in the required stoic manner.

As the count slowly rose, too slowly for the writhing girl in the frame, Eve found herself fascinated by the way her haunches seemed to turn in on themselves, as if trying to squeeze out the pain, then open like a blossoming flower, as if she might spit it out like a pip from an olive, the ripe split fruit of her vulva winking in the diamond gap at the top of the thighs. The sight of the plump plum recalled her suddenly to her own and she realised to her shame and shock that she was reacting to this scene with wet arousal.

Bettina had reached six by now, six dark bars packed tightly in beneath her widest part, reaching down to the division of thigh and buttock, the portion of her anatomy on which she would have to put her weight to sit. Eve thought this punishment, was intended to be felt and learnt from long after the stick ceased to fall. At seven Bettina's gasps changed to a shrill yelp of agony. She seemed about to rise, her fingers fluttering on the bottom rail, her feet stamping as much as their confined position would allow, her hips twisted tightly to the right as if to try and escape the extra bite to her flank, where the tip of the rod achieved its highest penetration, leaving purple blotches. For a moment it appeared she might lose her battle with her rebellious body, which had had enough of the cruel cane, but she rallied and straightened, though her panting breath was almost a sob.

Lady Jane was impervious to her distress. With careful concentration she set herself a trifle further back from the weeping buttock and pranced forward a full stride to deliver the coup de grace, sending the whippy rod into the mass of bruised flesh that had resulted from the seven previous measured strokes. It parted the air with an appreciably higher note, that sent shivers down Eve's spine, and probably all the other female backbones save, perhaps Lady Jane herself, then impacted with an awesome 'sluck' into the flinching buttocks held helpless by the rigidity of the frame over which they were bent. Bettina 's body shook with the blow, her buttocks clenched and unclenched like a pair of grotesque lips gulping air, the fatty pout of the vulva beneath mouthing its own protest. She gave out a long groaning howl of pain, then her body shook with a deep sob, as she clung to the frame, for support now, not restraint, as the remaining delinquents stood in shocked silence. Bettina was no stranger to the rod, and a strong healthy girl besides, and her reaction confirmed that Lady Jane was indeed on form tonight and their own prospects correspondingly dismal.

"OK, you may rise," Lady Jane pronounced, "I trust you felt those adequately."

Bettina straightened slowly, her fingers now seemingly

reluctant to leave the bar she had had so much difficulty in holding onto during her chastisement.

"Intensely, Ma'am," she acknowledged, as she rocked her hips from side to side, her hands fisted in front of her. One did not rub ones welts in public in this house, Eve understood.

"Now for your forfeit."

Lady Jane was holding out a matter of steel links and buckled leather. Bettina looked at it without enthusiasm but took it from her, and fastened a band tightly around her hips, until it sank into her waist snugly. She parted her legs with a groan and reached for the chain that dangled down the divide of her hot and throbbing buttocks. With the unfeeling links lodged in her weeping slit, she threaded the strap that hung on her belly through the curiously shaped buckle and drew up on it, sucking in her breath as the cruel metal bit into her tender female parts.

"Tighter than that, girl," Lady Jane commanded, "I want to see it in deep. Up another notch. The ten pound flag isn't showing yet."

Bettina groaned and pulled up again, almost yanking the chain into herself. Something flashed in the centre of the buckle and the centre disc turned red.

"Good," her Ladyship commented. "Now I hope I may expect you to put your disgusting underwear out of sight in future, and get yourself to breakfast before noon."

"Yes, Ma'am," the red-faced young woman replied emphatically, as she wiped a tear from one eye and waddled painfully across the room to stand face to the wall where the remaining offenders could contemplate her ravaged buttocks as they awaited their own turn to be called to judgement.

One of the naked nymphs from the pool was called next, a lovely girl of nineteen, whose reckless driving had left the family Mercedes scored from hood to trunk, with an ugly scratch along one side that would need a near complete respray. She had been confined to barracks for the next month, with a weekly dose of stick to improve her driving. She had already swallowed two such prescriptions, which were writ in her pert pale mounds, six angry looking stripes from the previous week, six fainter, but distinguishable tracks from the week before. Undoubtedly someone wielded a searching rod in her home, but now it was the first Friday of the month and it was thought that the trip over to Ladyswood, and anticipation of Jane's expert correction, would do the young tearaway's body and soul a power of good, and Lady Jane did not disappoint her. The half-dozen cuts that the young person received had her whining and panting as she bent over the bar, then hopping from foot to foot as she tried to control herself on her way to join Bettina and display the thick throbbing results of Lady Jane's imposition to the remaining accused. It seemed to do little to cheer them but, once again, Eve felt a surge of inner warmth as she contemplated the rich soft feminine flesh, so blatantly marked by suffering.

The widow, the subject of such filial devotion, was next to come to judgement.

The pangs a son can cause his mother are many and various but, Eve thought, few as various as those her offspring was about to deal out to the still elegant and desirable widow Trevelyan.

Called out by Jane and made to confess her reason for being present to all the females, young and mature, in the room, her humiliation was intense. Her son might be young, but in Eden young men learnt quickly from their elders the finer points of the management of women, be they sisters, wives or mothers.

A hot flush of embarrassment flooding her neck and cheeks, she murmured in a low voice that her son had sent her to be punished for going against his instructions.

"Speak up woman," Lady Jane admonished. "Let everyone hear what you've been up to. What did you refuse him?"

Looking even more humiliated, Mary announced in a firm voice, "He wants me to allow Peter Manners to sleep

78

with me."

"Very interesting," Lady Jane observed, "and does he have any particular reason for that?"

Despite her confusion the widow managed a spark of indignation.

"As everybody knows," she said, "Peter and he are good friends and he says he owes it to their friendship."

"Is that all? I think there is more."

Mrs Trevelyan hesitated before answering.

"He has had his eye on Helen Manners for some time. She's much older than him, nearly my age, but she's a very attractive woman still and I believe they have a bargain, that he will have Helen when I agree to sleep with Peter."

"Don't you fancy him then?"

This time both her confusion and her colour reached new heights.

"Well, yes, but...."

"But what?" Lady Jane urged, as each ear in the room waited eagerly to catch her reply.

A hot silence followed.

"There's something you've kept back isn't there?" Lady Jane said accusingly, "Come on, out with it."

"John wants me to have a child," the writhing widow blurted in a rush of words, "He insists that I have unprotected sex when I sleep with Peter."

Lady Jane raised one of her elegantly plucked eyebrows, although Eve felt sure she must have known all along what lay behind the committal.

"And how does Peter feel about that?" she inquired.

"I believe he was the one who suggested it; he rather fancies the idea of having a mistress and baby tucked away, now that his own children are grown up and Helen does not want any more herself."

Now the cat was out of the bag, the words came fast and indignant.

"But I think, as well, John has always resented being an

only child and wants to have me give up my career and have a baby sister for him, to compensate for what he regards as my selfishness."

"Didn't you and Frank want any more children then?"

"Well, I suppose Frank would have liked a large family," Mary conceded, "but I wasn't prepared to give up my career and I kept putting it off until he dropped the subject."

"Hmm. It seems to me," said her judge after a moment's consideration, " that you have no objections in principle to sleeping with Peter and that your reluctance is a combination of resentment of men's authority to dispose of you sexually as they think fit, and dereliction of duty in not providing them with a child, when it is their express wish that you produce one. In view of the seriousness of these offences I cannot award you less than ten cuts of the cane for each, a total of twenty strokes."

Mary Trevelyan opened her mouth as if to protest, then thought better of it and remained silent as Lady Jane continued.

"As you will be aware, we like to reinforce the efficacy of punishment by some little keepsake or reminder, just in case the lesson should be lost once the sting fades. Your son has very kindly sent over this nice tight chain cincher," she held up a band of interwoven steel links some three inches wide, equipped with a formidable and complicated form of fastener, "which you will wear continuously night and day until such time as your pregnancy test comes up positive. Now bare yourself and get over the bars."

As the reluctant mother pinned up her pinny, revealing a succulent pair of tight round buttocks, seemingly unaffected by maternity, Eve again sought Joyce's ear.

"How does that contraption work?"

"Goes round your middle and pulls it in four inches," came the whispered reply, " you sure know it's there every time you move, but it doesn't get in the way of sex, like Bettina's crotch-strap," Joyce added. "My slag of a sister is going to have to do without the delights of the prick for a while, which won't please her, but Mary Trevelyan will be able to take the cock that swells her belly, until she's confirmed in pod."

The widow Trevelyan had now taken up her position, her firm buttock cheeks spread and tautened by her bent posture, hands gripping the rail in front. Lady Jane repeated her performance, striking hard and accurately into the creamy meat, each cut seemingly directly behind the cunt, though she was too just a judge to take advantage and strike short, letting the tip 'whip in' and catch the delicate vulnerable tissues of the vulva. Perhaps if there had been some element of sexual betrayal involved she might have given this extreme unction, a girl caught deliberately trying to 'steal' another girl's man, or having sex with another man without her sponsor's permission, but Mary Trevelyan's case fell short of such treachery and her sex was spared.

But nothing else. Stroke after stroke, the rod bit into the soft yielding flesh of the bared buttock, lacing it with hot dark welts that rapidly filled and thickened until they stood out proud, finger thick and purple hued. Eve marvelled at the woman's stoicism as she absorbed each fearful lick with no more than grunts and gasps, the occasional groan forced from her in the intervals allowed for the pain to rise to its maximum before the next was delivered.

She marvelled too, at her own reactions.

Funny, Joyce had made some remark about a lovely pair to whip, in a tone that implied she'd love to be the one to whip them, and Daphne had hinted at similar reactions to bent beaten buttocks; now she was feeling an unfamiliar desire herself. It was all wrong of course, how could she look on a female being chastised in this way? A male perhaps, just recompense for millennia of oppression of the superior sex, but the thought of the rod on hard hirsute haunches held no appeal. It was these bared female buttocks that seized her attention, smooth, elastic, spread wide but not flabby, the compulsion of weekly work-outs seemed to have ensured that even these mature and pampered hinds kept their shape and did not offend the eye. More than that, they positively cried out to be whipped. Eve caught herself longing to seize the rod herself and feel the shock of the strokes vibrate back up her arm at each cut into the slabby mounds. She wanted to break this proud female, to make her scream and promise to let her lover impregnate her, to hear her pain. My God, she thought, what is happening to me? On this strange, disturbing, magical island for little more than a week and already succumbing to its ethos, its perverse practices. She shook her head to clear it of the raw sexuality of her thoughts but they refused to go away. She moved uncomfortably as she felt wet warmth suffusing her crotch.

Ten strokes delivered, ten scorching bands of anguish written across the straining hinds, and the woman was allowed to straighten and get her breath. The tight bending position was enough in itself to leave the victim panting; with a double handful of agonising cuts it would have been unnecessarily cruel to have held her there any longer.

It was a mixed blessing, though. Once relaxed, it was all the harder for Mary to rebuild her mental defence against the atrocious assault on her ravaged posterior. She was noticeably reluctant to go down again, when time was called, no more defiant dignity now, and soon she was puffing and blowing again, as the cane descended into her tender wounded flesh. No more than three were enough to break down her resistance. As the fourth stroke of her second tranche whickered in, slicing into an already angry weal, she gave a short shrill cry, then sobbed in shame at her weakness. Broken now, she cried out at each of her remaining dole, her shoulders heaving with sobs, her face streaked with tears and mucus from her dripping nostrils; a well-beaten female at the last.

At the first cry, Eve's belly had leapt, almost in spasm. She pressed her thighs together as the wetness oozed from her. Part of her mind tried to stop the thoughts that flooded in, part watched excitedly the writhing flesh bent over the brass rails, a secret hidden place in her brain imagined her own buttocks spread like that, her sex open to the eyes of all, the rod searing her flesh. She shook her head to drive away the thought.

Allowed to rise, the well-beaten widow and mother was made to don the steel linked girdle, with its strict, relentless fastening. The belt, adjusted, round her waist until it fitted, snugly the catches were thrown. Mary gasped involuntarily, then stood panting as she adjusted to her new stern regime, which squeezed her middle until her breath was curtailed.

"Hmm!" Lady Jane remarked with satisfaction, "You won't forget that in a hurry. My advice to you is to get Peter to stuff your belly instantly. Better a baby than that friendly hug I'd say."

Mary gave no answer but shuffled off to display her wounds alongside the others who had already been dealt with. There was a growing line now of tiger-striped bottoms on display, a sight Eve was finding increasingly, and ambiguously, disturbing.

Dolly Nicholls was next to come to judgement. The Major's svelte wife had been 'put on a charge', as he expressed it, for 'conduct unbecoming a lady' and a general need for a 'livener'. Eve remarked to her friend that 'liveners' seemed to be a regular fact of female life in these parts, and was assured, in reply, that she was only too right, the men of the island being somehow convinced that an occasional dose of stick, for no particular reason, was an excellent way of keeping a girl on her toes.

"And who's to say they're wrong?" she finished. In the interests of diplomacy, Eve bit down the angry retort that sprang to her lips and turned her attention to the details of Dolly's failings. As Lady Jane recited the charges from her black book, Eve could almost hear the Major's booming voice.

"The little lady's been getting a bit above herself, don'tcher'know. Nothing specific a bit frisky, feeling her oats. Needs a good livener to bring her back in hand. One thing you could look at. Her gait's gone to the devil. Strides around like a ploughman. Filly should trot dainty, what! See what you can do."

What Lady Jane could do was award a dozen stingers that had the vivacious Dolly reduced to tears as she stood with bunched hands, willing herself not to add to her disgrace by grasping her burning buns and squeezing the blazing agony from the brands burnt into them by the stick. She looked anything but lively, but no doubt that would come later when the first fires had subsided. Eve had already seen enough of local behaviour to know that, once the shock of a thrashing had passed, the women and girls of Eden seemed truly to be invigorated and 'livened' by the experience.

As Dolly stood with tear-streaked face, her make-up failing to match up to its claim of being waterproof, Lady Jane addressed the Major's other request.

"What's all this about galumphing about like a stableboy?" she demanded in a loose translation of the Major's words,"what have you been up to."

With a sniff of her weeping nostrils and a most unladylike wipe with the back of her hand, Dolly explained.

"He doesn't like to see me striding out in flatties," she said, between sniffs. "If he had his way, I'd wear heels at all times, and four inch ones in the evening."

"And why don't you?"

"They're so damned uncomfortable," Dolly burst out, with a return of some of her usual spirit, "My toes ache after a while and flat sandals are much more comfortable"

"But your husband wants it, and what a husband wants, he should get. You'll wear hose and heels at all times until the next monthly meeting, in bed as well unless Harry objects, and somehow I don't think that's likely. Just don't put a stiletto in his scrotum, or your next visit here won't be as easy as tonight's little tickle. Moreover, you'll put a teaspoon of baked rice in each stocking, just to remind you why you're wearing them."

Dolly groaned on hearing her fate, but nodded her head in acceptance and was dismissed to add her own blazing buttocks to the expanding row of well-marked bottoms lined up along the wall.

Another girl from a neighbouring estate was next, a little overweight and pudgy and accused of greed and failure to diet. Since parental admonitions had failed to curb her appetite and indolence, she had been sent to Ladyswood for expert diagnosis and treatment of her condition. Apart from the inevitable dose of stick, a stinging sixer for a soft young bottom, Lady Jane prescribed some treatment to be applied more directly to the seat of her problem than the seat of her pants. Released from the bars, the girl was made to lie on her back on a long padded bench, while Fleur and Pamela Harringer, still awaiting their own judgement, were deputed to hold her wrists and ankles. Stretched supine, her flabby stomach upwards, the girl received her six all over again, but this time with a wide leather strap, that had her howling and writhing as her pale white belly turned to fiery red. Released at last she half crouched over her aching bulge while Lady Jane added to her prescription a diet of bread and water for the next month, and ordered her to request her parents to have her fitted with a training corset. Once more Joyce enlightened her new friend's ignorance.

"Beastly tight, but nothing like as bad as a cunt cutter or even the widow's cincher. Solid steel boning from your tits to your thighs, back and front. Double laces that pull you in and keep you tight. That girl will find dieting easy once she's knotted into those stays. The way they press on your chest and belly you don't have room for more than a nibble at the best of times."

Fleur was next in for the 'house'. Her Aunt looked up from her redundant scrutiny of the black ledger to observe that she had missed her weekly appointment at the health club a fortnight previously. Fleur agreed that she had, but pointed out that she had already received the statutory penalty on her next visit, and still wore the stripes.

"That may be so," Lady Jane observed, "but we have a rule here, as you very well know, that all punishments earned outside the house are reviewed and repeated, to make sure the lesson is driven well home, not to speak of the affront to the dignity of the house that such public misdemeanours cause. How many did you get?"

"Six, Ma'am," Fleur advised her, "They accepted that I had tried to attend, but that I couldn't find transport."

"Because you had put your car in for service and forgotten to ask if you could borrow one of the others," her Aunt reminded her, "an excuse not acceptable here. You'll get your six strokes again and, for the next week, you'll run to the flagstaff and back every morning at dawn, buck naked, bare-arsed; barefooted too."

The mention of cuts had not caused any change in the girl's expression. Clearly they were expected and a sixer was a routine occurrence in this household, not to speak of in the island as a whole, but the imposition of a morning run seemed to dismay the nubile young woman disproportionately.

"She doesn't seem keen on early morning exercise," Eve remarked quietly to her neighbour.

Joyce gave a little hollow laugh.

"I should think not. Damn chilly in the dawn, in your birthday suit, and the flagstaff is over a mile away, up hill and along a main road where the early motorists will have fun watching her flash her cunt and bounce her boobs. But that's not the half of it. It's a half mile down the drive, and a half mile back. Any idea what those chippings feel like under bare feet?"

Eve winced at the thought. Young Fleur was going to be real sore when she came to breakfast.

Execution was swift and, to Fleur's credit, well taken. The young lady was as Eve suspected, experienced in these matters and as nearly took it in her stride as one might hope, given she had to take six biting slices from an Aunt on peak

86

form. When she took her place in the display line, the welts stood out clear and angry against the fading tracks of her earlier correction at the club.

CHAPTER 5 ....AND DESSERT

The original half dozen delinquents had been reduced to just one, the rest now lined up in hot arsed display along the wall. Lady Jane had reserved her sister-in-law's case for last, to give it the attention she thought its seriousness deserved, for Pamela Harringer had protested at her new sister-in-law being given charge of female discipline, which, before her arrival, Pamela had dispensed herself. It was a hardy perennial and she had recently renewed her complaint, arguing that she, at least, should be exempt. Sir William and her husband had been unreceptive and had jointly committed her to Lady Jane's justice with a recommendation that, since she was so fond of all things 'horsey', a riding crop might be the best implement to mete it out., and a public chastisement might 'encourage les autres'. Lady Jane called on her sister-in-law to stand forth. Reluctance showing in every movement Pamela complied.

"Mrs Harringer has been adjudged not only to have mutinied against legitimate, that is to say male, authority, but in so doing, to have brought this house into disrepute. For each offence she is sentenced to a dozen strokes across her bared buttocks and, by special recommendation of those males most qualified to know her physical capacities, these to be delivered with the same crop she is so fond of exercising on her mounts.

"The affront to the house," Lady Jane continued, as the Junoesque figure of her sister-in-law quivered in shame and mortification before her, "may be regarded as an internal matter, to be settled here and now, and you will bare your bottom at once for your first dozen at my hand. The question of mutiny is a different matter altogether and I propose that you join the others in displaying your stripes, until the men rejoin us, when you will take your second dozen in public.

Moreover, since you are having difficulty with accepting their disposal of you, I shall also recommend that the dozen should be dispensed by one of the men, to be chosen by them as the most suitable for your case."

Smiling cat-like at the obvious dismay on the older woman's beetroot hued face, she went on.

"Taking all considerations into account, my own suggestion, for what it is worth, would be that your pride would be best served by putting the crop into young Roger's hand. My only reservation is that he may not have the skill and experience to wield it to its maximum effect, when my choice would fall on the Major. Either way you may look forward to a hot time underneath."

Mrs Harringer still showed a spark of mutiny, despite her dire fate, and snorted in defiance at her sister-in-laws remarks.

"Still stiff necked, Pam? We must see what we can do about that. Ah I have it. A soda enema. That should take some of the stuffing out of you."

Where threats of crop and welts by the dozen had failed to move the proud maturity, this last broke down her defences.

"You can't do that Jane," she cried, "It's too much."

"You'll address me as Ma'am when I'm exercising my official duties," Lady Jane said sternly, but her joy at her victory belied her strict expression, "anymore protests from you and you'll be given your flushing in front of the men. As it is you'll have to hold it until they join us, or take another. Now be quiet, and put that big rump of yours over the bars."

Pamela pursed her lips tightly and reached to pin up her dress. The buttock she displayed would not have disgraced one of her own mares. Eve felt a resurgence of her earlier strange responses to bare female flesh, about to be thrashed. Moving with dignity the woman advanced to the bars and draped herself over them. The movement spread the broad haunches even wider, great slabs of saddle-exercised meat, though far from obese. The thighs were still firm enough for a thick black mat of wiry hair to protrude, not quite concealing the fatty lips of a notable vulva. Before this display of formidable female portions Eve had entertained some lingering doubts about the severity of the punishment prescribed. A crop seemed a trifle harsh for mere girl flesh, but this was prime mutton, not lamb, generous in its proportions and fully adequate to sustain even a riding whip, such as Lady Jane now produced.

"Recognise it, Pam?" she taunted waving it before the bent woman's eyes, "Percy picked it out specially as your favourite. Let's see if you're still as fond of it after you've had a taste."

Allowance made for the amplitude, the sheer mass, of the great buttock it was a severe and searching ordeal for the gasping grunting woman, as the crop bit deep, again and again, into her slabby cheeks. Eve gazed fascinated as she watched the ridges rise where each stroke had fallen, awesome purple welts with, on the sorry right flank where the tip bit deepest, inky blobs that threatened to burst, so tight and plum dark were they with trapped blood. Pamela was tough and sustained by pride and hatred of her sister-in-law's hold on her but even these defences could not hold out for ever. After the ninth stroke had whunked its way into her hot and swollen cheeks, she howled in simple agony, and her sobs continued until the next stroke sent her whining and mewling again. She kept up the musical accompaniment through the remaining strokes of her private punishment.

"Thirteen down and a butchers to come," Lady Jane pronounced with undisguised relish, Eve had long learnt that a dozen in these parts was always a butchers, "you can take a break until the men join us. No!" she cried, as the unfortunate sister-in-law let go of the bar, and made as if to lever herself upright, "Soda water wash for you, before you join the line."

The bent woman sobbed in humiliation as a maid was sent to bring the necessary apparatus; enema bag and bardex nozzle, and a litre of chilled soda water fresh from the refrigerator.

Without ceremony the nozzle was stuffed unlubricated, through the shrinking sphincter, drawing another whine of protest, and then pumped up hard, so that its inner bulb restrained it immovably in the reluctant rectum. The bag was filled, the clip released, and the cold aerated fluid flooded into the unhappy woman's quivering bowel. At first she merely sobbed in her shame but then she began to groan and gasp. Spasms could be seen working her belly and she shifted her considerable weight from one muscular leg to the other, her buttocks moving like a trotting mare as the cramps began in her aching bowel. All at once she straightened and stood, mouth gaping and hands clasped to her belly, which could be seen working. Incoherent sounds came from her mouth which finally resolved themselves into cries of, "No more! That's enough!. Oh God, my guts!"

"Hold still," Lady Jane barked,"You'll take it down to the last drop."

Her aching belly visibly clenching, Pamela had no choice but to obey, until the bag showed slack and empty, its bulging outline transferred to the wretched woman's straining stomach.

"I'll just seal you off," her sister-in-law announced, as she detached the trailing tube, "Now you can join the others in the chorus line."

When she was finally allowed to rise she presented a face so twisted with the pain still at its peak in her hinds, and the cramps that wrenched her belly, and so blotted with tears and the runs from her nostrils as to be unrecognisable as the proud and haughty aristocrat who had first bent over the hated bars. She waddled over to join the rest, holding her belly in both hands, the perfect picture of female penitent, and it was there that the gentlemen found her when, two minutes later, they filed into the room. Their timing was not as perfectly coincidental as Eve supposed, aided as it was by a discreet message Lady Jane had sent to her husband via a maid.

As the gentlemen entered the room, glasses in hand, they directed admiring comments at their women folk, lined up, bare and hot of arse, facing the wall, their still raised attire exposing their numerous and varied stripes for inspection by experienced male eyes.

They were regaled by the sight of six hotly decorated female posteriors lined against the wall, from the simple six of the impetuous young motorist, to the blazing butcher's of Pamela's writhing rump.

"By George, Dolly!" the Major exclaimed, looking fondly on his bride's well striped bottom, "Jane has toasted your bottom. Done you to a turn, what. Feeling more inclined to pace like a thoroughbred are we?"

It was clear that Dolly would have preferred to remain silent, but duty, not to speak of a desire to avoid any more of that biting rod on her still-sore arse, dictated she make at least a token reply, and she admitted she was.

Meanwhile Roger was stroking his sister's brightly burning buns.

"Must say sis," he declared, as she vainly tried to twist out of his touch, "Lady Jane has done you proud, but I'll enjoy it even more when I can lay them on myself, and watch you jump about."

Fleur made no reply, but bit her lip in mortification.

Meanwhile the Major had moved over to join Sir William and Percy Harringer as they contemplated the once arrogant jut of Pamela's well-fleshed mounds, now writhing helplessly under the influence of the icy aerated belly filling that cramped her bowels and forced groans from her lips.

"Jove, Percy," he brayed, "You're a lucky beggar. What a pair. Not that my little woman hasn't a nice round bottom, but your missus must be a great ride. And you'll find the saddle even softer tonight, I'll wager."

Lady Jane addressed her line of hot bottomed penitents.

"At ease girls," she said, "drop your skirts and tidy up. You can put that colonic down the pan now Pam, but I want you all back in ten minutes."

"Since you admire Pam's rump so much, Major, you must have a try some day," Percy offered generously, "though I think I'll reserve her for myself this evening. She'll be hot to trot. Jane, you've done us proud."

"Not done yet, Percy," Lady Jane informed him, "The Hon. Pam has still to get her second dose," and, as the subdued, but not cowed, females drifted back from their ablutions she explained the nature of his wife's sentence, and her suggestion that it be completed by the men in a public session.

"My dilemma was to choose between youthful enthusiasm and the Major's military muscle. I leave it to your judgement."

Her husband did not hesitate.

"A little of both, will have double the benefit," Sir William declared," but of course the choice must be yours Percy. She may live under my roof, but she's your woman, so you shall decide."

"Nothing simpler," Percy replied, "six from young Roger, here and seven from the Major."

The judgement was greeted with enthusiastic approval, not least by young Roger and Major Nicholls.

Pamela looked to her brother and husband for some hope of reprieve but found only an eager gleam of anticipation in each. As her brother moved his head slowly from side to side in a definitive negative, she gathered what dignity she could and moved to stand to the whipping frame.

"Bare and bend," Jane commanded and Pamela obeyed. With her feet set carefully in the lower slots she bent over the top rail and reached behind to lift the back flap of the penitent's pinafore onto her back. With an absence of underwear she was almost ready, needing only to reach down and grip the lower bar in front for her great mare's buttocks to be spread and lifted for the rod.

Before handing over the crop to the spotty Roger, Jane

let the Honourable Pam display her rump for a moment longer, to please the men and add to her discomforture. Truly a magnificent pair of buttocks, worthy of a mare, and one in training for the track, for they were as firm and muscled as they were large.

Roger's assault, when it came suggested he had been receiving some coaching in the gentle art of female correction for his youthful zest did not dissipate itself in wild inaccuracy but beat a natural rhythm on the already sore and seared rump meat. In a last desperate effort to salvage some dignity from the humiliation of submitting to this callow youth, Pam had set herself to endure without crying out, a defiance that cost her all her remaining strength, as she groaned and gasped, puffed and whined through a half dozen biting cuts of the crop, each adding its own distinct and burning track to the already furrowed and swollen buttock. Though he had not extracted a real cry from her, Roger seemed well pleased when he finally stood back and passed the whip to the Major.

This was mature male muscle at work, and it showed. Pamela could no longer hold out. Her groans became howls, her gasps yelps of pain. She suffered and writhed under seven lashes of the crop as hard as any she had received, and this on already tenderised flesh. At the end of this monumental cropping even the massive buttocks deployed by the Hon. Pamela were showing considerable signs of wear and tear, several little trickles of red showing where the skin had parted under the vicious tongue on her flank.

Given that she already knew about the code by which women had to conduct themselves after a beating as if nothing had happened to disturb their usual routine, Eve concluded that Mrs Harringer could look forward to many days of groaning equestrianism, and to a whole new meaning for the term saddle-sore. For the moment though, her husband required her saddle for more sporting activities and Eve was beginning to understand the ways of this strange place enough to know that she would, far from resenting the use of her hot and sensitised body, welcome the attention, which would ease her own sexual needs, and that her marital relations might well be repaired by the experience.

The others seemed equally keen to find their beds although, since the younger ones went off in pairs ostensibly to help with the application of soothing creams, it seemed equally probable that their immediate plans did not lack a sensual element as well.

In her own lonely bed Eve found that the excitement of the day had left her exhausted, languid but troubled. As she lay half sleeping, one hand straying unconsciously to lightly stroke the swelling pearl at the top of a warm moist crease, the images of bent and squirming buttocks swirled in and out of her half conscious mind, partly in remembrance of those hot lustful yearnings to seize a rod and lay into soft girl flesh but, more disturbingly still, an ache to spread her own bare buttocks over the brass rails and feel the clean hard bite of rattan in her own tender flesh. Washed over by thoughts of strokes delivered and received, flooded by hot waves of sexuality from her crafty fingers pursuing their way of their own volition it seemed, she let the mounting tide wash over her until her belly spasmed, the contractions of her oozing vagina squeezed sticky libations onto her hand and she drifted off into sleep.

Not far from where Eve thought her troubled thoughts, a singular scene was taking place. In her luxurious bedroom, Lady Jane, no longer the elegant hostess, and ice cool dispenser of justice, bent bare as a slug over an identical set of bars to those in the drawing-room, while her lord and master addressed her, rod in hand.

"An amusing evening," he pronounced, "but now we must come to reckon how far you have maintained the discipline of the house. We can disregard the girls sent in by our neighbours, they are hardly your responsibility, but Pamela and Bettina certainly qualify and the Major has been our house guest for so long that I think you must consider Dolly as under your wing as well. Together with Fleur that makes a tidy total, what! Good for a dozen do you think?"

"I think that's fair," the bent bare beauty replied, her voice somewhat muffled from her head down position, "Do you wish me to pay any form of forfeit as well?"

"Hmm. Apart from the obvious," and here Sir William slid the tip of the rod between the spread white thighs to nudge the pouting labia, with their glistening beads of honeydew "I think twenty-four hours in a cunt cutter, a fifteen pounder, might not come amiss, but that can wait until I've taken my personal fee. Brace yourself, my love; I am about to begin."

The fine white buttock halves clenched involuntarily, then sheer strength of will forced them to relax to receive the burning kiss of the cane. The execution was slow, steady and very thorough. By its end the proud aristocrat was panting and writhing as hopelessly as any girl she had thrashed that night, her shoulders heaving from time to time when a strangled sob escaped beyond her control. Before the hot surges of rising anguish in her riven hinds had passed their peak even, Sir William's trousers had hit the floor and his engorged and mighty member had thrust deep into the wet and willing slot the bending woman's posture offered so conveniently.

Conscious of her needs, he thrust deep and rhythmically into her clenching tunnel, sometimes straight as a die, sometimes varying his stroke to slide along one wall or the other, to probe the roof of the slippery tube, or plough its floor. Holding back on his own rising lava flow he waited until he could feel the first spasms of her orgasm then let all go, his belly slapping against the raw welts on her splayed buttocks, ignored by both in their mutual ecstasy. As the flood of his seed pumped into her belly he collapsed onto her back, his arms around her, his hands cupping her dangling breasts with their turgid rock hard teats.

For several minutes they lay like this in the warm companionable after glow of sex, his softening penis still embedded deep and making little affectionate nudges with its last fading strength, pressures answered by equally friendly squeezes of the now satisfied female muscles. Slowly the shrinking member, but a shadow of its former glory, slipped from its cosy bed until, with an audible 'shluck', followed a second later by a humiliatingly flatulent 'parp' from the pumped up sexual tract, it fell free to let a dribble of their combined ooze fall to the carpet between her feet, a complement to the sticky secretions already running down the insides of her thighs.

Sir William slapped his wife's well-welted rump affectionately as he stood.

"Don't forget the fifteen pounder," he admonished as he pulled up his pants and left the room.

Dawn came sudden and late in this latitude and Eve woke still restless and found her way down to a deserted breakfast room. As she waited for a maid to bring fresh coffee, she took in the ravishing view of park and curving drive, the hills beyond, crowned with the skeleton finger of a flagstaff on the crest of the right hand peak, the sea glinting in the first fingers of the sun in the U shaped hollow of the hills. as she watched a tiny figure appear from where the carriage drive disappeared in the trees. It was running, but with a ragged and interrupted gait. As it drew nearer Eve recognised Fleur, quite naked, her bare skin rosy with the effort of her run and the nip of the pre-dawn air. She moved purposefully but painfully along the stone chippings of the driveway, stumbling slightly at every second step, when some particularly sharp and vicious stone found a tender spot under her bare pink toes, causing her heavy naked breasts to bounce wildly on her chest. Eve could feel the girl's relief as a physical thing, as she left the cruel chips at last and ran more comfortably on the smooth kindly flags that passed outside the breakfast room window. As Eve looked after the retreating figure she was able to admire Lady Jane's handiwork; eight ruler straight livid welts, still hot and dark against her pale hide, placed true and parallel right under the nubile jut.

As she turned away from the tasty sight, she was joined by Lady Jane herself, bright eyed and bushy tailed, who greeted her warmly and hoped she had found the previous evening educational. As she talked, Lady Jane brought her orange juice over to join her at the table, and Eve was startled to see her make a characteristic 'moue' of pain as she settled her denim covered rear on the straight wooden chair. Surely it couldn't be? But she was beginning to learn about these things and that seemed the unmistakable act of a woman whose bottom had recently received whip, rod or strap, and was treating her wounds with the respect their tender state deserved. Suppressing the urge to comment, she took refuge in the subject of the previous night's activities and, especially, the case of Mrs Trevelyan.

"Surely," she protested, "It's not appropriate for a nineteen year old boy to insist his mother becomes pregnant. I mean forcing your own mother to have unprotected sex, that's got to be going too far."

"Well, you heard some of the background last night; how John has always resented having no brother or sister. Then there's the fact that Mary is leading a rather racketty life, besides not giving up her career, which John would rather like at this stage. Then there's Peter Manners," Lady Jane went on, "he'd very much like a mistress and a baby, and John would get to sleep with Helen Manners, so one way and another it would be very handy all round."

"Not for Mary Manners," Eve put in indignantly.

"Oh I don't know. Surely you realise it's very good for a woman to surrender herself completely, and what could be more complete than that; to have an inexorable seed take over your body and run its course regardless? You've been going through a bad time yourself I understand," Lady Jane observed thoughtfully. "Perhaps the inability to surrender yourself might be part of your problem, as well as offering a way out of it."

"I really don't think so," Eve replied hurriedly," I'm just not made that way."

"Really? Well we shall see. It's amazing what women find in themselves on this island. Their true natures have a chance to blossom here."

The arrival of more early risers cut short the conversation, much to Eve's relief, for Lady Jane's observations had produced a most uncomfortable feeling. Dolly Nicholls came in on her husband's arm as he offered her a considerate support for her high-heeled, stocking clad walk. It was clear not only that she was obeying her instructions from the first moment, but that baked rice had been procured already. Each mincing step was obviously painful, even at this early stage. Bitter rice indeed; a few hours of this granule plagued pedestrianism and she'd feel as if she was walking on nails. Eve could only hope her feet would become hardened rapidly. Her obvious discomfort though, could not totally disguise her other feelings. She had that look that Eve was beginning to recognise; the well-serviced look of a whipped woman whose husband had done his duty by her, to soothe her stripes.

The younger element seemed quite recovered from their ordeals of the night before. Well not quite ALL their ordeals. Puffy smudges under eyes, and that included Joyce, who had not been on the receiving end this time around, suggested that the buttock creaming sessions had indeed progressed to certain girlish practices designed to relieve frayed nerves and stressed limbs. Well she could scarcely blame them for that. She would have liked some friendly tongue or fingers herself in the night, rather than her solitary frotting, but their need was obviously greater than hers and she did not grudge them their little indulgences.

Mrs Trevelyan looked thoughtful, but unworried. Perhaps Lady Jane was right, and she only wanted to have the responsibility for her fate taken from her to accept it without resentment, or even welcome it.

Even Pamela Harringer, who had taken the severest beating, not to mention her ice cold belly cramping enema and the humiliation of being thrashed in public by a boy of seventeen, seemed almost serene. It was clear that she had benefited from her husband's admiration for her rosy rear cheeks, and she bore all the marks of a woman who had been well serviced by a vigorous mate. As the now docile wife and sister placed those meaty buns on her chair, she too could not quite suppress the same comical twist of the lips that had betrayed each of her sisters in tribulation as they had sat at the table. Eve wondered how she would react during her morning ride, and found herself making excuses to herself for wishing to be present when the lady returned.

At Joyce's urging, Eve stayed on. After the first evening, and breakfast the next morning when duty insisted that all those disciplined the night before must attend on time and be on their best behaviour, the only reference to the condign corrections was that written in the barely clad bikini bottoms that continued to lie around the pool, play tennis on Sir William's carefully tended courts or, for those whose normal life-style included frequent horse-riding, the somewhat vocal mounting and exercising of their favourite mares.

A less public but equally valid recognition took place in honeyed bedrooms, where nubile nymphs assuaged each other's bruises with soft touches of cooling creams and hot licks of eager tongues in healthy juice laden vulvas, where teeth nibbled gently on swollen clitoral buds to bring that easing of soreness that led to innocent slumber, all guilt for past crimes paid for in full in pained buttock flesh.

Eve enjoyed her stay and it was by mutual consent extended to a week, a time in which she consolidated her friendship with Joyce and became more intimately acquainted with many of the other girls.

During the week a docile Mary Trevelyan returned to her son, presumably to open her bed and her womb to her progeny-seeking lover, thus earning John the delights that a well preserved and sexually talented older woman can bring to an enthusiastic but untried youth.

The plump dieter went to taste bread and water for a

month, and the impetuous motorist to count the days until the next six stinging cuts would be laid across her tenderised young rear. Once Bettina had been permitted to remove the cruel chain that cut so savagely into her crotch, bruising delicate clit, tender perineum and shrinking anus alike in its horrid traverse of her pudenda, she had resumed her normal grace-ful gait and sought solace in the arms of various willing male helpers, though Eve rather fancied she'd exercise a little more discretion in that direction for a while, and make sure the sludgy evidence in her underwear was not conspicuously dis-played. Aunt Jane might prove even less gentle on a return visit.

Dolly Nicholls, of course, still limped on nylon clad toes tormented by the fiendishly hard grains of rice, that now felt like tacks driven into her feet, but discipline was winning out, and she was beginning to control herself to the point where she could walk with some dignity, to her husband's great sat-isfaction.

Fleur's dawn pink body, lush scarlet nippled breasts bouncing wildly, still stumbled up the chippings of the drive each early morn, on bare feet, and passed, all rosy from her exertions, below the breakfast-room windows, and Pamela still gave the odd betraying groan as she sat.

Still these were the only signs of the mayhem wrought among the females of the house, and the rest of the week passed in an atmosphere of peace and relaxation, only broken for Eve by a series of strange disturbing dreams, recalling varia-tions of the scenes in the drawing-room, sometimes with her-self as a protagonist about to lay the rod into anonymous dis-embodied buttocks bent over the bars, sometimes bent her-self, her nates spread for correction, displaying her fatty vulva through her gapped thighs. Each time she woke, with a sense of loss, before her arm could fall, or the rod bite her own cheeks.

As she dressed for the ride back to the Borenson estate, she paused to look over her shoulder and contemplate her bare buttocks in the mirror, gently smoothing a hand over the fading lines. It was almost with a sense of loss she realised she would not have the excitement they had caused her on the way over, when she had deliberately squeezed her cheeks together to feel the soft sore glow of the stripes.

With so much to do, and so many congenial companions, Eve had little time for introspection and analysis of all she had observed during her stay. The solitary ride home was another matter entirely. She had time to think and to try to make sense, not only of the ostensibly barbarous treatment of women here in Eden, but also of her ambivalent feelings when forced to watch. Why was she more aroused than outraged? Why did she watch fascinated the play of flayed buttocks, writhing under the rod, instead of protesting or, if her status as a guest precluded that, at least turning her head to look elsewhere, instead of letting her eyes rest of the squirming victim in excited interest?

So much lush female flesh, such pretty pouting pudenda winking in the gaps of creamy thighs, such incoherent gasps and moans of pain, indistinguishable from the sounds of passion, had left her wet and trembling. Unable to reconcile her thoughts she took refuge in conjuring up a surge of forgotten feminist outrage, and arrived at Daphne's home convinced that she had been truly disapproving all through her stay, and only silent out of courtesy to her hostess.

"It was monstrous," she declared to an amused and tolerant Daphne. "You just can't treat women like that in the twentieth century. It's quite unthinkable that men should oppress us like that."

"Oppress us did you say darling? Did Sir William order you stripped and thrashed then? Were you seized by the spotty Roger and put over his knee, your panties ripped off and your bottom spanked until you howled? Oh how horrid for you."

"Oh do be serious Dee, of course not. I wouldn't have allowed it," came the instant indignant reply.

"But those women you called abused and oppressed allowed it didn't they? Perhaps they connived in their own discipline, knowing it was for their own good."

"I don't believe it," Eve retorted vehemently, "No woman in her senses would."

"Are you saying those women were all out of their minds, then?"

"Er. Well perhaps not entirely, but they must have been conditioned to think that way."

"You don't think that perhaps you have been conditioned to think the way you do? Feminist dogma, political correctness and all the rest of the mantra?" Daphne asked innocently.

"Of course not. That's acquiring awareness," Eve replied.

"Perhaps those women are more aware than you realise," Daphne suggested. "They accept the occasional excess as going with the territory, just a minor part of an overall scheme of things that supports and sustains them rather better than a feminist wonderland."

"But you can't believe that," Eve exclaimed, "you're an educated modern woman."

"Educated means taught how to think," Daphne said firmly, "and we women here know which side our bread is buttered. We have it damned easy, really. We get everything we want, except the trappings of power. You don't think the men are so stupid that they would go so far as to make our lives a misery do you? We're the most valuable thing they have, and they know it. It's just that they are still taught how to ensure that the relations between the sexes are brought into balance; male mastery against female mystery. The balance of nature."

"I really don't see it. What about spotty Roger? Do you really think it's right that he should get to have Fleur bare her bottom whenever he orders it, and take a thrashing from a callow youth five years younger than her?"

"Not just any youth. He's her brother and head of that branch of the family. Of course he's a pain, young men often are at that age, but he'll grow out of it. Remember, girls ma-

102

ture much earlier than boys, and they've a lot of catching up to do. If the girls are left to exercise their female power unchecked it can be highly detrimental to their male siblings. Admittedly Roger is rather an extreme case, and Fleur is not likely to enjoy the next year or so, but he'll learn and there will be plenty of older men looking over his shoulder, and not just to enjoy the delights of Fleur's ripe young bottom under the rod. They know that the happiness and stability of society here depends on women continuing to accept the bargain, and they'll make quite sure he doesn't go too far before he comes to his senses. Meanwhile Fleur will just have to console herself for the raw state of her bottom by the knowledge she is having it skinned in a good cause."

Eve tried another tack.

"Alright, so Fleur has to take her welts in the name of education. What about Mrs Trevelyan? It's not even her brother that has control over her, it's her son. She's not only old enough to be his mother. she IS his mother."

"Ah yes, very interesting," Daphne agreed, "But, again, you haven't got the whole picture. Neither John nor Peter would push her this far if they didn't think she wanted to be. Well, perhaps they might just go this far, but no further. Get her a good beating to soothe their male feathers, after all an extra judicial thrashing once in a while never did any woman any harm, but they wouldn't push it to the limit if they didn't believe that, deep down, she wanted to be pushed that way."

"I can't see how you can say that," Eve burst out, "anyone with half an eye can see she's terrified of having this baby they are going to thrash her into bearing."

"Really? You know her that well?" Daphne inquired.

"Well, er not that well, of course, but it's obvious."

"You think so? Let me tell you, Mary Trevelyan has been agonising for years over having another baby before the biological clock ticks on too far, but she's always shrunk from giving up her career, and the status she thinks it gives her. Those who really know her, and that includes her son and her married lover, know that what she wants, deep down, rather than what she says aloud, is for the decision to be taken out of her hands. To be stuffed, plugged, spermed, without benefit of rubber or pills, until her belly is bulging beyond recall and she can lie back and enjoy it."

Eve gave up.

"OK, let's forget about women's rights and wrongs for now," she said. "How have you been getting along. Bottom all healed up by now I hope."

"Since you ask, very nicely thank you. Just some colourful decorations, but the bruising has all gone down, as you may see for yourself at bedtime, if my lord and master doesn't insist on keeping me in his bed all night. Actually he's far too considerate of me, and fond of you, not to allow us a little reunion tonight."

Eve had the grace to blush but didn't reject the implied invitation.

"Besides," Daphne continued with a grin, "he'll want to start conserving his strength for when his mistress arrives."

Eve gaped at her and Daphne laughed. "Yes, he's taking Daisy, my sister to his bed. And frankly I can't think of anyone I'd rather share him with. She's lovely."

Eve could simply think of nothing to say in the face of Daphne's calm acceptance of this display of absolute male dominion. Daphne seemed to realise that maybe she'd gone too far too quickly and steered the conversation onwards quickly.

"Now, much as I agree with you on the desirability of keeping my arse out of reach of rods and their like, I may not be so lucky," she told Eve, "Ladies' night on Saturday. You just came home in time."

Like the local rainy season, the reunion was hot, wet and intense and served to make Eve forget her friend's earlier, astounding revelation. Gordon was generous as usual, and sent Daphne off to Eve's room as soon as she had drawn breath again, after a panting writhing orgasm. A minute or two were devoted to mutual inspections of colourful but fading spoor from beatings nearly two weeks old; visual checks that soon led to a more hands on approach which, in turn, inevitably spread its sensuous tentacles to other, more sensitive parts. Much play of tongue and touch brought healthy young bodies to a fine arousal that only repeated convulsions could assuage. Dawn found their naked sweaty bodies locked together in sticky slumbering embrace. And Gordon laughed aloud at the smudged eyes and swollen lips that faced him across the breakfast table, when he stuck his head in to say goodbye, before leaving for the office.

CHAPTER 6   LADIES' NIGHT

Unusually they were to go out for the evening without Gordon.

"Ladies' night is special," Daphne had warned her, "you'll need to wear your best bib and tucker."

Not quite sure of what that might signify but still not possessing anything in the way of underwear that could remotely be called glamorous, Eve paid another visit to Daphne's room to beg or borrow something sexy to put her most feminine portions in.

She found her seated at her dressing table, applying the finishing touches to her make-up. A blue silk sheath, whose simplicity shouted designer dollars, lay over a chair nearby as she sat in her underwear before the mirror. Six hawser taut suspenders hauled smoky nylons high up succulent white thighs, gold sandals encased her feet and curled their straps in a loving embrace around her ankles. She wore no bra as yet, but it was not the luscious mammaries, with their thick succulent teats, displayed so proudly, that caught Eve's eye and interrupted her request for dainty underthings, but the sight of the tensioned spandex that covered the ample buttocks, compressing their twin and deeply riven halves into a single drum tight hemisphere, the twin globes seemingly welded into one.

"My God, darling," she blurted out," what are you wearing? I didn't think they made them like that anymore."

Daphne swivelled on the soft fur covering and followed her gaze down.

"Oh. I forgot. Ladies' night; full dress code. No bum cracks, no visible panty line, not a bra strap in sight. Everything all prim and proper. Hats and gloves too; the full Emily Post," she added, waving one hand vaguely towards a corner of the vanity where a pair of elbow length gloves and a neat cocktail hat lay waiting.

"Oh. you might have warned me."

"Didn't need to, darling," Daphne assured her, "I'll just explain that you're a visitor and my guest, and you're excused."

Eve looked away a moment, chewing it over in her mind then turned back to her friend.

"Look, I'm tired of being the odd one out, the curiosity from 'out there'. I'd much rather accept the dress code and be like everyone else. Only thing is, I don't have a girdle. Actually I thought they went out with the Ark."

"Well that at least is no problem," Daphne assured her. "We've always been the same size, and I've a spare pair in the drawer you can have; never been unwrapped. Better borrow a pair of French knickers to go with them too. Remember, no visible panty line."

The box from a well known New York store was unsealed and Daphne went back to her make-up while Eve threw off her wrapper and tried to get into the tough elastic tube.

"My God," she wailed, as it gripped her at the top of her thighs and refused to be tugged any further, "I must have put pounds on my bum. I can't get these anywhere near me."

Daphne turned and burst out laughing.

"I should have remembered that Englishwomen threw away their girdles in the swinging sixties together with their

106

chastity," she chuckled. "It's quite obvious your mummy never taught you how to handle one of these. It's a roll-on darling, and that's just what you do. Roll down the top edge a few inches, then cross your legs to make yourself as small as possible. Pull it up as far as you can tug it, then unroll it the rest of the way."

After a couple of false starts the deed was done, and Eve stood panting regarding herself in the mirror. She was jammed, crammed, stuffed into the tightly gripping tube, which squeezed her arse cheeks so tight together they seemed as one. The front panel pressed on her belly and the top and bottom edges bit into her thighs and waist, the lower edge forming a pelmet over the tight curls of her bush, part concealing, part framing, that secret and alluring thicket. She felt in the grip of a remorseless force, part discomfort, part reassuring support, but totally and emphatically female.

"How's it feel?" Daphne asked, gently smearing eye shadow with the tip of one manicured finger.

"Tight but nice in a funny way," she replied. "Makes you feel secure and yet feminine, though it does squeeze your bum a bit, doesn't it."

"You wait until you've worn one over a good caning," Daphne warned, "Gets real hot and sore, I can tell you. Although even that's a comfort in a funny sort of way," she added in a dreamy sort of tone.

The nylons were a struggle. Eve hadn't worn fully fashioned with seams before and found them a totally different kettle of fish from the normal sheer seamless sheath she was used to. She sat herself on a stool and tried to draw them on as best she could, standing to apply three garter tabs on each thigh.

Daphne took one look and cried out in despair.

"Those'll never do," she exclaimed, looking at the twisted and strained stockings," Turn up at the Ladies circle looking like that and you'll be taking them down for a dozen with the strap on the back of each of those lovely thighs. I wouldn't recommend it. Come and stand over here with your legs apart, and I'll do them for you."

Standing, feet apart as ordered, Eve felt Dee's fingers loosen the tabs, then gently stroke the nylon upwards, straightening the seams as she went, until her fingers reached the tabs where they lay against the sensitive white skin at their tops. The touch set off an instant warmth in her belly that spread quickly to her womb and brought glistening drops to the engorging labia. Suddenly she was overcome by a wave of lust. Her belly cramped with desire, but not this time for her feminine friend, whose gentle fingers strayed so near her aching female bud. This time only maleness would satisfy her. Reaction to the months of chastity she had endured since parting from the too sensitive and understanding Roger hit her like a blow in the solar plexus, a feeling of nausea and need that nearly overwhelmed her. What she needed now was not consideration but total savagery. Her mind saw a hot fleshy shaft ramming her to the gills, filling her belly, soaking her womb in fertile seed. As Dee finished her self-imposed maid's duty, Eve's belly gulped hungrily for male meat and she broke away and sought her own room in a turmoil of confusion. It was only when she reached its sanctuary that she remembered the French knickers that she had gone to borrow in the first place, before this alarming rush of lust had wiped her brain clean of any other thought. Sheepishly she crept back into Dee's room and retrieved them while her friend regarded her with a speculating look.

Ten minutes later, carefully made up, the lustful vulva decently covered in silken lingerie, the loosely fitting crotch gusset already well soaked in female dew, the rest of her body cased in a smart 'little black dress', the fashion-conscious traveller's trusty friend, she returned to Dee's room to find her pinning on a smart little pillbox hat, complete with veil.

"A hat!" she exclaimed," I haven't worn a hat for years."

"You will this evening," Daphne assured her," unless you want to ensure yourself a hot buttock. Put this on," handing over a small straw designed to be worn over one eye," and these too."

'These' were a pair of elbow length white cotton gloves.

"You'd better not let them get soiled," Daphne warned her," Six on each palm with one of our whippy canes is not very comfortable, and the bruises mean you're sore for hours."

"Wow!" Eve looked herself over in a tall mirror. "What a get-up. I've never had so many details to get right, or so many things to look out for. And this girdle keeps you conscious of yourself every minute."

"Exactly so," Daphne agreed,"that's the whole point of course. All those points to score or have someone else score against you. You'll see."

"Actually, I think we look like a pair of thirties Hollywood movie Queens," Eve observed with a smile, "old fashioned but very smart. I kinda like it in a way."

"That's just how it's meant to be," Daphne explained, "we're very traditional here on the island, and this goes back to the foundation of the circle. Actually it started as the Emily Post society."

"Who she?" Eve demanded.

"Columnist and author who laid down the rules of dress and etiquette for American females between the wars. We still follow her rules and anyone who spots an infringement is entitled to deal out summary justice on the spot."

"By which, of course, you mean on the bum," Eve remarked.

"Not just the bum, darling," Daphne assured her."Any place goes at the Ladies' circle. Let your bra straps show, and your tits get it. Scuff your shoes and it's the strap across your soft white tootsies. Now let's get on or we'll start the evening baring our bums for lateness."

In the car, cruising decorously towards the Capital, Eve raised the object of the evening's expedition again, and in particular, the ultra-conservative nature of the dress code.

"Seems a bit odd when you consider the generally relaxed sexual mores here. Rules like that generally go with Puritans."

"Well," Daphne explained," in the first place that relaxation is very much one for the men, we are expected to be obedient and accept whatever they give us, but not initiate affairs ourselves, but there are a couple of other reasons why this dress code persists. In the first place, it gives a wonderful opportunity to catch out a friend from time to time and ensure she gets a tight thrashing. The dress code committee is very hot on any infringements referred to it, so there's little real scope for appeal, once someone 'calls you out', as it's known, although the theoretical right exists, of course, as it does for all discipline. It's just that one's very unlikely to succeed and there are severe penalties, usually a doubling of sentence for failed appeals. Besides, it's just not done, which is the greatest deterrent."

"You said there were a couple of reasons."

"Oh the men are the other, as usual, round here. Apart from the fact that most of them seem to like the idea of bums put into tight casings and hawser taut hose attached, they seem to think it's a good idea if welted bottoms are compressed in hot spandex, to ensure maximum soreness for the maximum time. They're right of course," she said ruefully. "Having your cheeks pressed together like this really does increase the soreness and keeps you hissing when you walk or bend for quite a while longer than if you were free to let them move in the open. Very good for the feminine soul which, as they are very fond of reminding us, is traditionally held to be housed in that part of our anatomy. And, of course," she added," they are not averse to maintaining a system where sisters conspire to discipline each other. Saves them the bother, lazy beasts.!"

"Dee, isn't that high treason, or something like that?" Eve laughed.

"Well, perhaps. We don't really resent them you know. Taking the rough with the smooth we come out well in credit compared with poor benighted 'enlightened' women in so-called civilised countries, and I don't think there's a woman here would change her lot for the discontented, depression laden, angst ridden, eating disordered existence of the main-landers. Anyway, you weren't thinking of reporting me for the satisfaction of seeing these thrashed again, were you?" she grinned, slapping her ample spandex-wrapped posteriors.

"Well. it's a temptation," Eve admitted, with a matching grin."Perhaps they might let me thrash them myself."

"Bravo!" Daphne cried, "You're beginning to get into the spirit of things. You'll make an Eve in Eden yet. But be warned, the dress code covers literally everything you can think of, and more besides. You'll have to keep your wits about you, and your nose clean, if you want to escape with your bottom intact and, by the same token, look out for every detail, how-ever small, if you've ambitions to have some other woman take down her pants for you. Look out for things like bra straps on view and inappropriate colour of underwear, especially if showing through. Grubby straps showing count as two viola-tions, while offences based on bums, panty line, cracks vis-ible and so on, are rewarded on buttocks, dirty bras are paid for on the boobs. Chipped nail polish has its place too, on the palms and scuffed shoes, etc. on soles of the feet. Worse than it sounds I do assure you. The last time I was caught out I went on my knees for days. Couldn't bear my soles on the ground."

"Sounds like you can never be free of danger," Eve re-marked doubtfully.

"Yes, that's the joy of it."

"The joy!!"

"Of course. Just think of it," Daphne urged her," We have this privileged life here; no money worries, the men are all stinking rich, and provide all the luxuries a woman can de-cently ask for. We'd be bored stiff and committing murder or worse if that was all there was to it. But the constant uncer-tainty is what keeps us alive. You never know when one of your friends will spot a dingy bra strap and make you strip to the waist and hold your own nipples, while she cuts you in the fold with a whippy stick, or if one of your husband's friends he has given 'visiting rights' to, will turn up demanding head, or turn you over and bugger you."

Before Eve could think of some appropriate comment on this example of men disposing of their women's bodies in this cavalier manner, they pulled up in front of the club where the Ladies' night gathering was to be held

It was just as Daphne had described it. a flower filled hall, a cloud of scented females sporting hats and gloves, heels and hose, not a panty line in sight, not a trace of bum cracks, every seam ruler straight. Over and above the genuine friendliness of their greetings there hung an air of expectation, a sense of some competition about to take place. Eyes darted critically here and there, searching out each fellow female for signs of less-than-perfect dress.

"I don't understand it," Eve confided. "How can you all remain friends and yet be looking for any scrap of excuse to deal out punishment?"

"But that's the whole point darling," Daphne explained," It's in every females nature to be competitive about her appearance; it's only natural. The dangerous thing is for it to be suppressed and driven underground. We do things then we regret later, when we wake up and realise the hurt we've caused our friends. This way is all out front, nothing hidden; all lusts displayed openly and given back with interest. You wait until you meet the crowd at the Club tomorrow, and for a month after that as well. Licking their lips like kittens after cream, and nothing but affection all round."

Eve's further doubts had to wait to be expressed. A large handsome woman, in immaculate crepe frock, and the obligatory hat and gloves came to the microphone to welcome them all to this gathering to celebrate the great Miss Post, and enjoined them to enjoy the evening in a spirit of give and take. After she had stepped down conversation became general and the guests began to circulate from group to group greeting acquaintances, exchanging news and gossip and darting piercing glances at each others' rig for signs of any departure from perfection that might give excuse to 'call someone out', as the expression was.

At first things moved rather slowly. The first sign of things to come was when a rather flustered blonde entered the hall, full of apologies for lateness and telling anyone who cared to hear how her car had let her down. She might have saved her breath. The club secretary, guarding the doors with eagle eye, swept her into the cloakroom, leaving the door ajar. From it came the now familiar sounds of whippy rod striking elastic woman meat. Six sizzling cracks later, each accompanied by a gasping whine, and the blonde, now red-faced and sweating, shuffled out of the cloakroom to join her sisters, walking with that unmistakable gait that speaks as clearly as if broadcast on air, of hot aching lines across sore swollen buttocks.

The incident seemed to break some invisible restraint and all over the room women began to point out those little errors of deportment and dress code that needed rigorous and immediate correction. Next to where Eve was standing, a hawk-eyed female accused another of having more than the conventional two buttons of her elbow length gloves undone. Wincing painfully with every cut, grunting and whining, she was made to strip each glove in turn and hold out her hand, palm upwards to take six slashing cuts across it, before exposing the other hand for its own ration of misery. As the rod rose each time, she was seen to flinch and several times had to be reminded to hold her hand out properly or receive extra strokes. After the first cut or two, she was reduced to holding up one hand with the other to force it to stay in place. It was quite clear that it was taking all her willpower to raise each pink palm for torture after the first stroke had reminded her of just how painful this form of punishment was, not to speak of the humiliation of being beaten as a child might be at school. The weals rose thick and red across her palm and the whole hand seemed swollen and inflamed. Eve wondered if she'd even be able to hold a consolatory glass afterwards. By the time it was over she was weeping unrestrainedly, burying her wounded paws in her armpits for comfort. Nevertheless, Eve noted, she had no hesitation afterwards in kissing the rod that had cut her so cruelly, nor in thanking her accuser and executioner for pointing out the error of her ways.

No sooner had the woman expressed her gratitude for her correction, than Daphne pounced.

"Lillian, would you mind turning towards the door darling. Ah, just as I thought. Do you know that your zipper pull it sticking out?"

The redhead's fingers went instinctively to where the seam of her skirt ran up the invisible divide of her rear to the small of her elegant back, finding the metal tag protruding from the pleat.

"Oh damn you, Dee. Trust you to spot it. OK. What's the score?"

"Six of the veriest, of course darling," Daphne purred, and Eve could have sworn she licked her lips as she said it. "Just ask at the door for a penal will you, then come here and bare your bum."

Lillian was well constructed, Eve thought, beginning to find her own tongue inexplicably starting to wander across carefully painted lips. With the skirt removed, and the knickers lowered to the knees, she displayed a generous bum encased in drum tight spandex.

"You can keep that on for three extra," Daphne offered generously. "There's plenty of room for me to work your thighs below the belt, as it were."

It was hardly an inviting offer under the circumstances, and Lillian wisely, Eve thought, elected to snap open the garter tabs on each white thigh and roll the belt up to the fullest part of her pneumatic posterior, hoping no doubt that Daphne would be attracted by the generous expanse of buttock flesh and spare the tender thighs. Again Eve wished her luck. In the mood that was beginning to overtake her friend, and indeed all the women in the room, mercy was the least likely consideration.

"Grip those ankles tight and don't let go," Dee commanded and stood back to watch with satisfaction, the stretching of the ivory globes, now partially restored to their individual rotundity from the solid hemispherical mass confined within the elastic girdle.

The flesh was white but firm, elastic and smooth, just crying out for the cut of cane. Despite her reservations about this fearsome feminine festival, Eve found herself wishing it was her that gripped the solid length of yellow rattan that Daphne was flexing absent-mindedly as she waited for her victim to get into the desired position. Desired by all but the victim herself of course. Lillian quite obviously had no wish to be bent and bared like this, anticipating the bite of the rod into her sensitive buttocks.

A flush of feverish red creeping up Daphne's neck spoke volumes about the lust to punish the pale meat that coursed through her veins, but she was not going to spoil a second of it by rushing the process. She measured off her position by a light tap of the rod on the right cheek, just below the widest part, and drew several deep breaths to steady herself, breaths echoed by the bending victim as she waited for the first cut. The rod hissed, flesh leapt in elastic reaction, and a whiter line, rapidly filled with red, seared the stretched skin. As it darkened and the weal began to rise, Lillian let out a long groan, followed by a hissing through her clenched teeth. Eve knew enough about the timing of such a stroke, and its aftermath, to know that the woman was now feeling the true agony of the cut. When it first impacted, the nerves were temporarily numbed by the shock, a mercy that lasted no more than milli-seconds. After that came a swift and steady rise, each second passing adding its dole to the searing hurt, until the owner of the abused flesh could not believe it could get worse. After which inevitably it did. Lillian's knuckles whitened as she gripped her slim, strapped ankles and tried to ride out the pain. As she seemed to relax a little, holding the pain in check for now, Daphne wound up the spring of her body and unleashed another scorcher a hair's-breadth below the first.

Again the woman rode it out, rocking backwards and forwards a little as if to try and balance herself against the terrible forces working their evil in her behind. Daphne waited until she stilled and drove in another. This time she dropped her aim and found the slight crease between buttock and thigh. Eve watching with mounting arousal had marked this spot out for herself, mentally willing her friend to drive the rod into that soft succulent spot. With the pressure of the rolled up girdle above, the lower buttock halves were pushed firmly down and accentuated this crucial divide, and the rod sank almost out of sight into the soft sensitive mass, springing free after seeming to cling and burrow into the white meat. Lilliam visibly shook, and a small howl of distress escaped her lips.

"Felt that did we darling?" Daphne asked unnecessarily. "Then I think we'll work that spot some more, shall we?"

Lillian was too engaged in coping with the raging fire still rising to a climax in her beaten tush to make any answer and Daphne seemed to assume she had her agreement as the next stroke fell directly into that same scorched suculus. Lillian howled again. Four down and two to go. Eve caught herself wishing it was a dozen, as she watched the half imprisoned hinds work and writhe together as Lillian shifted her weight from toe to toe to try and ease her agony. Five fell, as Eve had half foreseen, on the resilient, but less generously covered, thighs, fully an inch below the tortured trench of the buttock crease. If Lillian was grateful for the removal to a distant clime she did not show it. Her head came back and she mewled like a cat.

"You might at least cane my bottom," she protested. "That was half way to my knees."

"Patience, patience, lovely Lily," Daphne purred, more cat-like than ever, "you shall have your wish," and lashed the last stroke with her full weight behind it into the now ripening spoor of the first strokes, swollen and hot, raised a finger thick above the smoothness of the rest of the alabaster bum flesh, and tender as all hell.

When Lillian had regained a little of her composure, together with her knickers and, of course, the girdle hoisted tightly over the burning welts, the garter snaps once more tight and true, she kissed the rod Daphne offered her, and offered thanks for her correction in tones that Eve could have sworn were almost sincere.

"Now that's what I call a well cut bottom," Daphne remarked in tones of considerable satisfaction as she watched the tearful Lillian shuffle off to seek what comfort she could in the powder room, "I doubt there's any woman in the room who could have caused more grief with just six strokes."

"You certainly hurt her," Eve agreed. "Did you see how she jerked at the last? I rather thought she might have broken position at that one."

"So did I darling, so did I, but we must all face disappointments from time to time."

"You'd better take care to stay out of her way the rest of the evening," Eve warned," she'll be hot for revenge after what you did to her."

Daphne looked genuinely shocked.

"Oh darling," she said," I thought you understood. There's nothing like that about it. No one harbours thoughts like that here. It's a kind of sport. Like tennis you know, or golf. A battle of wits and mind over matter. Besides," she added," it would be against the rules. You can't call out someone who's already beaten you. Mind you, Lillian would do well to make sure she's A1 before she ventures out of the ladies' room again. She's still fair game and I fancy another dose on top of my handiwork might be a tad uncomfortable. They should be ripening to their best about now. I bet she's locked in a stall, gripping her bum and hopping from leg to leg."

"Hi Daphne who's your friend?"

While they had been discussing the state of the unfortunate Lillian's burning backside, a small blonde girl, with a dainty, but athletic build and an angelic expression; had come over to join them.

"Oh Hi Denise. This is my old college friend, Eve. She's staying with us to mend a broken heart and see how we live here. Eve meet Denise Smiley."

Greetings exchanged, the conversation returned to the burning issue of the moment, to wit, Lillian's hard hewn buns.

"Great show," Denise congratulated her friend, "I don't think I've seen a better sixer at one of these catfights."

Daphne acknowledged the praise almost coyly.

"Thanks. I did put in my best effort."

"Oh, I can see that," Denise replied sweetly. "In fact you put so much effort behind it I do believe your bra strap has come adrift."

Eve's eyes flew to Daphne's generous cleavage. A telltale sliver of white bra strap just barely showed against the blue of her dress.

"Oh damn," Daphne said, without any great concern. "You would spot that. Okay I suppose you want my pants off for a sixer."

Clearly she didn't rate the diminutive Denise's prowess with the cane as anything more than a minor infliction which her meaty and well practised buttocks could accommodate without undue distress.

"A sixer, yes," Denise agreed, "but you can keep your panties. Prayer time for you darling."

A shadow of fear passed over the culprit's face.

"Oh no, Denny. you wouldn't do that to me. Or would you?" she finished doubtfully.

"Just watch me. Untidy bra means bruised boobs. You know the rules," Denise said without a change of tone. "Now stop wasting time and let's adjourn to the oratory."

The oratory proved to be an alcove, furnished with a 'prie dieu', one of those combined kneeling stools and bookrests on which devout ladies of times past knelt to say their prayers

118

and bring their bulging bosoms to a level where their swains, or their confessors, if they were not the same, might look deep into the cleavage and if heaven were with them, just glimpse the edge of a brown areola, or the pinkness of a tender dug. From a padded base to soften the pressure on delicate knees, the carved wood stand rose to breast height but, instead of the sloping rest, on which a pious lady might lay her breviary, the top was horizontal, though its front edge still carried a serrated raised ridge like that provided to hold a book from slipping.

Daphne stood in front of it with little enthusiasm evident.

"Alright, Dee. Get your top stuff off and assume the position. You know what to do."

Daphne lowered the zip between her shoulders and peeled down the top of her dress, then unhooked and removed the offending bra. Her slightly pendulous mammaries jounced softly on her chest as she dropped to her knees on the 'prayer desk'. As she did so, the full implication of what was happening finally came home to the watching Eve. This 'prayer stool' was designed for the support, not of holy text, but very carnal breast meat, which would then be thrashed excruciatingly.

"Okay. Lay them out," Denise ordered rather more forcefully than usual, her voice thickened a trifle by a lust that Eve found infectious and crotch kindling.

Dee put a hand under each heavy dug and lifted them onto the shelf of the prayer stand, sliding her hands out from under the luscious mounds which lay on the shelf like stranded sea creatures on a rocky ledge. They flattened slightly under their own considerable weight, causing the fat teats to thrust even more emphatically forward. Eve noticed with surprise that, despite Dee's obvious apprehension, and the warmth of the room, the teats were stiff and engorged, and the areolae that surrounded them were puckered and swollen, and darker than she recalled during their hours of amorous play, as if the blood had built up in them.

Denise came round behind the kneeling penitent and took hold of a heavy leather strap attached to the top edge, pulling it tight behind Dee's back.

"Breathe in," she commanded and yanked the buckle up another couple of notches until Daphne's chest was crushed hard against the curve of the carved timber top, making it impossible for her to withdraw even a fraction; her quivering dugs effectively anchored in position, however much she might wish to remove them from danger later.

With both women panting from the effects of this last effort, Denise was still not finished.

"I'd better cuff your hands behind you," she said, "I'm going to really hurt you this time, and I don't think you'll be able to keep your hands from straying to these luscious boobs without a little help. It'll only cost you a couple extra."

"I can take it," Daphne retorted quickly. "Six will be quite enough, thank you."

"Have it your own way, then," Denise replied, and reached into the inside of the prayer stand to come out with a length of clear plastic tubing.

"Oh God! Denny! No!" Dee burst out at the sight of it. "Not that, please."

Up to this point she had seemed to has faced her coming ordeal with relative equanimity but the sight of the slightly yellowish hose, swinging loosely in Denise's tiny grip seemed to have unnerved her. She was almost whimpering as she pleaded with her tormentor.

"Oh please, Denny, you don't know how that hurts," she begged. "Not the hose, please. Use the strap. I can take that."

"Ah but I do know," her fair haired executioner replied, "I got it with this several years back now, but I still remember it as if it were just last week. You don't forget this in a hurry."

Eve looked with renewed interest at the diminutive blonde. Beneath the soft material of her dress two compact, but significant cones strained to push the thin silk aside, nicely separated globes that didn't appear to have the benefit of a bra. She tried to picture them bare with the hose snaking across them.

"I ached for days afterwards," Denise assured her captive audience," and so will you. I told you I was going to hurt you, and the beauty of it is, I'll know exactly what you'll be feeling. And not just tonight either. I'll think of you nursing your aching boobs as I have breakfast in the morning. Come to that at tea and dinner too. You won't spend a minute without being conscious of your bruises for the best part of a week, I promise you."

Daphne made a brave effort to tough it out, which deceived nobody.

"I can take it," she ground out between gritted teeth, and grasped one wrist with her other hand in a vice-like grip behind her back. Eve knew enough about local conditions to guess that to bring one's hands to one's wounded teats would at best invalidate the stroke, at worst lead to having to take the whole punishment over.

Denise draped the clinging length of flexible plastic lightly on the slumberous flesh laid out so invitingly. As she lifted it Daphne turned her head away and squeezed her eyes closed.

"Oh no you don't," Denise called sharply," chin up and face the front, and don't you dare close your eyes again."

With a small moan of defeat she faced forward again, and lifted her chin high to clear the hose, when, as it inevitably would, it cracked across her tender bubs.

"That's right darling," Denise murmured, reverting to her normal sweetness, lust temporarily in hand, if not entirely stifled, and brought the stinging length of piping cracking down onto the soft white globes laid out like a sacrifice before her.

Daphne's head jerked back violently and her mouth gaped in a silent scream. For a split second she hung in rigid silence, then from her throat came a long low mewling sound.

On the altar-like shelf in front of her, the soft sensitive flesh of her breasts had nowhere to go. Held up firmly by the unyielding wood, it had to accept the full passion of the hose's kiss, bruising it to the core. As the narrow tubing bounced back, the pale groove of its impact rapidly darkened to a blood red. Daphne's breath returned in a hissing intake and the hose lifted again.

Daphne snorted and moaned, hissed and whined, but held to her task. Though her upper body writhed in pain, her breasts never actually left the shelf on which they were laid for their terrible immolation, and her hands stayed clasped together as if welded tight. Thirty agonising seconds later, three throbbing stripes lay across the blazing boobs, close packed and parallel, nearly touching Daphne's heaving chest. Denise may have seemed too slight to have inflicted real damage to her backside but she was accuracy incarnate when it came to breasts, and wristy with it, causing serious havoc to the tender boobs from the first.

Four was a beast. It fell exactly across each teat, where it stood out like a baby's thumb from its swollen and inflamed dug. Daphne shrieked at the unexpected change of direction and her hands shot forward as if to clutch and protect the tender points. Just in time she checked and fought a savage battle with herself, her fists bunched and quivering by her ears, her riven nipples screaming for ease, while that part of her mind still rational amid the pain was shouting equally loudly not to touch at any price or there would be even more of the same. Prudence won out in the end, but it cost her dear, and she was sweating freely before her hands eventually went back behind her back.

"A wise decision," Denise commended her, and cracked the hose across the bursting bulbs in exactly the same place.

This time Daphne just plain howled. It was almost too much. Again her hands came free and she fought the battle all over again, emitting strange honking noises from the depth of her throat as she tried to keep her hands from the aching orbs. The teats were now as hard and round as Morrello cherries and about the same colour. As her struggles and cries subsided Denise remarked in her sweetest tones," have you finished darling. Ready?"

Too overcome to speak, Daphne nodded dumbly, her lips peeled back from her teeth in a rictus of pain. Snot and tears ran down her cheeks, and her body shook from time to time with the effort of keeping her hands from her ravaged breasts lying on the shelf below that hideous length of pipe. The sullen looking heaps of beaten flesh lay quivering gently for the last. Eve waited tensed for it to crack across the bulging nipples once more, wondering if they might not split. It was almost with a sense of disappointment that she watched the hose flash down again to meet the leaden lumps of breast meat across their fullest width.

CHAPTER 7 MORE LADYLIKE BEHAVIOUR

"Another satisfied customer," Denise remarked, a little smugly Eve thought, as Daphne stumbled away a minute later, her arms cradling her wounded jugs, the dress still hanging about her waist, her bra thrown over one shoulder by a dismissive Denise.

"The thing is they think I can't hurt them, being a bit on the small side. Well there's one that knows different now."

"Do you think I should go after her, and make sure she's alright?" Eve asked, full of contrition for the way she had allowed herself to be swept along on the waves of hot uncontrollable desire that had filled her belly during the breast lashing.

"I shouldn't if I were you," Denise advised, "A girl likes to be alone with her tears at times like this. Time enough for your sympathy when she comes back. If I know our Dee, she'll have mended her mood with her make-up, and be chipper as usual when she does come back."

Well not quite, Eve thought, watching her friend's return, some fifteen minutes later. She managed something near a genuine smile for friends who greeted or condoled with her, but there was something a little stiff about it, as in the way she moved. Her bra was back in hiding again but the deep cleavage was crossed by several angry dark bruises, that not even Max Factor's best cover-all could disguise, and there were still hints of red rims around her eyes.

Once more the circus roared around them, bared woman flesh of all description regularly called upon to accept rod, strap or paddle, to expurgate those sins of dress and deportment that their friends pointed out so helpfully. By now they had been joined by a tall athletic brunette, who Daphne introduced as Lavinia.

"Larry comes from the other side of the island," she explained, "You'll have to visit some time. They have interesting activities of their own over there. Make your hair curl. Regular tartars, and that's just the women."

"Take no notice, she's only jealous," Lavinia advised, "but do come and stay. The races start next month. Come over for the opening meeting."

"Love to," Eve agreed. She liked the look of this tall friendly new acquaintance.

The three of them moved about from group to group, chatting here, watching there. As the evening wore on Eve was finding it more and more difficult to distinguish between winces of sympathy for some choice hurt suffered by a bare and bending delinquent, and spasms of hot desire that rippled through her belly and set her cunt weeping, though not exactly tears of sympathy. Daphne seemed almost completely recovered now, but Eve fancied she saw the occasional trace of fear flicker across her face if an acquaintance seemed to be inspecting her visually a little too deeply, and from time to time she caught her looking down at her heels, running a hand over her stocking seams on the back of her thighs, or trying to catch a glimpse of herself in a mirrored surface. She did not think the latter was a matter of vanity.

Watching her friend, she failed to observe that Lavinia was watching her.

"You must be one of the few not carrying some marks by now," Lavinia remarked suddenly. Daphne covered Eve's confusion quickly.

"Oh Eve's a visitor," she assured her, "she's excused."

"I may be only a visitor but I certainly don't wish to be excused," Eve answered hotly, "I've just been lucky; that's all."

Late in the evening Lavinia found her way over to where Daphne stood with Eve, having a last drink before getting ready to depart. The two friends stood chatting for a while, comparing their various and numerous stripes and bruises, laughing over the comical fates of some of their mutual friends. Suddenly Lavinia turned her whole gaze on Eve, where she stood quietly taking in their discussion.

"And what about you, darling?" she asked, "did you collect some mementos of our little soiree?"

"I stayed lucky," Eve replied, "I managed to avoid attention all evening."

"A picture of perfection," Daphne chimed in, "not a mark on her; clothes or bottom."

Lavinia's eyes did not waver for a moment from their fixed stare locked onto Eve's own.

"Is that so?" she murmured thoughtfully. "Well we'll soon see about that."

A sly smile flicked over her lips.

"Good little girl are we? Put on clean knickers just like mummy said?"

"Of course," Eve replied, "everything trim and nice, just as Dee prescribed."

"Show!"

Lavinia almost snapped the word and Eve looked at her puzzled.

"Get your pants down and show me your gusset." Lavinia demanded.

Eve hesitated a second then reached under her dress It was a snug fit, and she had to ruck it up tightly before she could reach her pants. Thumbs hooked into the elastic waistband, she slid the silken garment over her hips and stood on each leg in turn to release it and hand it to her interrogator, feeling cool air on exposed moist membranes as she did so. Lavinia took the proffered scrap of exquisite lingerie and turned it inside out, applying the gusset to her flaring nostrils. Eve blushed deeply as she saw the moisture was not confined to her crotch. The gus- set gleamed with her secretions.

"Smells of old fish and sticky with it," Lavinia declared. "Ripe and soaking; as soiled a pair of skimpies as I've ever tasted and an utter disgrace."

Daphne stepped in to defend her friend.

"Come off it, Larry, you know damn well there's not a woman in the room who hasn't wet her pants by now. You can smell musk everywhere you go. You can't call Eve out for that."

"But I just have," Lavinia replied sweetly. "Unless, of course, your little friend wants to hide behind her status as a guest?"

Eve had no doubts as to what lay ahead. Penalties were always dealt out on the nearest part of the anatomy to the offending dress item, and there could only be one place in contact with that ripely soaked scrap of cloth Lavinia was waving at her accusingly. But she wasn't about to hide behind her status as a guest. She had already committed herself too deeply for that to be an option.

"OK, you win," she said. "How do you want me?"

"Sure you don't want to appeal?" Daphne asked anxiously. "You've got a good case, Larry means to strap your cunt. You do realise that, don't you?"

"Would you appeal?" Eve challenged her.

"Er, well, perhaps not. But then I'm a resident," Daphne said lamely.

"Quite so," Eve replied grimly," No. No appeal. Lead on

Lavinia and let's get it over with."

Lavinia led the way to a low narrow coffee table.

"Hike up your skirt, and put your bum on the end," she instructed. With her dress pulled up onto her hips, Eve gingerly placed her buttocks on the edge of the polished wood, placing her feet slightly apart to steady herself.

"Now lie back and put your arms down and grip the legs that end."

Eve obeyed, then was ordered to put her feet further apart and spread her knees to open up her thighs and put her vulnerable pudenda on display. Strangely, although by now she was beginning to feel real fear, her vulva was wetter than ever. Lavinia leant over her and pushed the gusset of the offending panties between her teeth.

"This is going to hurt," she said, "and you'll be better off for something to bite on."

In view of what she expected lay ahead, Eve accepted the moist rag almost with gratitude tasting herself salty on her tongue, the musk of her sex strong in her nostrils. Her fears were doubled when Lavinia unclipped the suspender on the front of her girdle, so that she could turn back the front panel, leaving the tender female meat totally open and exposed.

Lavinia hauled up her own dress above her waist and threw one long shapely nylon-clad leg over Eve and the table until she stood astride her waist, facing her feet. Looking up Eve was treated to a view of a tightly packed girdle, covered by a pair of panties whose crotch was patently as soaked as her own offending garment. Below, a series of livid welts from some earlier adventure adorned the soft white flesh of the thighs, where they sprang bare from the stocking tops, hauled hawser tight by the constricting roll-on. Despite her own fear and danger she felt a sudden rush of lust as she watched the play of the firm muscles under the welts.

She could also see a long narrow black leather snake dangling from Lavinia's hand as she positioned herself, a snake that disappeared as Lavinia brought her hands together in front of her and raised them high.

"Stand by for six scorchers," she announced and the strap whistled as it descended. With an audible 'thuck', it fell across the wet slot of the pouting vulva. Eve screamed behind her impromptu gag and jerked her legs together, blasted by the searing agony of the assault on her most tender woman's parts. Lavinia let her writhe for thirty seconds or so then called her to order.

"You have to keep your legs open," she declared, "That stroke won't count, and nor will the next, if your thighs aren't wide open when the following stroke is due. Do I make myself clear?"

Eve moaned in assent and forced her reluctant legs to part and offer up her aching mound for the next awful belt. When it came she could not hold out, and jacked her thighs closed again, but had sufficient mind left, not to speak of fear of incurring even one extra stroke of that cruel leather, to make her muscles obey her and open up after only five seconds or so.

Lavinia was almost purring as she raised the strap again. This time, when she brought it down, she leaned forward with it, and let the thong go a touch deeper, so that the tip found its way into the bottom of the buttock crack and seared the anal bud itself. Once again Eve went into convulsions, strange whining noises coming down her streaming nostrils, bubbling through the spattering mucus. It took longer to regain control, but she laid herself open again in time to avoid further penalty and Lavinia struck again. Once more the strap fell full on the swollen vulva, its liquidity apparently undiminished by the pounding, judging by the wet smack of the impact, and the liquid spray it shot onto the inside of the splayed thighs. Three equally wet and weeping strokes later and Eve was at the end of her tether, her belly filled with anguish and heat, writhing uncontrollably on the hard bench, snorting with pain, her face a mask of snot and tears, her make-up in ruins, but she had won through. Tenderly Lavinia prised the panties from her clenching teeth and used them to wipe away the disgusting film from her face, before bending and kissing her full on her bitten lips.

"You were wonderful, darling," she breathed, "I've never enjoyed whipping a cunt so much in all my life."

Eve, returning her kiss with interest, her belly and genitals burning with arousal as much as with appalling agony, could only wonder how often she had indulged in this awful but electrifying sport.

A minute later she was allowed to sit up and adjust the tabs of the girdle to haul the nylons spinnaker taut again, before attempting to stand. She found she could not close her legs properly, so sore and swollen was her sex and, as for panties, she threw decorum to the winds, and the saturated underpants in the trash. Daphne and Lavinia helped her waddle, legs aspraddle, to the powder room, now taking on the appearance of a casualty clearing station in some particularly desperate battle zone, where she joined a knot of other women repairing the damage of the action, all moving stiffly in one way or another. As they were leaving, Lavinia kissed Eve again, this time with not quite the same hot inflamed passion, but warmly enough.

"Remember, you must come over and stay with us soon," she declared. "There's so much to see on the other side of the island, and I'm sure you'd enjoy it. I'll give you a ring once you've recovered."

Despite the fact that this woman had just whipped her cruelly on her genitals, Eve found herself responding as warmly, and promising to visit soon.

Their homeward progress was stately and sedate. Daphne was making sure no pot-holes or other obstacles set her aching breasts leaping in their nylon hammocks. As the car hummed quietly along, Eve remarked on the ferocity with which the women sought out each others' weaknesses, and punished them so severely.

"It's just a healthy outlet for our natural competitiveness," Daphne explained," all women look on each other as potential rivals and this is a way of letting those feelings come out without doing any damage to relationships."

"No damage! They must all hate each other by now."

"Really? Is that how you feel about Lavinia?"

"Well perhaps not," she admitted, "Yes, I see what you mean, although she did half pulp my cunt. I don't think I'll ever be able to take pleasure from it again."

"You want to bet? I guarantee that before the night is through you'll be howling like a bitch in heat."

"Oh Daphne, what a ridiculous idea. Anyway," Eve added semi-hysterically, "I suppose you could say we were damn lucky."

"What on earth do you mean?"

"Well, when you were shooing me out of the house, you remarked that we'd be damned lucky to come home with less than a dozen apiece on our bums and, just look at us. Not a scratch between us. Battered boobs and a ruined cunt, but not a mark on our bums."

Daphne's prophesies proved right on one point though. True enough, the throbbing in her cunt drove sleep away, and she lay tossing on her bed, unable to settle. At first it was pain, but soon the old feminine alchemy turned it to ever hotter desire, especially as she caught the sounds of Daphne's orgasmic howls from the bedroom at the far end of the same balcony on which her own opened. All those thoughts of hot masculine gristle filling her aching void returned, with interest. For a long while she tried to drive them away, but they would not be put down. Her own fingers failed her too. Apart from the fact that her swollen tender love bud was too sore to touch, her mind was set on hard shafts and male dominance, not dainty feminine ministrations. Daphne's howls had long since silenced into satisfaction, but still she could not sleep. She threw off the sweat soaked sheet and wandered naked onto the veranda, hoping desperately that the cool night air and the quiet sounds of the nightlife in the bushes might soothe her enough for her to return to bed.

Quite bare, she rested her arms on the wooden rail, flinching momentarily as the rough timber brushed her nipples, then deliberately letting them rub along the harsh bark, generating part pain, part pleasure that did nothing to cool her mood of arousal. Somewhere to her left a small bright red eye opened and shut at the far end of the veranda, where Gordon and Daphne's room lay. Someone, it could only be Gordon, was leaning there smoking a cigar.

Her first instinct was to flee back to her own room, but the raging demon between her legs was having none of that. She had heard Daphne receiving her share of 'consolation' earlier, as she had tried in vain for sleep, and now it was her turn. Slowly she began to walk along the long bare boards towards that beckoning eye. When she was about half way along, the eye became a shooting star, describing a high parabola into the air before falling to the shrubs below the balcony. Gordon had seen her pale white form moving in the starlight and was coming towards her. She stopped and waited with unwonted docility for his approach.

"Couldn't you sleep either? Dee was very restless at first, although she's sleeping sound enough now."

"I should think so," Eve replied, jealousy lending an edge to her voice. "She howled like a cat through at least three orgasms."

"You wouldn't deny a girl her consolations would you?" Gordon remarked coolly.

"It wouldn't be so bad if we all got them," Eve replied bitterly," there are some of us who have certain needs."

"What can you mean?" Gordon mocked her.

It was too much. The dam burst. Molten lava swept all caution away.

"Damn you! You know perfectly well what I mean. I need prick, I need a man. I need you. Fuck me, stuff me, cram me, ram me, do anything you like to me but shove that great shaft

131

of yours right up me until I choke on it. I can't go on like this any longer."

"You're desperate for it, aren't you," he observed.

"God Gordon, yes. I've just got to have it. Please Gordon. It's not fair. You saw to Daphne so she could get to sleep. Do the same for me. After all," she concluded with an insane giggle, "I am your guest, and it's a host's duty to satisfy a guest's wants."

"OK, you win, but I caned her first, to settle her. She was as rabid as you."

"Then cane me too. I don't care. Anything you like, but fuck my brains out. I can't take any more of this."

"Spoken like an Edenite," Gordon said approvingly. "Go back to your room while I hunt out a cane."

Almost crying from a heady mixture of lust, fear and need she scuttled back to her room and threw herself on the rumpled sheets again, her hands instinctively clasping her aching belly. Thirty seconds later Gordon stood in the doorway, flexing a serious looking rod between his fists.

"Hands and knees, please, with your back to me," he dictated. "You're getting eight this time"

She didn't care or rather, was past caring. All she wanted was that enormous bulge that tented his dressing gown in front, and she didn't care what it cost to get it.

The first stroke almost sent her flying. She hadn't remembered what a penal felt like in her rush to get fucked. Now it all came back in spades, but her need carried her through. She howled and squirmed as each hot lick bit into her flaming buttock flesh, but her beaten hams were always back in place for another stroke before he had to remind her. Cut after cut slowly mounted, forming a tight hot swollen ladder of rapidly darkening welts, nearly four inches wide by the time eight were packed in.

He was right though. It steadied her. She was half mad with desire when she started; by the time the last had fallen she had calmed sufficiently that she was aware of the coming sexual act for its own sake, though still aching with her hunger for it.

As Gordon laid down the rod, she made as if to turn, but he checked her with a word. Suddenly she felt a hard object nosing at her tight sealed sphincter.

"Not there, please," she pleaded, "in my cunt."

"You'll have all you can take later. For now this is my fee for servicing you," Gordon said thickly, and thrust his hips forward brutally.

She screamed, but the rod went home, and the filling of her belly was relief in itself. Her heat was such that she could ignore the new pain of her stretched anus and concentrate on the feelings generated by this male penetration. As he began to ride her those feelings rose rapidly in a screaming crescendo. She had been sodomised once or twice before, usually at the beginning of an affair, when she would have done anything to please a new lover, but, for the first time in her life, she could feel an orgasm building from her buggery. Gordon caught and nurtured it with careful timing, until she howled like a bitch, just as Daphne had predicted, then withdrew his smoking rod without discharging himself. Only then did he let her turn onto her back, and plugged her needy vagina, forcing the massy rod up to the hilt in the swollen sopping orifice. He pumped her vigorously, as she squirmed and howled under him, clasping her legs about him as she went into a second belly-churning spasm, then allowed himself to discharge into her gulping womb as she crested her third orgasm of the night.

Her arms and legs relaxed, and she lay, panting under him. She looked up sleepily.

"Thank you, Gordon, that was wonde....." she began. As he withdrew his softening shaft from the slick tunnel he looked down at her sleeping body, limbs thrown wide open to reveal the inflamed and engorged vulva, still swollen from its thrashing, a thin stream of their mingled seed and juices seeping stickily down to stain the sheets between her open thighs.

"You'll do," he murmured softly.

It was noon next day, when Eve tapped gently on Daphne's door and went in to return the clothes she had borrowed for the previous evening.

"Er," she hesitated, holding out the stockings, the gloves, the cheeky little hat, the smart suede pumps, "do you mind if I keep the girdle a little longer. Actually," she added, with

unusual coyness, "I thought I might try wearing it all day."

Daphne grinned knowingly.

"Nice and comforting, isn't it? Even when it squeezes the welts on your arse together. Or should that be, especially when it squeezes them."

"Er. Yes. Actually, Gordon caned me last night. Did he tell you?

"I already knew."

"How!"

"Well, apart from the fact that I heard you howling like a pig, and not only when he caned you, I just caught sight of the welts sticking out under the edge of that girdle you're so keen to wear."

Blushing furiously, Eve dropped her other bits and pieces on Daphne's dressing table and retired in confusion.

Gordon returned that evening to find two calm, attentive and seemingly content young women waiting for him, though he did note that both were very careful how they set their buttocks on their chairs when it was time for dinner.

"Met an admirer of yours at the club today," he remarked, turning towards Eve. She looked at him blankly.

"An admirer?" Daphne was all curiosity, "do tell."

"Angus McKensie," Gordon obliged, "You remember. Your Scottish friend from the airport."

"He's no friend of mine," Eve retorted hotly, "a real MCP if ever there was one."

"Don't you want to know what he said?" Gordon asked, winking at his wife.

"I can't stop you if you insist on telling," Eve replied

rather unconvincingly.

"The club was buzzing with the dark deeds of your witches coven last night," Gordon informed them. "All the husbands and others reporting what they'd been told by their wives and mistresses. Seems that we weren't the only household with confessions and absolutions last night," he added with a grin. Daphne and Eve chose to ignore the allusion.

"Anyway, it seems our Eve was quite the heroine. Everybody was full of praise for the visitor, and the way she entered into the spirit of the thing, allowing Lavinia to call her out, and taking a cunt busting with considerable courage."

Eve looked down modestly at her plate.

"Anyway, it served to increase Angus's already high opinion of you, from your short time together and knowing you were under my wing, he sent his compliments on your behaviour."

"The cheek of the man, and how typically patronising of him!" Eve burst out indignantly, "he can stuff his compliment. The man means nothing to me."

Daphne and her husband exchanged knowing glances over her bent head, as she studiously concentrated on her steak tartare. Both were thinking of the Bard's dictum about protesting too much.

Lavinia was as good as her word. Her call came just a week after the gathering, and by then Eve was beginning to walk without spreading her legs wide, in imitation of a duck, to keep the pressure off her pussy. It was still sore, but a companionable soreness. It kept her wetly conscious of herself, but not so much as to distract her completely from what was going on around her. In accordance with the unwritten law of the island, she and Daphne didn't try to hide from the world, and visited with neighbours, lay by the pool, their stripes and bruises little concealed by tanga bottoms, and discarded tops. Daphne's swollen breasts excited universal admiration, with their livid bruising, now turning rainbow coloured, and her battered nipples, still refusing to resume their habitual baby pink.

Eve was even persuaded to sit a horse before the week was up. She moaned a few times from the pounding of her bruised pussy on the hard leather saddle, and Daphne cut the ride shorter than she would have done merely on account of Gordon's stripes that radiantly adorned both bottoms. All in all it was a quick recovery as healthy young women can make in such circumstances.

"Come over tomorrow," Lavinia urged. "Pack for a fortnight at least. There's the races coming soon, and you wouldn't want to miss those."

After she rang off, Eve reported the gist of the conversation to Daphne, who smiled enigmatically.

"Oh no," she said, "you mustn't miss the races. They're something special."

"In what way special?" Eve wanted to know, but Daphne told her she'd find out in due course, and wouldn't add anything further.

Eve tried another tack. Was Lavinia wife or mistress, and what was the difference in this peculiar society?

"Not a lot," Daphne admitted," most women are both, in any case. Lavinia is married to Mark, as it happens, but I'm pretty sure she is the regular mistress of one of Mark's friends as well. That's apart from the occasional use of her that he offers to guests and other acquaintances."

"Don't the women get a say in these things?" Eve asked indignantly.

"Well, in theory, we are completely at our husbands' disposal, and just do as we're told, but it's not exactly unknown for a woman to indicate that she's interested in some man, in which case a sensible husband will permit the liaison, even formally instructing her to go to him. Sometimes there's a price though."

"There always is," Eve remarked dourly. "Don't tell me; let me guess. Something to do with rods and bottoms?"

"Got it in one, though by now I'm not surprised. You've seen enough of our ways. Yes, they may be expected to pay in the local currency for the privilege. Many a man finds his dish spiced with a fresh hot sixer each time he has her, which does nothing to diminish the enthusiasm of either party to the affair."

"A month ago I wouldn't have believed you," Eve admitted. "Even a week ago, I'd have said you were exaggerating but now, after my own ....experiences," she flushed slightly as she recalled how hot she'd been when Gordon 'took' her after first lashing her bared buttocks with a penal -"well I can see there might be something in it."

"Don't play the innocent with me, young lady," Daphne said laughing, "I know just what you're thinking. Well I'm very happy for you that Gordon striped you and stuffed you that night, and I'm sure you learnt a lot from it. And the previous evening's events too. You're beginning to appreciate the finer points of our way of life, like the pleasure of seeing a woman well beaten, as well as the satisfaction of being that woman yourself."

"You've got it all wrong," Eve protested. "I wouldn't get the slightest pleasure from seeing a woman beaten. It does nothing for me."

"You lying little hussy," Daphne cried without malice. "You even wanted to see me beaten. Not that I blame you," she hastened to add," a woman bent over the bars is beautiful, all buttock, lovely female flesh; with any luck, a plump pudenda pouting through the gap. And then the cane cutting into it. The flesh lifting as if of its own accord. Maybe a grunt or a moan. Perhaps she'll lift one hip as she goes up on tip-toe, to try and keep the rod from her flank. It's a test of fortitude and a struggle against the rod. Pure poetry. You're not telling me you're not moved by it, if it's only to wet your knickers."

CHAPTER 8 TWENTY-FIVE

The south side of the island was even more scenic and remote than the wooded hills where Daphne and Gordon lived. Some hours from the Capital, the hills here could legitimately be called mountains, and the woods more wild and extensive.

Mark and Lavinia's home was an old plantation house, from the days when the island depended on sugar and pineapples for a living, before it became the refuge of men with serious money, wanting to create a world of their own, free from outside influences. For the first day or two Eve was content merely to laze by the pool, drinking in the scenery that lay before them and meeting Lavinia's friends, all anxious to greet the rare phenomenon of a visitor from 'outside'. Moreover a visitor whose reputation had gone before her. Those who had been at the Ladies' night, and seen her cunt whipped, had brought back inspiring descriptions of her ordeal. Actually Eve was constantly surprised at her own reaction to the woman who had so cruelly whipped her pussy. From the moment they had met again she had felt not resentment, but affection, and it was not long before this had become intimacy. On her first evening, settling into bed, bare to take advantage of the mildness of the night, she was joined by her new friend, sent by a generous husband to fulfil the duties of a hostess. At first it was just a matter of apologising for taking advantage of her at the Ladies' night, and asking to see how her wounds had healed. This led to a kiss of atonement on the afflicted spot, a kiss that prolonged itself into a gentle nibbling, a sensuous licking, a volcanic eruption, that sealed their friendship.

Perhaps it was something in the air, but Eve became aware that all the young women she met around the pool, or taking drinks in the cool of the evening, playing tennis at the club or just chatting in each other's homes, had an air of healthy sexuality about them. She could feel it in her own vulva, which seemed constantly moist and plumper than before she had

138

come to the island, and she could see the same symptoms in the pudenda of the others on the frequent opportunities when those delightful parts were on view, in showers or poolside, since there was no false modesty among these hale and whole-some young women, and their bodies were constantly without benefit of clothing.

The exception, surprisingly, was Lavinia. Not to start with; during the first week she displayed something of the same vibrant animal health as the others, but then came a rapid deterioration. She became withdrawn, nervous, taut in every fibre. Finally Eve asked if anything was the matter.

"PMT," Lavinia replied tersely.

"Oh you poor dear," Eve commiserated," is it always this bad?"

"Not usually. We don't get too much of it here, but two or three times a year my hormones seem to go haywire," her friend replied.

"Is there anything I can do? Have you seen a doctor about it?"

"Don't worry. Mark knows how to handle it. He'll straighten me out. I'll be all right, you'll see."

At dinner that night Lavinia remained tense and withdrawn. Mark was quick to notice her condition.

"That time of the month again, old girl?" he asked sympathetically.

Lavinia nodded.

"A bad one?"

She agreed that it was.

"Better sort you out then. Tonight, after dinner," he said, kindly. "No point in delaying. Soonest dealt soonest mended. Your quarter century I think this time."

Lavinia seemed to hesitate a second but then nodded her agreement once again.

Quarter century? Eve was puzzled. She was sure Daphne had told her Lavinia was her own age, twenty-seven. Must be something else. She put the thought aside and concentrated on trying to kept up an intelligent conversation with Mark, to cover Lavinia's taciturn mood.

After dinner Mark rose from the table and declared briskly, "time we took care of your little problem, Larry. Are you coming to watch this Eve?"

She still hadn't any exact idea of what was afoot, but that phrase 'straighten me out', had an ominous and familiar ring to it. Out here in Eden things were generally straightened out on a woman's bare bottom. This was a marital matter she didn't think she had any part in.

"Eh. I think I'll pass on this one," she said. "Mustn't come between husband and wife. It sounds like a private affair to me."

"Oh please, Eve," Lavinia pleaded, seeming to rouse herself from her lethargy, "I'd like you to be there. Besides," she added, with something of her old spirit, "I promised Daphne you'd see how we lived, warts and all, and she'd never forgive me if I let you duck out."

"Put that way, how can I refuse?" Eve replied with what she hoped was an encouraging grin, and not the embarrassed smirk she feared. "Where are we going?"

They went to a room she hadn't entered until then, a closed door next to Mark's study. It was an austere chamber, stone floored, bare walls, adorned by only some ringbolts, a tall narrow closet and a ladder.

The latter, which captured all Eve's attention, sloped at forty-five degrees from the stone flags to the angle where the bare wall met the equally plain ceiling. In the angle a hook fastened it securely in place. The ladder was of the type used by window cleaners and fruit pickers, the rails two or three feet apart at the base, converging until they met at the apex.

"Perhaps you could get your things off," Mark suggested, and Lavinia stripped slowly and, Eve thought, rather reluctantly. She was not surprised when, although the chamber was not particularly chill, the naked woman seemed to be shivering a little as she waited. Her husband opened the closet and selected a particularly nasty looking yard of thick yellow rattan.

"Up you go," he ordered and Lavinia stepped to the ladder and began to slowly climb up, until she could reach the peak. Fastened to this point, where the tapering rails met, a pair of leather cuffs dangled invitingly. Lavinia buckled them around each wrist and then let herself slide back, until her arms were stretched taut above her head, carrying part of her weight, the other part resting on the harsh timber of the ladder, her voluptuous breasts hanging through a gap. By now Mark had retrieved a narrow strap from the cupboard. Tucking the wicked length of cane beneath one arm, he advanced on his buck naked wife where she hung in her bonds.

"Legs up, darling," he ordered and Lavinia took her toes off the bottom rung and clasped her thighs around the ladder higher up. She had to lift her thighs high to find a position where she could bend her knees and bring her feet together on the other side of the bars. Mark wrapped the strap around her slim ankles and fastened it to the rung above, pulling up tightly.

It must have been an uncomfortable position Eve thought, watching the straining tendons in the inner thighs pressed tight against the unyielding wood while braced to try and take some of her weight off her arms. The frog pose lifted her full bare buttocks off the ladder a little, and the angle of the support meant that a cane could sweep in from underneath with perfect freedom, the whole lower buttock, from thigh top to nearly the top of the bum's deep divide firmly held for its impact.

"Twenty-five would do it, we agreed, I think." Mark remarked without emotion, and Lavinia said almost inaudibly,"yes Mark."

Twenty-five! Now she understood the mysterious reference to a quarter century. Twenty-five strokes to Lavinia's bare but tocks! What a cure for PMT she thought, a little hysterically. She only hoped for her new friend's sake that it was efficacious. It would be a pity to endure a flogging like that and still end up with an aching belly.

Mark did not rush things. It was evident he took his obligations to his wife's well-being seriously, and did not wish her to miss out on any part of the treatment. He took his stance with care, laying the rod on the raised naked buttocks to assess just where to position himself, then, satisfied he had the flinching posteriors lined up accurately, paused again to roll up his right sleeve. Again he measured his mark and seemed satisfied. He drew back his arm, turned the rod back behind his shoulder and let the coiled up energy fly.

A thrumming of parted air and the rod thucked meatily into the cringing mass of perfectly presented posterior. Lavinia let out a short pained 'Ow', and hissed frantically as she sucked on the fierce fires lancing through her abused hinds.

Mark let her have the full benefit of the stroke, then repeated it, drawing another aching searing line right in the sitting-place set up on the ladder at the optimum height for its correction. Full benefit drawn from this cut also, he went on to drive in a third and a fourth.

Eve marvelled at first at how little Lavinia moved under what were obviously strokes of a severity beyond the norm, but soon realised that, although only fastened at wrists and ankles, a woman in this position could make but little movement. Her own weight held her down, especially as she became exhausted by the trauma of a beating such as this, while the way her knees were wrapped around the rails made it very difficult, as well as painful, for her to try and lift herself, even if she still had the strength. Actually, she realised, to be left on the ladder in that position for any length of time would be a severe torture in its own right, never mind with a penal weight cane, wielded by an obviously skilled and experienced male, cutting into your buttocks.

At five the suffering woman got the benefit of a slight pause, while Mark changed his position. Not only was he skilled, but truly ambidextrous it appeared, for he moved the rod to his left hand, and himself to Lavinia's right, and delivered the next five measured cuts from that side with as much force and accuracy as he had the first.

Another pause, and he was back on her left. She was beginning to feel the weakening effects of so much pain now, and cried out at each cut. Eve noticed that she tried desperately to twist her body away from the rod each time, and remembered what Daphne had said about trying to keep the tip of the rod from her flank. She remembered too what Dee had said about the beauty of a naked beaten woman and flushed as she realised she was already wet between the legs. Worse, she caught herself craning forward to see each cut's impact into the flushed and welted flesh, and even resenting the time spent changing sides, so eager was she to see another cut, hear another moan of agony, watch the buttocks clench together, as Lavinia tried to fight the pain.

By the time Mark changed sides for the last time there were twenty livid welts competing for space in the hand's span of once white flesh between the faint outline of the stretched succul fold and the anal level. They looked hot and swollen, though only on the flanks, where the tip had raised thick plum coloured bruises, was she showing signs of significant wear and tear. Still, if her skin had not broken, her spirit was near to it. She lay limp now, like butcher's meat, while the last five awful strokes 'wunked' in with as much force as the first. She cried out at each one, thoroughly beaten in both mind and body, and Eve felt each howl stoking the fires in her own belly. Later, in her room, some of the passion cooled by time and lustful finger play on her aching clitoris, she became ashamed at her feelings but, in the heat of the moment, the cries had been music to her ears, and she had mentally urged Mark to strike even harder. Daphne was right; pure poetry.

Lavinia did not appear for breakfast and Eve, peeking cautiously through her door after Mark had departed, saw she was still sleeping soundly, and sensibly left her to rest. She was on her feet again the next day though, apparently 'cured', though she moved very stiffly, and avoided sitting most of the time. At first Eve was hesitant to raise the matter of her health, not least because of the guilt she still felt, but Lavinia's increasing animation helped to break the ice.

"Much better, thank you," she replied to Eve's nervous enquiries, "I told you Mark knew how to handle me. An ache in the bum, I will admit, but no belly ache now and, if past form's anything to go by, I'll be good for a few months now."

"Seems Daphne was right then, that you Eden females are always at your best after a good flogging," Eve remarked, with a tentative smile.

"Good, you're beginning to become human again," said Lavinia with a relieved smile, "I thought things might become difficult for a while, you seemed so reserved, but now I see it's going to be alright."

"Oh Larry, I'm so glad you're feeling better but I still feel guilty."

"Whatever for? It was Mark's decision and, as usual he was quite right."

"It's not that. While you were there, all splayed out on that ladder, with the cane cutting your behind, I was enjoying it. I actually got wet watching you. and I wanked myself off afterwards too."

"So why on earth should you feel guilty about that? You couldn't do anything about it, to make it better that is, so why shouldn't you enjoy it? We all do. Women have such lovely bottoms, and especially when they're being caned."

"Oh I'm so glad you see it that way. That's how Daphne described it, but I didn't believe her at the time."

"Actually, I'm quite flattered. Nice to know someone likes my bum," Lavinia said with a smile.

"It's a lovely bum," Eve replied emphatically, "though a bit battered at the moment, I'm sure."

"Nothing that a few days' rest, and a little TLC won't cure," Lavinia assured her. "Still a bit scabby on the sides, but that'll pass. One thing though. It's lucky the races don't start until next week. It might be a touch uncomfortable sitting in the stands in my present state."

"Oh yes, the races," Eve exclaimed, "Daphne was dropping large hints that they're somewhat out of the ordinary here, but she didn't say what."

"Then neither shall I," said Lavinia, "let it all come as a delightful surprise."

Mark drove them. Eve had expected the kind of scene she was used to elsewhere, open ground, parks filled with cars, horse boxes lined up, the smell of hay and horses, bookies shouting the odds, all stretched out over a mile or two of downland or heath. Instead they wound up a long wooded drive to a large gracious mansion. True there were cars galore parked round the front and sides of the house, and plenty of smartly dressed people moving about, but little else to betray the fact that a race meeting was being held.

They moved through the house and across the yard behind, to enter a long rather blank looking building. It proved to be a grandstand, filled with an animated crowd, and they emerged on a balcony overlooking a track. At first glance it seemed a standard athletics circuit, two broad straights, about 100 metres long connected by two long bends at either end. But it was what was on the circuit that distinguished it from any other Eve had seen. Moving swiftly round the track were a number of very light trotting 'surreys' skeleton tubular structures, with shafts and lightweight seats, and over-sized bicycle wheels to raise the drivers off the ground. It was not the drivers, conventionally dressed for amateur riders, but what was between the shafts that had Eve catching her breath. Each pair of tubular extensions was filled by a naked girl, her hair tied back in a pony tail, a bridle holding a bit in her mouth, with reins to the rider, and a heavy waistbelt connecting her to the shafts for traction, for her arms were folded and strapped behind her back, helping to thrust out her naked breasts provocatively. Each girl ran round the track with a high-stepping gait, her poise and pace controlled by the reins and the vicious carriage whip in the driver's hand.

145

"Well, didn't I tell you it would be a delightful surprise?" Lavinia said, laughing. She was still a little subdued from time to time, and generally exuded a softer presence than before her flogging, but she had recovered well, and today the promised outing had left her animated, and her usual happy self again.

"My god, isn't it just! Who are they, and how does it all work?" Eve wanted to know.

"Well all the girls you see today are amateurs, although some of them take it very seriously, and are almost as full time as the professionals. Oh, they're under starter's orders. Tell you more later."

Mark produced a race card, and began to recite the details.

"Audrey, 20, first time out so no form. She runs in lane 1. Caroline, 27, her third season. Lane two. Started nine times and won three. Bianca, 22. Ran three times last year and won once. I expect the bookies will make Caroline favourite on that form."

"Isn't she a bit long in the tooth," Eve remarked, rather unkindly," she's my age. Surely the youngsters will eat her up."

"Lot to learn young lady," Mark reproved her. "This is as much a test of fortitude as speed. That's why its so popular. No Caroline is just approaching her peak. The youngsters haven't hardened up yet, in body or in mind. Pity we weren't here a little earlier or I'd put some of my hard-earned money on that girl's delightful bare haunches."

The runners had lined up on the far side of the track by now, the starter's flag was up, and then down, and three whips cracked as one on bare female flesh.

"Not really necessary at this stage," Mark remarked, "the girls are ready to go without any urging, and they haven't tired yet, but the punters love it of course, so the drivers make sure they get their money's worth. You wait until these girls are sweating a bit, and their legs like lead. Then you'll see

146

iz and Katie shine
t Asian awards

Liz Hurley, the 42-year-old mode
Nayar, and Katie Derham, 37, the
gathered at the London Hilton on
Achievement Awards. The event

some fancy whip work to sting them into action."

The three surreys had sprung forward as if one and were racing round the track, the long bare legs of the 'ponies' flashing in a high-stepping gait, causing the big loose breasts to dance on their heaving chests, and revealing enticing glimpses of the secret grots between their thighs, plump and healthy as her own, Eve noticed; one shaved completely, the others neatly cropped to trim triangles.

"No one using the whip much," she remarked, as the girls raced by in front of them, heading for the finishing post, "I thought you said it was usual towards the end."

"Towards the end, yes," Mark replied, not taking his eyes for a moment off the delightful sight of naked female limbs flashing in the sun as they pounded round the track, "but this is 1500 metres. They've got two more laps to go."

Eve began to understand what Mark had meant about a test of fortitude, and found herself responding to the challenge being played out before her, with even greater excitement. Those girls would be hurting by the time they'd done three laps, and even more so with the whips cutting them to extract that last extra ounce of effort. She looked more closely as they came round next time. First time past the post, Audrey had been in the lead, her youthful enthusiasm carrying her that extra metre or two ahead of the others, who were neck and neck, but she'd gone too early, and was paying for it now. Her driver had the whip going steadily, but she could not stop the older girls from pulling past, even to escape the cruel lash that was cutting thin red lines into her naked back and shoulders, even curling round to catch her wildly flying breasts. Eve could hear her panting breath from the stand.

Into the last lap now, and Audrey was out of it, though that did not spare her the kiss of the whip, as her driver vainly tried to flog her back into contention. The other two were still neck and neck, several lengths ahead. Their drivers were flogging them unmercifully down the back straight, but neither could gain any advantage. Coming off the last bend, Bianca's driver called on her for an extra effort, and let his thong fly out that little bit more so that it cracked across her nipples.

"Get up," he shouted, "or I'll cut the tits off you!"

She tried her best, throwing herself forward for half a dozen paces, and winning a metre for her considerable pains, but wasting valuable breath in a frantic scream. The more experienced Caroline held her nerve and when her driver called on her in turn for that added burst of energy, reinforcing the message with a cunning stroke which cracked right between her

flashing thighs as they opened, burrowing deep into her furry furrow, she took back the advantage Bianca had won so painfully in three strides, then kept going, as the other girl tired, to cross the line half length ahead. The crowd went wild, and Eve turned a flushed face towards her host and hostess.

"Marvellous," she gasped, panting as if she'd run naked in the shafts herself, "I've never seen anything so exciting. I could do that you know. Just think of it. Racing on the track like that, with the crowd cheering you on, putting all you've got into it. Those girls make me quite envious."

"It's not all glory," Lavinia warned her." Think of the pain of those whips. The drivers weren't sparing them you know."

"I could see that," Eve retorted," but what's a whipping when you're really living out there?"

Three more races only served to stoke up the excitement she felt. While Mark was off looking up some of his business friends, Eve could only talk of one thing.

"Do you think there's any chance of someone giving me a race in one of those?" she asked.

"What makes you think you could do it?" Lavinia challenged

"Well, I'm the right age, according to Mark, and I've always looked after myself. At coll. I was the women's mile champion and I've always worked out regularly since. Even here I've been going to Daphne's health club with her, and

I've played a lot of tennis, so I've not got badly out of shape. No I could do it, if I could find someone to take me in hand and train me properly."

Lavinia looked doubtful.

"There's more to it, than just running round a track," she observed, "If I were to introduce you to a proper trainer, you might find some of their ideas a bit much."

"What sort of ideas?

"Oh, I don't know. It's a bit technical," Lavinia said evasively.

"Anyway, what do you mean 'if' you introduced me? Does that mean you know one of the trainers?"

"Well, yes I do, as a matter of fact, but I'm still a bit doubtful about you meeting him."

"Oh come on Larry," Eve coaxed, almost wheedling, "you owe me one remember. You nearly cut the cunt out of me that time."

"Ouch! That was a little below the belt," Lavinia complained.

"So was the flogging you gave my pussy," Eve retorted, "Come one. Where is he?"

"Outside the tack room when I last saw him," Lavinia admitted, "OK, on your head be it, and your bum and tits as well I warn you. Let's go look."

The tack-room was behind the stands, in an area where owners and trainers mingled to discuss the day's events, trade girls and equipment and generally do what owners and trainers do. Lavinia walked up to a small knot and greeted one of the group.

"Can I introduce you to my friend Eve," she said. "She's caught the bug, and won't let me rest until I ask you if you'll give her a trial between the shafts."

"We've already met," Angus said, smiling across at Eve where she stood dumbstruck.

For a moment it looked as if she might turn and run, then pride and ambition took hold of her and she squared her shoulders and stepped closer.

"Good afternoon, Mr McKensie," she said. "Would you give me a trial? I've been watching the races and I'm sure I could do it."

Angus swept an appraising glance up and down her figure, then concealed his admiration behind a strictly professional manner.

"And what makes you think you can run in a surrey, Missy?" he observed doubtfully, "It's a tough game and I don't mess with any girl I accept for training. No kid gloves. Plenty of stick, and not a lot of carrot, except the need to win. They all have to show they can take it. Could you?"

Eve looked him straight in the eye.

"Yes I could," she declared firmly.

Angus seemed to consider a moment, then called out to his chief groom.

"Come over here, will you, Ian. I want your opinion of this filly," he yelled, and Eve blushed as every eye in the neighbourhood turned to see who he meant, but she stood her ground, and waited quietly while the wiry stable man excused himself to the burly woman in tweeds to whom he had been talking and made his way over to where they stood.

"Think this one could learn to work a cart?" Angus asked.

The groom stood back and looked her up and down.

"Could be," he admitted after a long scrutiny. "Hard to tell with all those clothes on."

"Get your things off," Angus ordered without ceremony.

"What! Here, in front of all these people?"

"If you can't stand to strip in front of a crowd you'd be no use as a ponygirl," he advised her, "besides, I hear you've shown half the island everything you've got at one time or another. One more little show is not going to faze them."

Blushing even deeper she gripped the hem of her cotton frock and pulled it up over her head, standing docilely in her bra and pants, with it hanging from one hand. Ian walked all round her then ordered her to bend. She set her feet a little apart, let the dress drop to the ground beside her, and bent in a pliant bow from her hips, to place her hands on the ground in front of her. She was determined to persuade Angus she had what it took, but he was still testing her.

"Pants down, girl," he ordered.

She started to protest, half rising from her bent position.

"I don't see that that's really necessary," she began, but Angus checked her.

"A filly's cunt is the best guide to her health," he assured her, "Get your knickers off and let Ian assess the state you're in."

This was not exactly reassuring; she was well aware of the state she was in and not keen to have this arrogant Scotsman and his dour assistant feel the hot wetness of her vulva or the thick engorgement of her clit, but she was not going to fail now. She reached behind, drew down the flimsy covering of her panties to her knees, letting the air strike cool on the mounting wetness of her labia and upper thighs, then bent back into position.

Ian was not long in discovering her state of health.

"A fine ripe one, this," he commented, his hand probing between her shaking thighs, his fingers exploring the delicate folds of her vulva, coming to rest on the pulsing bud of her clitoris. "Wet as a hound's nose and just as healthy. Nice muscle tone, too," he continued, transferring his touch to the naked, bending girl's great relief, from her genitals to the flesh of her buttocks and thighs and the muscles of her calves. She quivered again as he reached under her to weigh her dangling breasts in his large calloused hands, before pronouncing them, too, to be healthy.

"A well configured filly," he remarked, his inspection done," though her bud's a bit above average. May need some pruning there."

"Thank you Ian," Angus said, "you can straighten up now, lassie, and get those rags back on, since you're so shy."

"So what do you think?" she persisted, once she had recovered her clothes. "Will you take me?"

"I don't know. Lassie. I'm tempted, but I don't often handle amateurs. My girls are professionals. I wouldn't treat you any less severely. And then there's your build."

"Your man seemed to think I'd do."

"He also said your clit was full, fat and sensitive. He recommended gelding."

"What's that?" she asked, pretty sure she wasn't going to like the answer.

"Your clit is surgically removed, so that its sensuality doesn't interfere with training, sapping energy and diverting thoughts."

"Oh!"

There was a prolonged silence as he let the news sink in and she struggled with her thoughts. She wanted to race, but that!!

"You seem to be having some difficulty with that."

"Yes. You must give me time to absorb the idea. It's a big step for a girl. You know, to have her womanhood cut out like that."

"I understand," Angus spoke less sternly. "There may be a compromise. I'm not really in favour myself, but I'll be honest; I'd like to have you race for me. You're one of the best prospects I've seen in a long while."

"What sort of compromise?" She was grasping at straws.

"Some owners believe that it's enough to put the clit out of action for a few weeks during training," Angus replied

"Out of action?"

"Actually crushed so that it is too painful to touch, and there's no longer any temptation to masturbate. Actually there used to be a school of thought that it was a superior method, since it left the filly frustrated and raring to run, rather than just remove the desire altogether."

"And it would grow back? You guarantee it?"

"Oh yes," Angus assured her," with a fleshy organ like that, just a mass of blood vessels and nerve endings, you'd heal in a month or so. Probably be more sensitive than ever for a while. If you stayed with me though, you could look forward to it being burst again each season."

"How's it done?" The idea terrified her, but she had to know

"Special pliers. They are designed to fit round the bulb and close on it until the flesh gives way. Wouldn't work for someone less well endowed, but you have a beauty. Should burst like a ripe grape."

Eve shuddered, and stood looking down at her feet for a long pause then lifted her head and looked him directly in the eye.

"I'll do it," she said.

The Rubicon crossed, it didn't take long to arrange the few remaining details. The next races were in a fortnight. Angus conceded that, since it was close season for the professionals, and he and Ian could give her their whole attention, he might just have her ready to race by then, if she started her training at once. She could move into his stables that day, since she wouldn't need even the clothes she stood up in. Everything else she needed would be supplied by the stable. She said goodbye to a still doubtful Lavinia and got into the McKensie stable's box.

At the stable she was made to strip again, and her clothes taken away. After a thorough inspection by a man in a vet's white coat she was pronounced sound in wind and limb and installed in a straw lined loose box which, she was told, would be her home for the next two weeks. Ian informed her that it was usual for women to be given twenty-four hours' rest after the crushing out of their sexual organ and, with the short time available to them, the operation would be performed that night. After a light supper of wholemeal bread and apples, she received another visit from the vet, and was made to kneel on all fours in the corner of her box that contained the drain for her natural motions.

She nearly rebelled when she realised what came next,

then steadied and reminded herself that this was nothing thing compared with what came later.

The vet's fingers ran up and down the deep crack of her buttocks and pried them apart, another finger probed for the shrinking anus and, finding it in its hot moist trench, slapped in a chilly dollop of lubricant, followed by a cold metal nozzle that seemed to fill her whole belly, forcing it in deeper and deeper, until she thought it would choke her. Half a gallon of hot glycerin enema followed, until her belly hung swelling below her, and she found difficulty breathing from the pressure on her diaphragm. It was five full minutes, five minutes filled with stomach cramps and humiliating leakage from her sphincter before she was allowed the even greater humiliation of letting it all go in explosive eruption, watched dispassionately by Angus and his head groom. Then they did it all over again!

After she had finished humiliating herself in a second disgusting session, squatting and squelching over the drain in the corner, she was wiped clean and helped up onto a portable examination table, fitted with the kind of stirrups found in gynie departments, to hold the thighs well apart and give total access to a woman's genitals. Secured firmly in place, and her whole pubic area stinging from the spirit used to clean and sterilise it, she braced herself for the jab of the hypodermic that would numb her doomed clitoris.

It never came. Instead, she saw through the wide vee of her parted thighs, Ian, the head groom, lifting a curiously shaped set of stainless steel pliers from a covered sterile dish. As he began to manipulate her bud with his fingers, encased in surgical gloves, an awful realisation began to dawn. Here in this strict training stable, women did not get the benefit of anaesthetics. They had to face their ordeals fully conscious, and un-numbed!

Despite the rush of adrenalin the horror of her position induced, she could feel her secret pearl swelling under his touch. It had always been well formed, to her great satisfaction on

untold occasions, but in the heady atmosphere of Eden it had seemed to flower, like the pudenda of all the young women she had observed, and this evening seemed to fill her fork.

Even the dour groom seemed impressed.

"That's a fine fruit you have there, lassie," he observed, "I'm almost sorry to damage it. Still, ye canna race with a thing like that between your legs, drawing off your strength. It'll have to go."

She flinched as far as her restraints would allow as she felt the metal close around the tender bulb. At first it was not too painful, and the sexual surge it sent through her made her buck with lust, not anguish, as the jaws squeezed firmly on the base of the clitoral 'flute', ensuring it would not slip out, and forcing it to swell even more opulently, the blood throbbing in it, the pulse echoing in her ears.

"I'll not rush it," the grim-faced groom informed her, "I wouldn't want to tear the root. You'll have it back in a month or two, I promise you, as good as new."

She was grateful for the latter, but could have done without the former. The jaws had closed over the trapped bud now, and she was in serious pain. She would have liked it over in one swift burst, but Ian only tightened the grip in creeping increments.

The cruel iron took its awesome grip of tenderest woman flesh that would have shrunk from its bite but could not escape. As the pressure mounted and blood and nerves shrieked for release her lips went back in a rictus of pain. through clenched teeth a thin "yeeee eeee eeee" of absolute suffering forced its way. As the steel jaws slowly crushed her delicate bud her mouth opened without her volition, a shriek of absolute agony was torn from her throat, repeated and repeated as the unrelenting pressure forced the bulb of her clit into bulging prominence. The pain of the rupture when it came was no greater than the crushing that had brought it about but the sensation revolted her stomach. Her belly heaved and roiled, her head swam, a red mist closed over her eyes and for a moment she was lost to sense. When she was aware again, it was of the awful pain continuing in her groin, the nausea in her belly, and the stony faces of her groom and her trainer looking down on her.

"You'll do, Lassie," Angus said without emotion, "Ian will put a dressing on, and you'll have the night to rest. Tomorrow we'll start your training proper."

She thought she could never sleep with that terrible ache in her groin, and the awful sense of having lost a part of herself, but Ian dropped a couple of tablets in a glass and handed them to her saying, "drink these. They'll help you to sleep."

She was surprised at the softness of his tone, the same kind of gentleness she had heard other grooms using to four-legged mares, and took the glass gratefully.

In the morning she still hurt, but it was a bearable pain, though she could only walk with her legs well splayed. She entered her training as she was to continue it, quite naked. Her 'wound' was protected by a dressing in the form of a tiny tanga, thin tapes keeping a minute triangle of lint pressed over her vulva, preventing infection from getting in. After three days she lost even this minimum covering, as the crushed remains of her clitoris had scabbed over and would provide their own protection. She had thought that her mind could never concentrate on anything other than that lost, or rather, mislaid bud, but the intensity of her training, for up to twelve hours each day, kept her occupied for most of the time. She worked out in the gym, submitted to the rugged attentions of Angus's female physiotherapist, above all she ran on the track.

At first distance training. On her first morning, while she was still too sore to stand almost, she was put between the shafts of one of the lightweight surreys and driven at little more than walking pace, to accustom her to the sensation, though the high-stepping gait she was obliged to adopt at all times in harness, did nothing for the comfort of her groin. That was the only concession to her 'treatment'. From then on she was driven relentlessly,; long distance hauls through the local woods to improve her stamina, short sprints to get up her speed, tactical changes of pace up and down to make her race-ready, all enforced and encouraged by the relentless application of the thin stinging whip across her bare buttocks and shoulders, or curling round her sides to sear her freely bouncing breasts.

At first her feet troubled her, running barefoot on the fine cinder track. Ian rubbed them with spirit after every outing and they hardened rapidly. At the end of the first week she was beginning to feel at home on the track, and her body was criss crossed with thin red welts.

Angus had come to see her progress every day, and seemed pleased with how she was shaping.

"The master thinks you're doing well for an amateur," Ian confided, as he sponged her down after one of these visits, "I can't say you've done badly," he added, grudgingly," but we've a gae deal of work to do, if you're not going to disgrace us at the races next week."

She'd become well used to being harnessed in the surrey after two weeks of intensive training, even having her arms fastened behind her back had ceased to trouble her balance, though she was still a little sore from the way her heavy unsupported breasts danced up and down on her chest as she pranced along. She'd mentioned it to Ian, saying she thought he might have got more out of a girl if she was given some minimal uplift to check the painful bouncing.

"Maybe so," he conceded, but the regulations forbid it. Girls have to run naked. Besides, I think the fancy like to see you girls with your tits dancing. I'm not altogether displeased by the effect myself. Besides, this sport is all about female fortitude, so why remove a little test of character like enduring aching breasts?"

It was out of season for the professionals, so there had been few visitors, just Angus himself, the vet, physio and, of course the groom Ian. It was one thing to race naked, breasts flying, thighs flashing, her bare vulva open to the air with every stride, with only these to see, quite another to display like that before a crowd of strangers. Now it was race day though, and she found herself doing a warm up lap of the track, bare arsed, teats flapping on her chest, exposed to the gaze of a thousand spectators. Worse than that, she could spot immediately a dozen women she had met at various times, and was quite sure there would be many more she couldn't spare the attention to pick out from the crowd. She was pretty sure that Lavinia had spread the word of her foolhardy ambition to race in harness, and they had turned out in force to watch her. As she cantered past the stands she saw Lavinia herself waving from the front row.

Now they came up to the starter's stand, and lined up with the other two in her race. Just before he'd pushed the unpalatable discomfort of the iron bit into her mouth, and reduced her to the dumb beast she represented on the track, she'd asked Ian how he rated the opposition.

"You've drawn the short straw, lassie," he said, "both the others in your race have been here before, and one of them won handsomely the last race of last season, so the bookies won't rate you. Still, this is your first time out. Nobody will blame you if you can't win. Just try and put up a respectable performance, and not let Mr Angus down. He thinks a great deal of you, you ken."

Now she tried to size up the opposition. Outside her was a strong looking blonde with long lean legs, topped with a neat golden triangle, and very large loose breasts. Maybe that might help she thought. Her own boobs were a nuisance in the closing stages of a race, but they were firm and high. This girl seemed to be much lower slung and her tits had bounced up to shoulder height, even on the warm up lap. Perhaps they might slow her when the going got tough in lap three.

The other girl was dark where the first was fair, with a tight, tanned arse and neat compact breasts. There would be nothing to gain there she thought. Before she could gather more, Ian tightened her reins momentarily to warn her that the starter's flag was up. It flashed down and Ian laid the whip across her back to start her, though not with all the force he could sometimes put into it. He knew he had a willing runner, and didn't need to push her at this stage. Later, when she reached her pain barrier, when every breath burnt like fire, her feet were sore to every touch of the track and all her muscles were protesting, then he would flog her unmercifully, to help her find that last effort of will, but not now.

She was pleased to see that the other drivers, unlike Ian, were not professionals. They seemed to like wielding the whip for its own sake, delighting in the crack of leather on bare woman flesh, and the livid lines they left on straining flank, breast or buttock. Their arms were moving relentlessly from the first, flaying their charges, spurring them into action, but also draining their strength. She was grateful for Ian's superior driving ability and his restraint in the cuts he delivered judiciously to her straining haunches and sides.

There was nothing in it for the first lap, then the brunette on her inside began to tire under her driver's constant barrage of lashes. Whipped from the first stride, it no longer served to spur her on, only to sap her strength. She began to fall behind. Her driver lashed her even more furiously, a steady rain of cuts all over her sweating body, but she could not respond, and it was a two horse race when they entered the last lap.

Eve was sweating herself by now, and her back and sides were sore from the whip, her breasts aching from their furious oscillation on her heaving chest, but she felt intact inside, with just a little something left to give, when Ian's whip demanded it. The big blonde was still running well, but Eve could see her heavy breasts were taking their toll. They hung on her chest like plastic bags, each loaded with an Edam cheese. As she ran they leapt almost to her chin, then dropped with a sickening lurch, stretching the skin until they nearly reached her waist. Sometimes they merely lifted and fell vertically, at others, as the pace varied, one or other would swing sideways and then back in again, like a boxer trying to plant a hook on the girls jaw. She must have been suffering badly after over two laps of this punishment but her driver, a middle-aged woman in tweeds, was relentless at holding her to her work, and continued to ply the whip freely.

Into the home straight, still neck and neck and the pace telling. Eve ached all over, her feet were sore, her breasts hurt, her legs were on fire, but still she threw herself into it. Now Ian was helping her with the whip, lashing her in earnest now, each cut nearly drawing blood. As they came past the stands for the last time, she distinctly heard Lavinia shout, "Come on Eve. You can do it," and somehow forced herself to respond, but the tweedy woman was lashing her blonde steed unmercifully now, the whip snaking round the bound arms to slice into the dancing breasts. She just couldn't make any impression on the girl, and there was only a dozen strides left.

"Move your fucking arse," Ian shouted, with totally uncharacteristic brutality and cut her on the cunt.

It was the kind of stroke only a professional could bring off successfully, the long fine whip cord snaking out, then guided by a flick of the wrist to double back on itself and, with perfect timing, breach the flashing thighs as they parted in mid stride and seek out the feminine secrets between. It bit into Eve's still tender vulva, sending a lancing agony into her genitals.

She shrieked behind her bit at the suddenness and intensity of the pain, and leapt forward. Left, right, left, thrice more Ian found his target, on alternate strides, and then the finish line flashed past. The blonde's tortured breasts crossed it just a metre behind.

Lavinia had cheered herself hoarse as Eve had snatched that desperately narrow lead, stealing victory on the very line itself, paying a terrible price with her wounded pussy. She waited until Ian had driven into the winner's enclosure and then hurried off to meet her in the saddling ring behind the stands.

She arrived to find Ian pouring a bucket of cold water over her sweating and whip streaked body.

"Darling," she cried, "you were wonderful. I just knew you'd do it. Mark fancied the blonde, well men do, don't they, but you've just won me a couple of hundred. When you're decent again, I'll treat you from my winnings."

While Ian towelled his winner down vigorously, ignoring the sore streaks he'd just painted on her hide, Lavinia ran an eye over her body to assess her shape.

"My God! What's that?" she cried, catching sight of the black scab protruding from between the inflamed lips, swollen and bruised from those final 'incentives'.

Eve followed her glance down.

"Oh that," she said, with studied nonchalance, "a girl can't race with a tennis ball between her legs. I had mine crushed to put it out of action for a while."

Ian permitted himself one of his rare fleeting grins, as Lavinia handed over the fresh clothes she had brought to cover Eve's nakedness.

CHAPTER 9 OF PEGS, PENS AND PENDANTS.

The visit to Lavinia's had been a great success, but she was happy to be back with Daphne again after over a month tasting the delights of Southside. Her first breakfast back, she demanded news of the district, which she had begun to feel was almost 'home'.

"What's been going on, while I've been away?" she demanded, "and what have you been up to? No good I'll be bound. Good thing I'm back to see you don't get into trouble," she joked.

"Too late," Daphne replied with a rueful grimace, "the damage is already done."

"What do you mean?"

"Well, as you know, Friday afternoon's my weekly workout at the health club. I was feeling so good driving myself back the other night, I let it go to my head. Now it'll go to my seat. Collected a ticket for speeding; sixty in a fifty zone."

"Oh, Dee! How beastly for you," suddenly Eve was all concern for her friend, thoughts of feminist outrage lost. "And I suppose, being Eden, it means another dose of stick."

"You suppose right. Under the Discipline of Females Act, 1898, and in accordance with the Road Traffic (Female Offenders) Act 1970, I am required and obliged to redeem the said ticket in person, which means ON my person of course, within seventy-two hours, on pain of a doubling of the penalty prescribed, and that is something I do NOT intend to incur."

Tact fought a losing battle with curiosity in Eve's brain. As usual with this kind of female struggle, tact didn't stand a chance .

"What do you think you'll get?"

Daphne pulled a sour face.

"Not less than six, that's for sure, but the officer of the day is entitled to use his own judgement; what the conditions were like, any previous offences, whether his mistress was less than fully cooperative in bed that lunchtime; all that sort of thing. I've known women get a dozen for ten miles over the limit before now. God I hope it doesn't come to that. Besides, Gordon's almost sure to add his own punishment on top."

"Oh, Darling, you have been in the wars since I came to stay. I'm beginning to feel I'm a bit of a jinx."

"Of course you're not. It's none of it your fault and you're such a comfort afterwards. It's so helpful to have a woman friend when one finally gets back."

"Oh you won't have to wait till you get back," Eve said firmly, "I'm coming with you all the way."

"They won't let you do that. You get beaten in private. You'd have to stay in the waiting room for hours."

"What does that matter. I don't mind waiting all day, if I can help you when you come out."

Daphne looked a little uncomfortable.

"Well the seating in the waiting room is a little, shall we say uncomfortable," Daphne started, but Eve cut her short.

"Look, we may disagree on some of the finer points of female discipline but we're still best friends and I'm coming with you so I won't hear another word about it."

Daphne shook her head doubtfully but let her have her way.

There was nothing to distinguish the Traffic Department's Corrective wing from any other office building occupied by officialdom. A rather bleak little outer office, with a female clerk at a paper littered desk. There were two or three other women there already, none of them looking particularly cheerful. One by one, as their papers were checked, they disappeared through the door on the left, marked WAITING ROOM. The bored clerk looked at Daphne's ticket with no visible interest, compared it with some documents in her file, date-and time- stamped it and handed it back. She looked up at Eve and said," Ticket please."

"Oh, I'm just here to keep Mrs Borenson company," she said, hastily.

The clerk looked doubtful.

"Well I don't know....."

"It's not against regulations is it?" Eve demanded.

"Oh no," the girl replied, "it's just that.... Well the seats you know. Not many people care for them."

"Oh bother the seats," Eve exclaimed. "A sore arse is nothing to help a friend who's going to be a lot sorer soon."

"Well, if you're sure..."

"I'm sure," Eve declared firmly, cutting off any further protest, and turned into the waiting room door.

It was a bare forbidding chamber. Though the high windows let in a minimum of light, and the single bare bulb did little to improve things, she was still sufficiently aware of what she was looking at to stop short in the doorway, causing Daphne to bump into her back.

"My God!" she exclaimed, "I see what you meant when you said the seating was likely to be a little uncomfortable. Next time I'll listen to you."

What had caused her astonishment was not the lines of solid polished wood benches that filled three walls of the chamber, but the neatly spaced wooden pegs that jutted from them, spaced about twenty inches apart, just the right distance for a row of women sitting waiting their turn to be processed. Each peg was the size and shape of a fair size male penis, dark polished wood with that rich glossy patina that only comes from much use in contact with human tissue. If she had had any doubts as to their mode of employment, they were put out of her mind at once by the sight of three or four other women, who had entered the room before them, seated bolt upright on their pegs, their skirts spread around them on the bench, a glimpse of lowered knicker visible on their thighs. Their screwed up faces only served to confirm their condition. If any further explanation was needed it came in the form of the woman who had preceded them at the desk.

She had been only a few paces ahead on them entering the room, and Eve was just in time to see her lift her skirt in back, hook her fingers into her panties and draw them down to her knees, turn her back on the bench and, very gingerly, lower her rump towards it. As the phallus nosed its way between her plump arse-cheeks, she sucked in her breath and used both hands to drag the fat cheeks apart, feeling for the knob with her anus. She paused, as if trying to gather her courage, when she had it lodged, then let out her breath in a smothered whoop and let all her weight fall on the rod which immediately penetrated her to the hilt, and her slabby buttocks met the bench with an audible slap.

"There's someone who's been here before," Daphne remarked grimly. "Best thing to do, under the circumstances. Make sure you aim right and then let it all drop. Get it over with. It's damned uncomfortable either way you do it but that way at least it's over quick."

164

"OK then," Eve agreed, "we drop our pants and then wham! Straight up and no messing."

"You're forgetting something," Daphne cautioned. "You'll be dry as a bone down there. If you could get it in your cunt you'd probably make it but you can't use your twat. The angle's all wrong for one thing, and it's against regulations for another and you'd earn yourself extras or, in the case of visitors like you, a quick dose of cane you didn't come prepared for. As it is, your arse is different, and you could tear it. No, first thing it's down on your knees and suck that pole as if it was your favourite prick. Once you've slobbered enough to get it good and slippery, you can lower your knicks and sit down hard on it. Just make sure it's centred properly first," she warned."

They'd chosen pegs side by side, and, once the initial shock was over, could feel their thighs touching in companionable intimacy. Eve didn't care for the hard spike up her rectum, it was neither comfortable nor dignified, but she was glad to take it, for the opportunity it gave to support her friend.

While they waited, a door next to the one by which they had entered swung open, and a woman stood there, her face grim and twisted, her hands holding her buttocks, She seemed to be having a seizure of some kind, for her body was arched rigid, and her mouth gaped in a soundless scream. Then she relaxed and stumbled to the exit, moaning to herself, apparently blind to everything else around her. As she disappeared Eve leant closer to Daphne's ear and whispered, "do you think she's alright?"

"She'll live," Daphne replied laconically. "Gets you like that afterwards. You think it's all over, and it hits you when you're not looking."

Eve could sense the rising fear for her own fate, and dropped the subject.

As the stricken woman disappeared, a man's head appeared in the doorway through which she had just emerged.

"Next!" he called, brusquely. The woman at the end of

the line gulped and drew herself up off her peg, which left her stretched anus with an audible plop. As she hauled up her knickers, and walked towards the door, her abused sphincter let out a distinct and humiliating squelch of fetid air.

There were two more women in front of Daphne. When they had all been called, each summons heralded by a stricken female exiting, her dues paid, and still feeling them intensely, Daphne fell silent, lost in her own thoughts. With her own call, she pushed herself up from the unfeeling wood deep in her belly and, emitting a shaming fart of her own, walked stiffly and reluctantly to the fateful door. Eve mouthed, "good luck", as she crossed the floor.

Afterwards Eve was lost in thought, scarcely noticing as new recruits entered the chamber to impale themselves on their spikes, and wait for their own turn. Daphne seemed to have been away a long time, when she looked up and saw her friend standing speechless in the doorway, her face twisted with pain, her hands clasping her rump. Without thinking she sprang to her feet to go to her. Too late she remembered. She shrieked in surprise and pain as the rod ripped from her anus, almost turning it inside out. With the passing of time the sparse lubricant she had spat onto it had been squeezed out by the relentless pressure of her sphincter and the delicate lining of her rectal tube was all but welded to it. Her precipitous rise almost tore the tissue and she found herself facing her friend, their expressions matching each other in their almost comical distortions, their hands clasped to their hinds in identical poses, the one to squeeze the agony out of a mass of livid welts, the other to contain the burn of abraded flesh in her anus.

"Oh darling I should have warned you to be more careful," Daphne said ruefully, her mouth still twisted in her own distress.

"Never mind me. You must be in agony this close to a beating."

"God. They gave me a dozen. Said there were aggravating circumstances, whatever they were. I think he was just off

166

women today. Probably his wife is on the rag this week," Daphne informed her, "they strap you down to take them, which is a kindness really as a woman would find it difficult otherwise, and who wants extras on top of a dozen? But you have to stand in a corner for five minutes after they release you with your pants down and your hands on your head while the full burn takes place. More difficult than taking the cuts themselves, and you daren't let your hands drop or you could go back for a repeat performance. One poor girl did last year. She couldn't sit for a week and she didn't lift her eyes above waist level for months. I don't think she's dared drive herself since. Come to that, I'm not too keen on the idea myself, just now. Would you do the honours, darling? I'll just kneel on the back seat. That is, if you haven't pulled your guts through your arse too badly."

"I feel as if someone reached in there with a farrier's rasp, and reamed out my hole," Eve conceded," and I'm not looking forward to using the john for the next week or two, but I'm still in better shape than you. Now let's get cracking, before we get done for talking in the waiting room. Once is quite enough for both of us."

She proved a true prophetess. Daphne's welts kept her quiet and withdrawn for a week, but then she seemed to spring back quickly to her old bright self. As for her own fundament, though, she was nearly in tears when the call of nature became too urgent to ignore, and she tried shitting through her torn anus. The exercise in itself only served to put back the healing, and it was a week before she could relieve herself in any comfort.

But they were healthy, feisty young women fuelled by the sensual and life-enhancing atmosphere of Eden, and were soon back to their old selves, and throwing themselves into the social world of their peers.

"What's the matter with Penny, do you think?"

Penny and Douglas were old friends of Gordon, an hour's drive away. Gordon had driven them over one evening for cocktails.

The three of them were sitting exchanging gossip, Eve, Daphne, and Tina, a voluptuous redhead who, according to Daphne's surreptitious briefing, was the present subject of Gordon's roving eye. Her husband Nick seemed happy to let him, and Eve had seen him looking fairly interested in Daphne, himself. Perhaps there was trade in the offing.

Penny was one of those sleek, smoothly sculptured women, with raven hair to her shoulders, a type best suited to modelling swim wear than high fashion, Eve thought. No skeletal clothes horse, she; a truly female person with large firm breasts, and buttocks a man could rest on in comfort, with out fear of having his belly pierced by razor sharp hip bones.

Like a good hostess, she came over to where they were sitting, and Tina pulled no punches.

"What's the matter, Penny?" she asked without preamble." You look as if you're going to be hung in the morning. What happened to all that spirit? You used to be a ball of fun. I remember when you nearly killed us with your impressions of our husbands."

"Oh don't you start," their hostess protested mournfully. "Doug thinks it's all got a little out of hand, and that I need straightening out. It's not that I've done anything particularly dreadful, just a few drinks too many here, a bit lippy there, a touch extravagant at times."

"Well, aren't we all?" Daphne declared. "It's just called being female."

"Well Doug calls it, and I quote, 'a progressive failure of duty'. I'm really not sure if he means my duty, or his, but he's promised to straighten me out after the party."

Tina didn't seem impressed by the explanation.

"Well cheer up, Penny," she advised. "A good thrashing never killed a woman, and I'm sure you'll feel all the better for it afterwards."

"It's not a thrashing. I'm to have an all-nighter."

"Oh!"

Eve looked at Daphne questioningly, as all three women fell suddenly glum. Daphne didn't answer directly, instead she ad dressed the potential penitent.

"What does Doug use then? Wooden Pony is it?"

"Would that it was, although that's bad enough," Penny replied mournfully, and the other women nodded in agreement. "No he likes the cage. He says I always come out completely docile and don't lift my eyes from his toecaps. He's right too."

There was a moment of gloomy silence as the women all digested this dismal prospect.

"What's more, "she added in sombre tones," he thinks it might be good for you lot if you came to see it, so he's probably fixing that with the men right now."

The cage was constructed from sections of ordinary steel pipe, fastened at the corners and sides by standard fittings. It was no more than three feet long and less than two foot square in section. Eve wondered that even a fashion waif would be able to crawl in, let alone Penny's full-fledged femininity, posed nakedly beside it. Penny herself looked at the contraption with a distinct lack of enthusiasm.

Doug frowned slightly at this apparent reluctance to accept her 'treatment' in the proper spirit.

"I won't have you uptight about a needful correction," he informed her, "I think a little loosener is called for. Six should do it. Bend down and touch your toes."

With even less enthusiasm Penny did as she was told, stretching the pale white satin of her buttocks drum tight to receive the searing kiss of Doug's well practised rod, hissing as loudly through the air as Penny's breath between her teeth as she rode out each flaming burst of anguish as it flooded through her.

The six dealt out strictly, Penny was allowed to rise, where she treated them all to an agonised dance, clutching her beaten buttocks, where the half dozen hard ridged welts were already rising.

"Come on Pen. You're keeping our guests waiting," Doug admonished, "time to curl up in your comfy cage."

Penny looked as if she might disagree with this description but took one quick look at the rod still quivering in Doug's fist and thought better of it. Better enter the cage silently, with six searing stripes across her aching bottom, than argue and carry a dozen in with her.

"Don't hang about," her loving consort commanded. "Get in position. You know what to do."

Obediently she dropped to her knees, her back to the cage door, and gingerly put one foot back to feel for the front edge. With great reluctance, inch by inch, she backed into the metal framed crate. As her buttocks with their flaming stripes, passed into the enclosure, she put her arms behind her, feeling for the openings between the bars of the roof. It was slow and

uncomfortable work wriggling herself into the restricted space, but finally she was in, her buttocks pressed against the rear wall, her arms hooked over the bar that ran across the roof, her lush breasts crushed against her bent knees, her head projecting between the upper bars of the door, which Doug lifted into place and latched.

Now that she was safely in, and there was no way that she could escape, Doug attached the chain of an overhead hoist to the ringbolt welded to the roof of the cage, and hauled it up to chest level.

"No point in risking back pain," he explained to the watching guests, "I leave that sort of thing to Penny. This is the ergonomically correct working height as laid down by the Chamber of Trade."

He moved behind his concertina-ed consort, and she gasped as he forced her hands back through the bars, until her elbows were bent around the crossbar, and fastened a leather cuff about each wrist, linked by a chain beneath her belly, restricting her movements even more.

The true nature of this feared punishment was becoming

clear to Eve now. Every part of Penny's body was under strain, and she could do nothing to relieve it. With every passing hour in the long dark night, the ache in her limbs and joints would get more unbearable until she was weeping with pain that could only go on getting worse, until the long-distant morning. To add to her discomfort Doug prised open her jaws and set a thick rubber bar across her mouth, fastening like a horse's bit with straps behind her head, that stretched her lips back at the corners, and had her dribbling spittle from the first. With this constraint she could make little intelligible sound, and her breath snorted through her nostrils.

But there was worse to come she discovered. Penny's mouth wasn't the only orifice to be brutally forced. Doug produced a hard ribbed rubber dildo, a fair facsimile of a man's prick, and a well-endowed man at that, Eve considered. To groans of protest from behind the bitted lips, Doug presented the bulbous tip to the shrinking whorl of Penny's sphincter, obscenely and openly displayed against the rear bars, which pressed on the welt laddered cheeks until they parted widely. Penny recoiled from the assault as much as her constraints would allow, her groans now sharp staccato grunts, indicative of serious distress, mixed with panic. Doug paused in his efforts and considered.

"Perhaps she is a little dry," he conceded and his captive wife nodded her head vigorously in agreement, "Eve you're our principle guess of the evening. Would you do the honours?"

He held out the monster prick to her and she took it doubtfully. What was expected she wondered. Anything might go in this strange but exciting world. She put it to her mouth and began to lick it carefully.

"Oh come on, Eve," Tina cried, "you can do better than that. I bet you're a boiling lake underneath."

Eve looked at the other women for help, but none came. Blushing furiously she lifted her skirt and dropped her pants. Tina was right of course. She was soaking, and the sticky dew glistened copiously on her lips. Quickly she rubbed the tip of the phallus between the wetted lips, gasping as she went further than intended and touched the fevered button of her clit, sending a spasm through her belly.

"More, more," Tina urged. She threw all restraint aside and thrust the ribbed mammoth deep into her sodden sheath. Wrenching it out unceremoniously, she dropped her skirt again, leaving the knickers round her knees in her haste, and handed the dripping dong to the master of these dolorous ceremonies.

This time the added lubrication enabled him to gain a purchase more easily, but Penny still heaved and writhed, howling behind her bit, as the massive length was driven home without further finesse. Doug clamped the butt of the plug to the rear bars of the cage, adding yet another degree of restraint to the kneeling woman's predicament. Eve tried not to think of how that hard and unfeeling intruder in the woman's rectum would feel after a night of unrelenting pressure against tender entrails. As she speculated on the effect of rigid rubber on feminine bowels, Doug was completing the rearward arrangements. This involved placing a hideously strong clamp across the pouting labia, effectively sealing the vulva for the night, after attaching an elastic cord to the clit ring. Stretched tight, and fastened to the floor of the cage, this drew an even more vehement grunt of protest from the crouching victim. Doug went to the front for the final touches.

Bent as she was within the cage, her arms hooked round the top bar, Penny's heavy breasts hung pendulously below her, her kneecaps pressed uncomfortably into their under-sides. Doug hooked a light chain onto one of the gold rings she wore in her long thick nipples and passed it under the lower bars, bringing it back up to meet the other tautly stretched nipple, on which he was pulling heavily with his other hand.

Finally it was done. As they left the 'playroom', and Doug switched off the lights behind them, consigning Penny to the long dark night ahead, she could be heard whimpering in the darkness. Eve for one could not blame her.

Upstairs, there was a last drink all round, the men animated over the inspiring scene, the women a little subdued, as they contemplated Penny's fate, condemned to spend the long lonely hours of the night, cramped painfully in her cage, the bars pressed relentlessly into her knees, with no chance to alter or ease her position, the strong steel jaws gripping the fleshy lips of her cunt, the elastic cord pulling cruelly on her clit, the chain tugging against her tender nipples if she made any move at all to flex her aching limbs. Above all that monstrosity in her rectum, abusing her bowel. At least she would be spared the humiliation of soiling herself from that orifice, but she would almost certainly have to endure the shame of pissing herself as she hung there in the dark.

At one point, Eve found herself alone with her host. She'd last seen Gordon escorting Tina to his car, and Daphne seemed to have been appropriated by Nick at the same time. To try and lighten her mood she twitted Doug on how Penny's discipline would be his loss too.

"You've only yourself to blame if you've an empty bed tonight," she teased him. "You shouldn't have left her strung up like that if you didn't want to spend a lonely night."

"Oh, didn't Gordon tell you? He's offered me your services for the night to fill the gap, so to speak."

"Has he indeed!" Eve was taken aback by the news. "He never consulted me on the subject."

"Why should he?" Doug replied in tones of sweet reason, "after all he is your sponsor, and entirely within his rights to dispose of you however he pleases. It's the custom of the country, after all."

Eve couldn't decide whether to explode in anger or accept with the best grace she could. She had an uneasy feeling this might well be a put up job to test her real commitment to the Eden life. Playing safe, she nodded silently and followed docily where Doug led.

He led her to Penny's now deserted bedroom

She stripped without being told, and climbed onto the

matrimonial bed, lying on her back, with her thighs open to expose the hot sodden gash of her vulva. Doug looked up from freeing a solid length of penis from his shorts.

"Oh, not that way. Hands and knees please," he ordered.

"What do you mean?"

"Gordon specified anal only. He thought vaginal might be a little bit too personal at your stage in Eden so, as I've no objection to a touch of sodomy, we agreed back door only."

Eve looked at the great cock bobbing in front of his muscular belly.

"No way," she said. "Fucking not buggery if you please."

"'Fraid I can't do that," Doug was adamant, "Gordon and I have an agreement. I thought you understood. Here these things are decided by the sponsor. If Gordon says buggery then buggery it has to be."

Eve turned over without a word, but let out a yelp of outrage at the sharp pain as Doug tried to force her dry anus.

"You might at least put something on that monster." she complained

"Actually Penny rather likes it that way," Doug replied to her protest. "Says the pain adds spice to the spearing, but if you can't take it, I'll put some cream on it."

"Oh, if that's how she likes it, I suppose it will have to do," Eve replied bitterly, "seeing that I'm meant to be filling in for her."

A moment later she was wincing in protest as he renewed the pressure of the great organ against her tight tender vent. She buried her head in the pillow, lifting her buttocks high, trying to make it as easy on herself as possible, but there was no way that shaft was going to go in without hurting atrociously. Biting hard on the pillowcase, to cover her howls, she endured its remorseless advance. Suddenly she shrieked as the tortured sphincter gave way and the rod sank instantly to the hilt in her bowel. She continued to howl all though the long painful buggery that followed.

A month after Penny's night in the cage, and Doug had

entered her rectum, the island atmosphere continued to work its magic on Eve's body, which radiated health and vital juice.

"Problem is," she told herself, "a girl needs regular servicing under these conditions, and I'm not getting it."

She was standing in her stockings and heels, absently cradling her breasts in her hands, her thumbs stroking idly over nipples that stuck out like the proverbial organ stops. Between her legs, her fully restored clit throbbed and pulsed. She looked over one shoulder to see her tight pink buttocks jutting arrogantly behind her.

"And don't think I've forgotten you," she muttered, "what you need is a damn good hiding, and a thorough fucking."

Restlessly, she wandered, still naked, into Daphne's room, where she was seated at her dressing-table, getting ready for that night's party.

"Anything special going on tonight?" Eve enquired, "Do I need to look out anything in particular?"

"Just the usual glad rags," Daphne replied.

"My God!" she exclaimed suddenly, as she began to frantically search in her jewellery drawer, "No, it's a pendant night tonight. I almost forgot. Gordon has put me in Green. Don't know whether to be glad or sad."

"What's a pendant night when its at home?" Eve wanted to know.

"Didn't I explain? Sorry, there's been so much going on it slipped my mind. Pendant nights all the women wear pendants in various colours to show whether they're available or not. Like this."

She finally found what she was looking for, and held up a simple gold pendant on a thin gold chain. At first Eve took it to be a leaf design, then realised with a start it was a stylised representation of a vulva, and a very open and engorged one at that. It came complete with a small pearl where the point of the clitoris would come. Below that the mouth of the vagina was indicated by an oval green stone. It was a quality jewel and she was almost certain it was a real Emerald that closed the simulated sexual seam.

"Er, very pretty," she managed to say finally. "Does it have some significance?"

"Everything in Eden has some significance, as you must have noticed," Daphne assured her. "Pendant nights we all wear these. A ruby if your man puts you off limits, or has reserved you for one man in particular by prior arrangement. Green like this, and you're fair game for anyone who asks."

"You mean you can't refuse? You have to go with anyone who asks you?" Eve asked doubtfully.

"Just that. What's more, if he doesn't require your services for the whole night, you may have your pendant returned and have to wear it until someone else claims you."

"And you have to have sex with them, of course," Eve said indignantly.

"Any way they choose. Back, front or in your mouth," Daphne assured her.

"How degrading! Can't you refuse?"

"No way. Not if you're wearing Green. Amber's different."

"What's that then?" Eve asked, although she wasn't sure she wanted to know.

"Amber means any man can ask you, but you can choose whether to accept."

"Oh, that's better," Eve answered more cheerfully. "After all it should be a woman's choice."

"You think so?" Daphne said thoughtfully, "I think you have a little way to go in your education yet. Besides, it's a privilege that has to be paid for."

"Paid for?"

"Mmm. Yes indeed. Can't have us trampling all over the poor dears' delicate feelings," Daphne explained. "If you refuse a man he can, if he likes, and they always do seem to, claim some compensation. That means you have to assuage his hurt feelings by hurts of your own. To wit, a sixer with a penal on your bare bum."

"My God! It always comes down to that, doesn't it," Eve exclaimed. "A thrashing on the bare. Win lose or draw, we lose our drawers, and gain some fancy decorations too."

"Well a sixer never killed a girl," Daphne said calmly, "and men are such sensitive creatures underneath all that tough exterior. Anyway, as a visitor, you won't have to worry about that sort of thing."

Indignation at such patronage swept reason out the door.

"There it is again," Eve burst out, "treating me like an outsider again. Please, please, Daphne, let me be like one of you, even though I haven't applied to immigrate yet. It's horrible to be left on the outside of these events."

"So what do you want to do then? Wear one of my pendants?"

Eve drew in a deep breath. She let it out in an emphatic "Yes"

Daphne allowed herself a crooked smile.

"Atta Girl," she said. "Let's show 'em. Only thing is, what colour are you going in?"

"Er, well... actually, I hadn't really thought about that," came the lame admission.

"Then you'd better. Actually you haven't much choice if you're going to wear a proper pendant, and not some codged up thing around your neck. I've got the green, so you're left with Red or Amber. Better be safe and put yourself out of bounds. Be just as good a protection as claiming visitor status actually."

Afterwards, Eve could never decide if Daphne had said it to trap her into going to the party 'available' or not. Daphne was her friend, but, on Eden, friendships between women could take some strange turns. At the time she didn't even stop to consider if she was being conned into her selection.

"Nonsense!" she burst out. "It's got to be the Amber. I want to be one of you."

Daphne handed it over without a word. In the car Gordon regarded the winking amber lozenge with a quizzical eye, but held his peace. He knew his wife well enough to know she wouldn't have allowed her friend to take this step unless she thought it would be for her own good. He might be sponsoring this young woman and, as such, be authorised to dispose of her sexually as he chose, but he would not insist on his prerogative tonight. He did however make a mental note to reinforce his rights by printing some reminders on his wife's beautiful backside when they got home.

At first it was just a party like any other of the dozens she had attended, though there was the added piquancy of checking on the colours of the women's pendants, and speculating on how they would all fare. Later, couples started disappearing from time to time, returning later with that flushed and dishevelled look, the women especially, that spoke of hurried undressing and resumption of clothing, and vigorous sexual exercises. Several women too, she noticed, had lost their jewels temporarily, and she assumed some man had claimed his right to her, but would not enforce the claim until later. Meanwhile other men would recognise that she was spoken for.

She was looking round for Daphne, who had made a temporary exit with a muscular military man when a familiar voice at her elbow had her turn and confront Angus McKensie. He had been asking how she'd enjoyed the evening so far, and remarking how attractive she was looking, when he spotted the amber signal at her throat.

"Are you wearing that for show?" he asked, "or has Gordon really set you loose?"

"Gordon has nothing to do with it," she replied stiffly, "it is my own choice."

"Then I shall get great pleasure out of having you," he said. "Come with me."

If it had been anyone else or, indeed, if he had actually asked, instead of merely taking her for granted, she might well have agreed, but she still harboured resentment at his patronising attitude at their first meeting, and his arrogant assumption that she would meekly submit put her back up like a cornered cat.

"You obviously haven't been looking," she said haughtily, "my pendant is amber not green. I do not choose to accept you."

"Do you not, lassie," he said thoughtfully, "well, you will, you will. Meanwhile, since you choose to play by the rules, so shall I. Let us adjourn to somewhere where they keep a rod for your impertinent backside."

She said nothing but, putting her chin firmly in the air, stalked off towards the bedrooms, leaving him to follow in her wake. Her outward calmness concealing an inner consciousness of his eyes watching the elastic roll of her buttocks under their thin covering, flesh he would in a moment be carving with a whippy stick.

The vacant room she led him to, like all the others in the house, held all that was needed.

She handed him the cane that lay on the bedcover, and, still not speaking, went and knelt on the bed.

"You won't be needing your knickers, lassie," he informed her, and she dragged them down to her knees, before resuming her position on all fours.

The rod's tip flicked contemptuously at the pelmet of a skirt that covered her bared and stretched hinds.

"It's no a guid idea to wear amber, if ye canna deliver," he remarked, "I doubt you'll be becoming a trifle sore before the night's out, if you continue this way."

She had no doubt at all that he was expert in the whipping of women, nor that he would take out on her flinching flesh, every last drop he was owed by the rules she had so lightly

accepted. He did not disappoint her. When it was over, he threw the rod on the bed beside her and left the room without a word.

She had hoped she could carry off the episode without drawing attention to herself, but she was caught in the doorway as she re-entered the room, by a sudden rekindling of the fire in her behind. As she gasped and gripped her buttocks, Daphne came up to commiserate.

"I take it you had to pay off an unsuitable suitor," she remarked, "anyone I know?"

"Angus McKensie," Eve ground out through gritted teeth, as she kneaded her throbbing cheeks. "The patronising pig. I wouldn't have had him, if he was the last man in the world. I'll take another sixer from him, if he asks again tonight, and cheap at the price."

Daphne looked at her with a thoughtful expression.

"Is that so," she said, as if she had serious doubts, "well, you'll be relieved to know that that's not allowed. The rules of the game say a man, once refused, can't ask again if he's already been given satisfaction, so you're quite safe. Though I do think," she added, "that you might be wrong about Angus. Never mind. Let me find you a nice acceptable young man to kiss those burning buns better."

In the event Daphne was spared the trouble.

"Evening ladies," a strong male voice came from behind them.

"Is the whole Southside here tonight?" Daphne enquired, turning to face a smiling Nick. "And what have you done with Tina?"

"Turned her loose in green, just like you. I'm not expecting to see her again before breakfast."

"Have you seen anything of Penny since she was caged?"

"We were there just the other night. Totally malleable. Didn't lift her eyes once. Doug certainly has a way with women."

"A very backward way, I'd call it," Eve was remembering her painful buggering.

"Oh, hello, Eve. You're looking lovely. And that amber suits you. May I look a little closer?" he asked with a meaningful smile.

What the hell, Eve thought to herself, I've had the beating I promised myself, so let's get fucked, and complete the job. Aloud she said, "perhaps somewhere less crowded, if Daphne will excuse us."

"Don't worry about me, children," Daphne said, one carefully pencilled eyebrow raised in wonder, "I'm sure I won't be lonely."

"I'm sure you won't" Eve laughed, and led the way to the bedrooms.

Nick was everything she needed in a lover, she thought, careful, considerate and unselfish, holding back while she convulsed briefly in a rapid orgasm almost as soon as he penetrated her hungry gash, then coming with her in a less rushed climax, that left them both gasping. Why was it then that it was Angus's craggy face, and peremptory manner, that slid into her sleepy post-coital musings?

CHAPTER 10   TRIALS AND TRIBULATIONS

"If you're really determined to become one of us, it's probably time you set about making a rod for your own backside," Gordon remarked.

It was a week since Eve had worn her amber, and demonstrated a further commitment to the Eden way.

"Past time, I'd say," Daphne agreed, "A woman needs her own rod above her bed to remind her of her status, lest she forgets what she is. She can't feel comfortable and wanted without one."

"Is that why you have a cane hung over your bed, Dee?" Eve asked cautiously.

"Just so. I made that rod myself before I came of age. Every girl does here. Actually, I suppose, since you're what might be termed a 'mature student', it's not entirely necessary, but it would be nice to think you'd continued the tradition."

"And what does that imply?" Eve enquired with even

more suspicion. She'd come to know, over the past few months, that the 'traditional' things were often the toughest in the long run.

"Nothing very difficult," Gordon informed her,"You just get a length of prime cane and treat it to add strength, weight and stiffness; bring it up to penal standard, in other words."

"And how does one prepare a cane, and where does one get the material in the first place?"

"Nothing simpler. There are several places in town that sell quality rattan. The treatment consists of sanding down, drying out, applying repeated dippings in diluted varnish, to rack up the density and cutting power. By then it's up to full weight and strength, and ready for use."

"Sounds easy enough. What's the snag?"

Daphne laughed.

"You're becoming a right cynic in your old age," she grinned. "Actually there's nothing very great. First off there's a bit of a ritual involved. It takes at least a week to complete the process, and any time you're working on the rod you have to be buck naked. I mean really bare. No rings, no watch, no jewellery, not even a hair slide. A piece of string if, like you, your hair might get stuck in the varnish. No make up, scrubbed face and nail varnish removed. You even have to shave your pussy. The only time you can handle the rod with any covering at all is when you first buy it, when you can wear the minimum clothes that decency and the weather will allow, which can be very little out here, but no underwear and all the other provisions about make-up and so on apply."

"Thanks very much. It must be perfectly obvious to everyone you pass just what you're doing. How do you do the actual preparation?"

"First you buy a length of rattan, not less than thirty six inches long and half an inch in diameter. The store will make sure you have the right thing. They're used to women coming in and asking for material for a rod. You also need a can of varnish and a can of thinners. Don't worry about the things to put them in. Gordon has plenty of trays to soak the rod in."

"And then?"

"Then you strip and sand down the rod, taking particular care to produce a nice smooth hemispherical end. It's in your own best interest to put some real care into that bit as anything less than perfectly rounded and smoothed and it could dig deeper into your flank than you'd really care to have it. Of course, a woman is not usually expected to do anything to mitigate her suffering under correction, but it can leave unsightly marks, and we don't want that, do we?"

"Ugh! No," Eve agreed emphatically." So what happens when it up to standard, shape wise?"

"First you dry it out for twenty four hours, in a cool oven," Gordon explained, "then you start to soak it. Five days in a tray of thinned varnish, with a cover, so that the varnish doesn't set before it's soaked all the way in. You have to rock it backwards and forwards four times a day."

"And that means stripping and, later in the week, shaving, each time." Daphne reminded her, "Some girls just stay at home for the week, and never put on any clothes at all until the job's done."

"And that's it?"

"Oh no," Gordon continued. "At the end of five days you fish the rod out, and hang it by the end that is to be the handle. Most girls will have crocheted a string tube to put on at this point, so that the drying varnish attaches it permanently to the rod to give the user a good grip. The surplus varnish runs to the bottom, and it's allowed to dry. The surface will go quite nice and smooth and, with any luck, it will have formed a nice hard 'blob' on your carefully rounded end. When you come to taste it that blob will raise nice thick bruises on your flank, without drawing blood, so try to encourage it. Dry overnight, sand down lightly, apply a thin coat of undiluted varnish, sand again, apply two more coats at intervals of about six hours, with light sanding in between, making sure the blob is building up nicely, and then allow another day to harden."

"And the job's complete?"

"All but the testing."

"I knew it! There just had to be a testing, of course." Eve exclaimed, a slight acidity detectable in her tone, "where, and how many?"

"A butcher's, what else for a new penal, and where do we women get it most, and get most benefit?" Daphne asked mockingly, "Give you three guesses."

"Where we keep our brains, I suppose; our ass, our fanny, our can or, in good plain English, our bum. I'm surprised there are any women on this awful island that can sit. We seem to be getting it day and night."

"Now, Darling, don't exaggerate. We only get it when we need it; or just possibly, if our man needs to relax, which comes to much the same thing. Besides, if it's such an awful island, how come you're so keen to become one of us? No-one forced you."

"You win," Eve agreed, "After Denise's party, next week, I'll shave my pussy and go to town without my pants for the necessary."

"Good idea," Gordon agreed, "It'll give you something to keep you busy, while Daphne's away."

"Oh. What's up then?"

"I'm going to the mainland to see my gynnie," Daphne explained, "I'll do a bit of shopping while I'm there, so I'll be away about a week. I'll leave the honour of the house in your capable hands while I'm away."

"Nothing serious, I hope," Eve said, full of concern,."You seemed in good fettle in that department, the last time I was there."

"Well, you made intimate enough contact to know," Daphne laughed. "No it's just routine. We work our pussies hard out here, so it seems a good idea to have an annual check-up"

"Well hurry on back, darling, I shall miss you. Preparing a rod for my backside, as you so elegantly put it, doesn't sound as if it will exactly fill every waking hour."

The visit to town to purchase the necessaries was as embarrassing as she had feared. Wearing just a short print dress, in honour of the mild sunny weather, bare foot and with scrubbed face, her errand was obvious to all the residents, from the parking attendant who took her fee, to the man behind the counter of the hardware shop, and several hundred passers-by she had met in the street. Blushing furiously she had explained to the man what she needed.

"No problem," he assured her, "we have ladies like yourself in every day who are making their rods. I'll put up our standard pack."

As he handed over a long thin package, whose purpose and contents were the subject of knowing glances from several women making other purchases in the shop, the assistant remarked, "I'm sure you'll be very pleased with this rattan. We only import the finest quality, and I think you'll find its penetrative power very satisfactory."

Eve wasn't sure if satisfactory was the best way to describe what her feelings might be on tasting this boasted power of penetration, but kept her thoughts to herself, escaping from the speculative gaze of the other women present as quickly as she could.

Back home, she completed her ritual stripping and purification, before starting on the limber length of quality rattan. Conscientiously she sanded, dried, soaked and turned, smoothed and drained, while the rod formed slowly under her care. She began to find that the process took on a fascination of its own, drawing her to work on the end blob, building up the coats until she had a significant bulb. Daphne had told her that this added mass, leant strength to each cut of the cane, increasing its power to bruise significantly, especially on the tortured flank, but she didn't stint her efforts to improve its size, swept along by the urge to make the best, regardless of any future personal cost.

She was nearing the end of her task, the rod hanging

vertically, a last coat of varnish draining to add itself to the mass of the bulb, when the phone rang. Still in her scrubbed and naked state she picked it up to hear Gordon on the other end.

"Eve," he said, "I've a bit of a problem."

"Anything I can help with?"

"Perhaps. That's why I'm ringing."

There was a moment's hesitation, unusually for Gordon.

"May not be all that pleasant for you," he said.

"Go on. Fire away," Eve encouraged.

"It's like this. I double parked this morning, thinking I'd be out again in seconds. Unfortunately I got held up by some chap I couldn't put off. By the time I got out they'd towed the Merc to the pound. I need someone to collect it for me."

"Oh."

Eve knew exactly what that meant. A man would merely have to hand over cash, but thanks to that infamous Traffic (Female offenders) Act 1970, that Daphne knew off by heart it seemed, a woman would be subject to the usual penalty.

"I would have asked Daphne to do it, of course," he assured her, "but she's not due back for three days, and the ticket has to be paid off within twenty-four hours."

"But I thought men were allowed to pay a fine," she protested.

"They are, but it's usual to send one of their women to pay, sort of point of honour, you know. No self-respecting woman would let down the honour of the house by buying off for cash."

"And Daphne said she was leaving the honour of the house in my hands, is that it?"

"Actually, there's a slight complication. I've clocked up rather a lot of penalty points on my licence, and the car was parked on a spot reserved for official cars only, so I would very probably lose my licence if I were to admit I was driving. I can't afford to do that, so I'm afraid you're going to have to make out it was you that left it there."

"I don't seem to have much choice, do I? OK, I'll do it; for Daphne and the honour of the house."

Ten minutes later she was dressed as much as she thought necessary, in view of her imminent whipping, a bra, white blouse and short linen skirt. There really didn't seem any point in putting on underpants under the circumstances. She headed the little Renault down the gravel driveway towards the highway and the fate that awaited her in town.

She handed the Renault over to Gordon in exchange for the keys to the Merc, and set off to the Traffic Department offices.

The same female clerk was on the desk, and confirmed that she had come to the right place to recover the Merc. She inspected Eve's visitor's licence, filled in details on a printed form, handed it over and told her to take a seat in the waiting-room.

"You'll be called when they're ready for you," she was informed.

Nothing had changed in the waiting-room except the faces of the women seated in line on their pegs, although their expressions were exactly the same mixture of discomfort and apprehension she remembered. She had no doubt her own exactly matched theirs, as she settled herself reluctantly on a well-licked nozzle. This time, the discomfort in her rectum was aggravated by apprehension as to what came next. Other than an intimate examination of the sickening welts on Daphne's tortured bottom, she'd not extracted any details from her friend of exactly what had gone on behind that closed door, only that it had been painful, humiliating, and to be avoided at all costs. Now she was about to get first hand experience herself.

The waiting seemed interminable. There were only two other offenders ahead of her, but their processing seemed to take forever. When the second of them had staggered from the room, face beetroot red, body arched in pain, moaning through her teeth as she gripped her buttocks through the hastily donned skirt, Eve nearly wet herself with the strain of waiting for the command to enter.

"Next!" the voice called, and she levered herself carefully off her peg, mindful of the havoc she had wrought by her intemperent extraction previously. It wasn't exactly comfortable this time either, she still had to break the grip her sphincter had established on the inadequately lubricated rod, but at least she didn't tear her anus.

On legs of rubber she crossed the room, unminding of the pitying glances of the next women in line, and passed into the room beyond. It contained little more cheer than the bleak, forbidding chamber she had passed the last two hours in, just a small desk, a medical examination table and a straight-backed chair. Besides the male whose head had rounded the door to summon each delinquent to her doom, a second male figure in a civilian suit, sat behind the desk.

"Papers!" it barked, and Eve fumbled in her haste to hand them over.

"First time?"

She admitted it was.

"Then we'll try and ensure you do not wish to return," the official promised. "Take off your clothes and lie on the table there."

Not daring to hesitate, she stripped quickly, laying her clothes on the chair, while watched, apparently without interest, by the two men. It would seem they had seen too many female bodies stripped naked in this room, and no jutting buttock, swelling breast, or sweetly furred belly could rouse their interest anymore. It was all simply meat to be flogged and sent on its way, hopefully reformed, or at least, deterred from reoffending.

The suit approached the table and made a cursory examination of her naked body, ordering her to part her thighs to expose her vulva, and turn onto her front so that he could grip a cheek in each hand and stretch them apart after he'd palped her breasts. She could actually feel his breath on her inflamed anus. Finally he went back to the desk and wrote out some notes.

"You can get up now," he said without looking up from his work. "Leave your things where they are and go through there."

The uniform grasped her arm to reinforce the point and thrust her through another door, to confront another suit. Uniform passed him the first suit's notes, and the other papers.

"Seems you've been a naughty girl," he announced, after a brief perusal. "Double parked, and in an official area too. We can't have that sort of thing. The Medical examiner reports you're a strong healthy young woman, so there is no reason why you should not be made an example of. Six strokes for double parking and twelve for obstructing an area reserved for officials."

"Oh no! Please!" she burst out, as the awful tally sank into her consciousness. "That's too many, just for a parking offence."

"Are you making an official appeal?" the suit wanted to know.

Eve checked herself. She had to be careful. She was appalled by the sentence, but she was on dangerous ground, appeals on this island were almost invariably unsuccessful and the price of that failure was normally a doubling of the sentence. Even if it didn't lead to the full potential of a thirty-six stroke flogging, it was not a gamble she dared to take.

"No Sir."

"A wise decision," the suit said drily. "Carry on Officer."

Uniform turned her back, away from the desk, and her belly lurched as she took in the rest of the room. A bleak arrangement of bars occupied the centre of its stone-flagged width. She had seen the equivalent many times before in studies and basements in the homes she had visited with Daphne, standard female correctional equipment it seemed, though this particular example of the breed seemed just that little extra solid and intimidating. Two heavy cast iron uprights, seemingly cemented into the floor, four horizontal iron rails, one at crotch height, one to suit the knees, the other two spaced apart some six or eight inches horizontally, no more than four or five inches off the floor. Altogether a bleak and uninviting object for a naked woman to place her body on. She let herself be positioned with its top bar pressing against the furry triangle at the base of her belly then, on command, stepped inside the bottom rail, which ran across the back of her leg, a little way above the ankle. Uniform pushed her feet apart with the toe of his boot, and dropped a plate across the lower bars to ensure she couldn't close them again.

"Over!" he ordered, and she bent from the waist over the top rail, reaching down for the lowest rail on that side. The last pressed against her shins, just below the knees, ensuring she could not bend her legs. There was a sensation of cold steel, and a click, and her wrists were handcuffed to the bar. Now she was quite immobilised. Her bare buttocks were bent and stretched at just the right height for a rod in a male hand to cut into the fatty under-sides, where it would bruise most, and leave the sufferer sore for the longest; right in the Sitzplas and with eighteen she'd be lucky to be able to take her weight on those butchered hams for a week. Her imagination raced. What did she look like back there to these taciturn men, going about their business, as if they were dipping sheep? With her legs spread like this, she was only too well aware of her pouting pussy grinning through her gapped thighs, its light covering of hairy tendrils insufficient to conceal its moist seam, above it the wrinkled crater of her anus shrinking into itself. She whimpered in sudden fear as she heard the rattle of a rod, as Uniform picked it up off the desk.

He must have looked at his superior for permission for Suit announced solemnly, "you may proceed officer."

For an age nothing happened, then there was a thrrrrping sound behind her, a meaty sound as the rod impacted and then all hell broke loose in the hapless buttock flesh.

"Aarh!" she groaned as fire swept through her lacerated

hinds, and hissed like a snake as she tried to master the rising tide that followed. Biting her lip she rode it out and braced herself for the second.

Again she grunted with pain, adding a long drawn out moan as she tried to ride it, then rocked under the third, which had her gasping and panting in its aftermath.

She had only had three and, already, she was sweating and clenching. It would do her no good, she knew, but it was impossible to let her stung buttocks fall limp.

The toll mounted inexorably. Four had her rising on her toes as far as the bars would allow, at five she tried to twist aside. The rod's tip was boring into her flank, and she thought she could feel a small trickle there already. At six the presiding Suit called a halt.

"Hold off a minute," he ordered," With a dozen and a half the woman sometimes goes off into a fog, and doesn't feel them all fully. Give her a short break, and she'll clear her head and get to savour them all through."

It was not really mercy but, at the time, it seemed a blessing beyond price. Eve hung over the heartless rigidity of the bars, drawing in deep breaths, trying to steady her racing pulse. All too soon, Suit called time.

"Next six, if you please. You should be able to make her feel them after your rest," he remarked.

Uniform was a professional. A stroke from a long penal, wrapping round the flank, biting in on the hip, raising thick plum coloured blobs on the tender sides, was always liable to break the skin and let the blood flow. With eighteen it was almost a certainty, given the relatively small area that had to sustain a dozen and a half agonising impacts. The artist in him deplored too heavy damage to such delicate flesh and he compensated for the severer sentences by deploying an ambidexterity developed by long practice into perfectly balanced correction. The first stroke of her second tranche fell across Eve's cringing buttocks from right to left, sparing the martyred flesh, where six bluish black bruises graced her right hip, impacting instead on the hitherto unmarked left.

Though conscious of the mercy shown, when contemplating her wounds later, at the time she could only think of the searing pain of the stroke itself. She had collected her resources in the brief interval allowed her, and gave only an agonised grunt of pain as it struck, a sharp intake of breath a second later as the full measure of the hurt chimed in. To brace herself against the new angle of attack, she pressed her belly against the unyielding iron of the top bar, biting her lower lip, gripping the lowest bar in front as if to save herself from drowning.

Eight bit in deep, sending her writhing sideways again, nine had her rising and falling on her toes, her knees scraping on the rough metal of the bar that prevented her from trying to get relief by bending them.

Ten caught her much lower than to date, Exactly on the boundary between thigh and buttock swell. She mewled with the pain of being cut in such a tender spot. Uniform methodically completed the dozen with two more precisely on the line, leaving her whimpering and whining as she took the half minute break awarded her to enable her to appreciate the full measure of her punishment.

Uniform resumed where he had left off, though with the right hand again, precisely in the crease or, as Daphne was wont to put it, right behind the cunt. Two sizzling cuts to the line of raised bruise there and she yelped shrilly at each, her anguish heightened by fear that he would cut short and find the pouting vulva that would be menaced if the tip of the rod was allowed to enter the valley between the spread thighs and seek it out.

She had gone fourteen so far, and now sweated freely, her face a mask of pain and mucus from snorting nostrils and gaping mouth. Her lower lip was swollen to twice its normal size, where she had bitten on it as she awaited each stroke. She was sure she could taste blood. With four more to come, she was beginning to feel despair, as if she would never survive this awful martyrdom of her spread naked buttocks. Fourteen aching lines of blood filled welts stretched across them now. How in Eden's name could she endure the last quartet?

In fact, of course, she could do nothing but endure them. A woman, stripped naked, hung over those effectively constraining bars, cuffed to the rail in front, her feet trapped behind, was just so much meat behind, over which she had no control, merely slabs of flesh, which could feel but not resist. She must hang there and howl, if she could not suffer in silence.

Four more times the rod whirred and thumped, four times she went rigid, relaxed, howled her distress and outrage, slumped until the rod stiffened her again. When the final stroke had fallen she could only hang over the top rail and sob.

Released, she was forbidden, under threat of a return visit to the bars, to touch her blistered, bloated bottom. So sore she could hardly move her legs, she shuffled to the wall and stood, hands on head, her raw beaten buttocks to the room, facing into a corner for five minutes by the clock.

Finally released, told to get dressed, exit and be quick about it, she almost scampered to the next room in her haste to obey, pulling on her clothes as best she could, careless of her appearance, only wanting out of there. She made her own version of the unnerving entrance that all of her predecessors, and all of her successors made and would make; the rigid arching as she pulled open the stiffly sprung door, the rictus of pain on her face as she stood in the doorway getting her breath back to cross the waiting room under the gaze of those still to have their turn under the rod, the limping passage past the secretary's desk, and the hit of daylight after the dimness of the correctional establishment. She paused on the top of the steps, dimly conscious that the crowd in the street would all be aware of what she had been there for, and, no doubt, all imagining what lay beneath her hastily fastened skirt; the women with mixed sympathy and lust, the men with dry amusement and a certain satisfaction that a proper justice had been done. She was still blushing when she limped into Gordon's office. At his suggestion they garaged the Renault for the night and he drove her home in the Mercedes. It had the advantage that there was room for her to kneel across the back seat.

By the time Daphne got back, she was getting over the worst, though her bottom was still a disaster area, and she took care to position a soft cushion before she sat. Looking at the rainbow-hued welts, at four days old ripened into tight finger-thick ropes, hot heavy, still inflamed and too sore for comfort, Daphne was all concern.

"What rotten luck," she sympathised, "Of course I would have had to take them if I'd been here, for the honour of the house, you know, but it was damned brave of you to do it."

"But I had to," Eve explained, "You left the honour of the house in my charge, remember?"

Nothing more was said but, at breakfast the next morning, Daphne's reluctance to commit her buttocks to even the softest of cushions was more eloquent than words.

"For the honour of the house?" Eve enquired, settling herself just as carefully.

"Mmm," Daphne agreed, shifting uneasily in her seat, "Couldn't shirk my responsibility, y'know."

"You didn't have to."

"Oh yes I did. Besides, Gordon couldn't very well send me to the gynie with a bottom like a ploughed field. Didn't lay a rod on me for days beforehand and, by the time I got back, I'd been a month without a thrashing worth the name. A girl can't get by if she's neglected for so long."

Time passed. Nothing had been said about Eve's projected application for citizenship for a month. By now she had healed, save a few discolorations on her hip, that might well leave some small scars for a long while yet, and she'd recovered her normal good spirits, after a period of relatively muted behaviour.

"I imagine you've had enough of our ways," Daphne said

one evening, as they lay in front of a wood fire, lit to cheer the coolness of some of the island nights, "What do you plan to do when you get back to the UK?"

"I'm not going back," Eve said, "I still want to put in my papers. I needed time to get over that beating I took, but it hasn't changed anything."

Daphne looked thoughtful, but let it drop for the moment. The next day, though, she cornered Eve after breakfast, and told her to sit down and listen carefully.

"Gordon and I both love you dearly, and we're concerned that you may not know what you're letting yourself in for," she began. "If you put your papers in, he's only prepared to countersign them if you pass some preliminary tests first. Since a woman understands another woman much better than a man, he's turned that part over to me.".

"I would have thought the men round here know all about thrashing a woman. Anyway, haven't I survived enough beatings to convince you yet?" Eve asked acidly.

"Ah but the physical discipline is only one part of it, and in some ways the easiest to bear," Daphne assured her, "though you might not think so under the rod or the lash. but the course at the Initiation Centre is designed specifically to humiliate and break a woman's pride so that she can be remade as a suitable companion for men. We are anxious that you don't bite off more than you bargained for, and have to pull out. You'd never get over it, knowing you."

"So what has Gordon got in store for me?" Eve asked doubtfully.

"He's left the details to me; as I said, he believes quite rightly, that only a woman can get completely under another woman's skin, and really make her writhe. Here's what you'll have to do to get your application countersigned. First off, for two weeks, you don't get out of those clothes you're wearing right now."

"You mean I have to put on the same things every day?"

"No, I mean you don't get to take them off for a fortnight. You keep them on day and night."

"Ouch! I see what you mean by the female angle on this. A man would never think what that would do for a woman. Never mind," she said, pointing her chin determinedly, "I'll do it. I'll have to take them off when I shower, of course."

"No showers darling, no baths, in fact you'll not touch soap and water for a fortnight and that make-up stays put, just where it is, until it wears off too. And no brush and comb, not even a toothbrush, until your time is up. Oh, and one more thing," looking at Eve's sleeveless blouse, "No razor. You should have some nicely ragged tufts under there in two weeks, not to speak of a powerful perfume."

"I suppose I'll be allowed to take my pants down when I use the john," Eve said caustically.

Daphne seemed to consider the request, as if doubtful it could be granted.

"You can take your pants down, but no toilet paper. You'll be pretty ripe in this climate by the time you finish."

"You bitch! You really do know how to get a woman where it hurts, don't you?"

"See what I mean? You may be able to take a beating, darling, but a little humiliation and you fold like a wilting flower."

"Who said I'm wilting," Eve exclaimed indignantly, "OK, I'll do it, though I don't think I'll be leaving my room much of the time."

"You don't learn do you," Daphne reproached her. "Surely you remember the golden rule. Didn't you understand that here every woman must always continue with her normal social life after punishment, as if nothing had happened? You'll go to town with your clothes sticking to your back, and mix with the others at parties stinking to high heaven, and, just to encourage you, I'm going to cane you every morning before breakfast. Time that new rod of yours got an airing."

"I can't do it," Eve wailed, "you can't ask that of me! Not the beating, I don't mean that. I'll take three thrashing a day, if that's what you say, but I can't go out to your friends, looking like an alcoholic slag, and stinking like the public sewer."

"I told you you wouldn't be able to take it," Daphne replied, sadly, "Better you admit it now, and not have to be rescued from the Centre with a nervous breakdown. They'll put you through worse than that in there."

Eve drew herself up very straight, and set her jaw.

"I can and I will," she declared, "I'll show you I can do it. When do I start?"

"Right here and now darling. You can go and get that lovely new cane of yours, and I'll give it a test run before you bring it to me again before breakfast. Then it's bed on a burning bottom."

By the second week, Eve was as pungent as Daphne had promised. Even at the beginning, social life was a torment, and it didn't get better. Any benefit she found from familiarity with the situation was easily outweighed by the rapid worsening of her hygiene. One evening, as she set her crumpled and soiled once-white skirt moving and followed Daphne to the waiting car, the waft of thick body odour was so strong it hit her like a blow. Her underarms itched from their rapidly rising growth of scratchy stubble and contributed its own rich perfume to the stench emanating from her crotch. Try as she might to accustom herself to these shaming effluvia, not to speak of the dry skin and rubbed mascara, the worn and smudged lipstick, the dirty nails, with their chipped polish, she was never for a minute unaware of her condition and, much worse, that all those she came in contact with were just as aware.

Her bottom was sore and burning with the steadily rising collection of welts, old and new, that Daphne laid on in the chilly hour before breakfast. Religiously she unhooked her personal rod, and carried it in to Daphne's room, as soon as she heard Gordon making his early morning start to the office. Saturday and Sunday she had to take her stripes in front of him. She felt peculiarly humiliated to submit to another woman in front of him, and even more so when she had to peel off the stinking panties, with their disgusting streaks of excrement, and the acrid fumes of stale urine. She would have much preferred to take twice the strokes from his own hand instead.

And then the blessed morning came. She had taken her rod in to Daphne as usual, handed it over without a word, and bent and touched her toes. Daphne had laid them on with a particular emphasis that morning, and the tears welled in her eyes. When it was over, she lifted her up and held her close.

"That was lovely," she declared, "I enjoyed that one more than any other beating I've given you this last fortnight. Can you guess why?"

Eve could only shake her head against the full soft breasts it was pressed into. Daphne's nightwear, like that of most of the women of Eden consisted of a little perfume dabbed behind the ears.

"Because darling it was not part of your trial. You've become so intoxicated by your own stench you haven't been keeping count. Your fortnight was up last night. That beating was purely for pleasure. Mine that is," she added hastily, "I hope you found it extraordinarily painful. How would you feel about a bath?"

"You bitch!" Eve exclaimed, "You lovely bitch! I don't care, though. If I can just soak all morning in hot suds I'll forgive you anything."

That night, still glowing in the euphoria brought on by a hot tub, and fresh underwear, she was summoned to Gordon's study. She found him sitting at his desk. With a hand gesture he directed her to the traditional spot on the mat in front of it. She felt like a naughty schoolgirl in the Head's office. Perhaps he intended to cane her too. She didn't care; nothing mattered now. Besides, she was beginning to find a caning from a man part of the natural order of things; evolution's plan for stable relationships between the sexes.

"Daphne tells me you came through her test with flying colours, not to speak of a colourful bottom. It must have needed some grit, judging by the whiffs I caught from time to time."

"Frankly," Eve declared with feeling," I'd rather you had strung me up on a triangle and given me a bloody back, than go through that again."

"Hmm! You may well be getting that as well," he remarked grimly, picking up a sheaf of papers from the desk. "After what you've been through, are you quite sure you wish to go carry on with these?" he asked. Eve recognised her immigration application forms.

"Quite sure," she declared firmly, "the more so just because of what I've been through."

"You realise it will mean doing a spell in a Female Initiation Centre? They're not exactly renowned for their gentleness."

"So I've heard but I understand all the women here go through it, so it seems only fair that I should too."

"You've got the right spirit," Gordon conceded, "but don't forget, they've been bred to it from childhood. Watched their cousins and aunts and elder sisters go through it. It's second nature to them. Do you have any idea what to expect?"

"Oh Daphne has been giving me some lurid accounts," Eve replied," and what she didn't mention the other girls made sure was filled in in graphic detail."

"You know that at some point you can look forward to being flogged to the blood at the triangle, as you were suggesting in jest a moment ago?"

"I wasn't jesting. I'd rather that than go another fortnight without soap or clean knickers."

"Well, if you're so determined, who am I to stand in your way? I'll sign."

"Oh thank you Gordon. May I kiss you now please?"

"Hold your horses. Much as I'd enjoy such intimacy, we've a few more points to settle yet. Amongst other things I have to give my opinion on your suitability for treatment, your capacity for endurance, and the strength of your will. These will be taken into consideration in determining how long you will spend in the freezer, and the regime to which you will be subjected."

"The freezer?"

"The Female Reconstruction and Educational Establishment, but that's too much of a mouthful. You'll find the women round here all refer to it as the freezer. They've all been through it of course, though most will have done the minimum stretch. I can't guarantee what sort of stretch you'll have to serve."

"So it's not a standard course than?"

"Far from it. Well, there's not much variation in the treatment of youngsters who come to it at eighteen or nineteen. For them it's mostly a standard term, just like going to college, no more than a month unless their families have particular reason to suggest they require special treatment. That doesn't happen often here, given the healthy social climate young women grow up in, but sometimes a girl gets infected by pernicious feminist tosh and takes a little longer than usual to be shown the error of her ways. With mature students, as it were, things are different. They're much more likely to have picked up unfortunate habits in the outside world, or developed an assertiveness that needs straightening out, and their treatment is carefully configured to meet their individual needs."

"What do you mean?"

"Well, the course may be made harsher to compensate for soft living before they were brought to the island, or longer as well as harsher, if they show evidence of being particularly strong willed or used to getting their own way. Sometimes the standard course is inadequate for that kind of woman, and she needs to serve an extra novitiate, so to speak, before she is fit to take her vows."

"Are you two going to take all night to sign a piece of paper? I'm dying for a drink."

Gordon shot a bleak look at his wife's head, where it

craned round his study door.

"Charmingly put, my dear," he remarked, "remind me to thank you for your timely intervention in a tangible way, once I have dealt with Eve's problem. In the meantime I suggest you take a seat, while you still can in any comfort, and bring your woman's view to bear on the matter."

"What's the problem, then?" Daphne asked, settling her splendid haunches onto the leather of one of his armchairs, apparently unmoved by the thrashing that Gordon intended for them.

"Would you say Eve would be adequately covered by the standard course, or should I recommend an extended treatment? Is she strong-willed beyond the average and too used to having her own way, instead of deferring to men, would you say?"

Daphne contemplated her friend thoughtfully, as she stood at attention on the mat.

"Why don't you ask Eve?" she suggested, finally.

"Maybe I might just forgive your interruption," Gordon said admiringly. "A suggestion like that deserves some reward."

"Thank you, Sir," she replied without sarcasm. "Though I probably still have need of a thrashing."

Gordon smiled lovingly at his wife and turned to Eve.

"Well, what do you think? How would you rate your own character? I see you as a young woman who sees herself better than most."

Eve let her eyes drop for a second, as she gathered her thoughts.

"You're right of course," she said finally, "I am strong willed, and I have been used to having my own way too long. Of course, you can't run a successful business in today's world without it, but it plays havoc with feminine nature."

"That's pretty definite," Gordon accepted. "How about your treatment? Should I recommend the standard course, which means you'd be out in a month, or do you think you'd need something more? I have to warn you, you could be held for up to twice the normal stretch, with or without a spell on a chain-gang."

This was getting serious. Bad enough to have to spend two months living under the conditions Daphne and, especially her young friends, had recited with such obvious relish for her discomfiture and, she had noticed, little shadows of fear in their own eyes at their recollections of the experience. What about the chain-gang though!? None of the girls had been on one, so there were no first hand descriptions, but they weren't needed. She'd seen them for herself several times, since that first startling eye-opener on the day Daphne had collected her from the airport.

This won't do, she reproached herself, you were asked if you needed more than the normal ration of discipline to make you worthy to join the other women in Eden, and here you are already thinking about whether you could take it, not whether you need it, which is what you were asked.

Aloud she said, "I think you should recommend additional treatment."

"Oh Darling, I'm so proud of you," Daphne cried, rising from her chair and throwing her arms around her friend, "That was really honest and brave."

"I agree," her husband echoed, writing something on the forms in front of him, then signing it with a flourish. "Now, while Eve just countersigns here, accepting my recommendations, you may remove your knickers and fetch me one of those canes you love so much from the closet over there."

CHAPTER 11   THE FREEZER

At breakfast a week later, Gordon opened an official look-ing brown envelope, read the contents quickly and passed it over to Eve. It was a formal notification to Gordon, as her sponsor, that her application for citizenship had been accepted, subject to a satisfactory report from the Female Reconstruction and Education Establishment. That body would take her up as soon as a vacancy occurred. Meanwhile her sponsor should take steps to ensure she could be contacted at short notice at any time.

"So that's it," she said, "I'm in."

"Well there is just the little matter of the freezer yet," Daphne cautioned her. "You won't be told what sort of stretch you'll have to do until they've had you in and assessed you formally, so it could be a little while yet before you get your papers."

Staying in contact provided no difficulty; the housekeeper always knew where the women were going when they left the house. In fact the call came when the three of them were at-tending a smart reception for a visiting dignitary, a cocktail party on the lawns of the home of the Chief Minister. Gordon had gone along with his two women on his arms, Daphne to his right, as befitted the wife, Eve on his left, the place re-served for mistresses or guests. Dee had recommended 'best bib and tucker' again but not, to Eve's great relief, the full Emily Post drill that went with those painful memories of Ladies' Night. She'd chosen a tailored linen suit in dove grey, over a crisp white blouse, gunmetal nylons held tautly by a lacy garterbelt, part of a matching set of bra and high cut briefs. Polished pumps with three inch heels completed an outfit that spoke of money and sophisticated good taste, and she moved from group to group on the crowded lawn, with a quiet confidence in herself and her appearance. As she turned away from some acquaintances to cross to a girl she recognised from the visit to Lavinia, she found herself confronted by two large females in military style uniforms.

"Is your name Eve?" one of them enquired.

"It is," she admitted, more curious than alarmed

"And can you confirm that this is you?" the woman persisted, holding out a sheet of paper with a photograph attached.

Eve's belly did a quick somersault, as she recognised her own passport picture, and precise details of her physical appearance, down to her bra cup, and the size of her shoes.

"Yes. That's me," she confirmed. So it had come. This was it; her 'taking up' as the notice had promised.

"Please remove all your clothing," the officer requested.

Eve looked at her in astonishment.

"Here?" she exclaimed, "in front of all these people? Can't we at least go inside?"

Daphne was at her elbow.

"Don't argue, darling," she urged, "it will only make it worse. They are Freezers, FREE's security, and they take up entrants exactly where they find them. You could earn yourself a serious punishment if you resist. You could even foul up your chances of becoming a citizen.

Eve capitulated and took off her jacket, handing it to Daphne, then the skirt. With trembling fingers she unbuttoned the blouse. Why had she chosen this particular one this day of all days? The people around her had stopped their conversation to stare as she fumbled with the row of a score of tiny buttons that held the blouse together over her thrusting breasts, and more and more were turning to look as they realised something untoward was occurring. She could see the visiting dignitary paused with his glass short of his lips, as he drank in the scene. Even more embarrassing was the look she was getting from the eminent man's young wife.

She set her teeth and stripped off the blouse. Her fingers transferred themselves blindly to the clasp of her bra and the heavy globes of her breasts sprang free as she handed the scrap of lace that had been taming them to her friend. For some reason she chose to peel off the briefs from her glistening crotch and step out of them carefully, a foot at a time, leaving herself only her gartered stockings and her shoes. The pumps were soon at Daphne's feet, then each stocking was unhooked in turn and rolled down its shapely thigh to be passed over as a soft coit of flimsy nylon. Finally the garter belt joined the pile of feminine gear resting on Daphne's arms and Eve stood up naked as her namesake in front of the large and curious crowd.

Well not quite as naked as the girl in the ancient garden.

"Those too," the guard said with a gesture and her watch, her rings, the pearl studs from her ears, joined the rest of her apparel. Now she was truly naked; buck naked, nude as a slug, bare-arsed and pink titted. Proudly she stood upright, and disdained to try and cover her nakedness with her hands.

"Turn around," the guard ordered, "and put your hands behind your back."

The snap of the cuffs seemed to jolt something in her memory.

"Daphne," she called urgently, "Daisy will be here by the time I get out. Who's going to be my sponsor once she's Gordon's mistress?"

"Don't worry, Darling," Daphne reassured her, "we'll find somebody suitable before you get out. Trust me."

With that she had to be content for while she had been speaking the guard had fastened a heavy dog collar about her neck. It carried a brass plate with the number 213 in large numerals, and a leash, which the guard pulled harshly to indicate she should go with them. Flanked on either side by her formidable females, she walked naked and cuffed through the well dressed crowd, which parted to let her through, then closed behind her with a buzz of conversation, to watch her departing back and enticingly rolling buttocks.

The journey was a nightmare and seemed to take forever. She was made to kneel on the floor of a small van, on a fibre mat which chaffed her knees. Straps held her ankles firm and her cuffs were hauled up behind her and dropped over a hook on a short piece of chain hanging from the roof. Shoulders aching, knees sore, she groaned and moaned with every bump of the poorly sprung vehicle on the rough roads of the island. It was a relief when the van stopped and she had reached her destination, although she was under no delusion as to the nature of her reception or the harshness of her life for the next month or two.

The Female Reconstruction and Education Establishment was housed in a grim military pile, a relic of some long passed colonial administration that had felt the need to build this grim structure to house its brutal and licentious soldiery, and put the fear of God into the surrounding natives. As far as Eve was concerned it still achieved the latter purpose efficiently, even if she was not a native.

The only external concession she could see to its present incarnation was the motto of the service, carved deeply in large Gothic letters above the dark recess of the forbidding iron-bound entrance gates:-

IN SUBMISSION FREEDOM

Inside, the barrack-like building was revealed as a hollow square, its walls as bleak on the inside as on the outer face, except that the former carried rows of small barred windows where the latter had sported mere rifle slits. The sheer granite walls, and lack of openings, showed instantly the futility of thinking of escape, should the regime become unbearable. More immediately, their chilling grey aspect, and brutal strength brought home to her her powerless naked femininity.

She had little time to think of such matters though, or even to take in the groups of women, naked as herself, that were scattered about the vast parade ground, toiling at unknown tasks under the barked incomprehensible orders of female guards, all from much the same brutal mould as her own escorts.

These jerked on her chain to bring her through another forbidding doorway, into the dark bowels of the establishment, giving her little chance to take in the proceedings in the court-yard. A brief call at a reception desk, where the first guard called out Eve's name and number to the clerk behind the desk, and handed in the identity papers, then she was pro-pelled into a large circular chamber, its wall tiled to the ceil-ing. One of the guards went to the centre of the circle, where a hose and brass nozzle hung from a central hydrant. Number two pushed Eve into the room, then stepped back, closing the door on her, and watched the proceeding through a large glass panel, an anticipatory grin on her face.

"Time for a wash," the first guard said, and turned on a tap.

Instantly a jet of ice cold water sprang from the nozzle and caught her in the belly, driving her against the wall. The pressure was immense, and the jet felt like an iron bar. With her arms still fastened behind her back, she could do nothing to protect herself, and the jet moved from belly to breasts, hitting them like a whip. She cried out in shock and pain, as the awful force drove into her tender mammaries, pinned against the tiles for a moment, then the guard began to play the jet with the skill of long practice. With deadly accuracy she switched the aching blast of icy water from breasts to buttocks, waist to thighs, back to the breasts again, then into the divide of her buttocks, each time drawing a new cry from her victim, and each time moving her on in the desired direc-tion. Helpless under the agonising assault, Eve found herself spun steadily round, as she progressed around the outside of the bizarre circus ring she was trapped in. The guard used the jet to handle her like a baby, though no woman would think of treating a baby like that, sending her willy nilly round the circuit, hitting every part of her flinching body in the process. The jet blasted her pussy, leaving it throbbing and abused, knocked her head almost senseless, as it tore into her hair, loosening it and leaving it hanging in wet curtains around her face. It caught her breasts painfully, distorting them momentarily into weird caricatures of their normal delightful globes, the nipples hardening into aching rocks. It lashed her buttocks like a wet rope's end, leaving them sore and bruised, and drove the breath from her in hooting gasps as it hit her full in her softly rounded belly. By the time the guard switched off the hose, after three dreadful circuits of the wash circle, she was hoarse and exhausted from her cries, battered and bruised all over, and barely able to stand.

"No-one can say we aren't concerned for hygiene here," the guard observed in what she appeared to think a humorous remark. Eve was not amused.

Still panting and aching she was hauled on her leash to a bare walled room, with a medical couch, a desk and various cabinets of equipment.

They were joined almost immediately by a young blonde woman. She was tall, slim, pretty; no, Eve corrected herself, actually she was genuinely beautiful, with those high cheekbones and blue eyes, but something about the woman caused her to flinch. There was a hardness around the eyes and mouth that belied the beauty, something of the night, a cruel icy Northern night. Eve shuddered in her naked vulnerability before this threatening female.

She seemed to be the medical officer for she wore a white coat, unlike the military style uniforms of all the other staff she had seen so far, and this seemed to be confirmed when she pulled on a pair of surgical gloves.

"Get her ready," she ordered and the guards pushed her up to the metal table, until the edge pressed across the tops of her thigh in line with the gash of her vulva. Strong hands forced her over and down until her breasts, with their fear hardened nipples still chilled into rigid points, rested on the cold iron. A heavy boot kicked at the inside of one ankle, forcing her to move that foot sideways and, a second later, an equally painful knock on the other caused her to open her thighs widely. Something cold touched the gape of her labia, and she recognised the smell of KY. As the realisation of what was about to happen hit her, she at least consoled herself that she wouldn't suffer it unlubricated.

Latex clad fingers forced their way in, one by one, until the hand was bunched in a tight cone, the thumb supporting the others to make a spearhead threatening her cringing belly. There was a forceful thrust, she gasped, groaned, the arm thrust harder and she felt the hand entering deeply into her stretched vagina. One more vigorous shove and it was all in, and the woman's fingers were exploring her cervix, squeezing painfully on the neck of her womb. She gave a small animal sound of distress and her assailant rebuked her in a slight Nordic accent.

"You think this is rough girl. Wait until I check your arse. Then you'll have something to howl about."

At last she seemed satisfied and withdrew her hand. The exit was almost as painful as the entrance, for she used no finesse, simply pulling her hand free in one brusque movement, but at least it was a relief to have it gone. There was a short pause and the fingers were back, but this time probing the even more reluctant anus. A latex-wrapped digit pressed hard on the wrinkled whorl of brown tissue clenching tightly against it, forced the passage brutally, then was joined by a second. After some exploratory turning in the narrow passage, they made room for a third and them a fourth. Oh God! Was that her thumb? No no, she couldn't be planning that, surely?

But she was. The wedge of fingers formed itself again, the tips just lodged in the clenching sphincter.

"Give," the doctor cried, slapping hard on a bare buttock. Eve tried to let herself relax; it would be best she knew, but this was impossible. The doctor murmured something to one of the guards, who unclipped a short dog whip from her belt. There was a brief sound of air parting and a crack of leather on girl flesh, and Eve cried out at the sudden blast of fire in her rear. In the ensuing maelstrom of pain that followed, somehow she let herself go enough that the doctor's fingers pushed in past the knuckle. After that it was simply a matter of brutal shove, followed by a cruel screwing motion, and her wrist was through, followed by her arm up to the elbow. If Eve had thought the palping of her womb was bowel churning, this invasion of her rectum, followed by the opening of the penetrating fist into vice-like fingers that explored her entrails and organs ruthlessly, left her sweating and nauseous. When the doctor finally extracted the probing hand with no more care than she had evacuated her vagina, she could only howl in protest.

Weak legged she was made to stand, then given a cursory examination of her breasts, mouth, ears and feet, before being told she was in excellent condition, and would be reported as fit for all levels of exercise and discipline, standard, medium and hard. Feelings of satisfaction and pride in her physique were clouded be a certainty that this could only be to her disadvantage among the severe regimes of this bleak establishment.

"You can take her down to processing now," the doctor informed the guards, and in a minute Eve found herself in another bare and unfriendly chamber, where even worse humiliations awaited, though without the icy menace of the doctors manner to turn the knife. The operators here seemed bored and indifferent, but lacked the calculated cruelty of the medical woman. Eve hoped, without much conviction, that she would not have to encounter her again.

First to arrive was a monstrous enema. Forced over a similar table to the one in medical inspection, she had to brace herself while a gross, moulded rubber nozzle was forced into her stretched and sore anus, and two quarts of hot soapy water run in from a rubber bag hung from a drip stand. Her bowels writhed and roiled, her belly swelled. She wanted desperately to 'go' but the nozzle held her sealed immovably. Only after ten full minutes of belly cramps and pain was the nozzle none too gently withdrawn, and she was allowed to squat over a bucket and relieve herself, amid a cacophony of shaming belching from her bowels, liquid eruptions of the most disgusting nature, and spasmodic jerks of her belly. When at last she had quieted a little, she was made to go over the table again and take a repeat of the horrible irrigational procedure.

The uproar in her belly quelled enough for her to respond to instructions. For the first time since she had been cuffed, naked in front of the crowd at the reception that afternoon, her manacles were released, but only to be snapped shut again with her hands in front of her, but it was like a present from heaven compared to the increasing torture of having her arms secured behind her. She was told to mount the table and lie on her back, her knees first, drawn up tightly, then allowed to fall outwards, leaving her vulva and mons totally exposed. One of the civilian attendants produced a bundle of linen strips, an insulated bowl containing hot honey coloured grains and a wooden spoon. She heaped the hot unrefined sugar, as it proved to be, on the hairy vulva, working it in with the spoon, and pressed strips of linen tightly against it, ignoring the protests this scalding assault evinced. A warning cut with the dog whip on one tender white inner thigh sent a clear message of what would happen if she failed to keep herself fully open.

After some minutes in this painful and humiliating pose, her attendant returned and tested the result. Satisfied, she gripped the end of the first strip and, with a slow deliberate and inexorable movement, tore it from its place. The cooling sugar ensured that hairs and strip remained firmly together. Since something had to give, it was the lodgement of the hairs in the tender skin of her mons and vulva. Inch by inch the cruel extraction proceeded, until Eve could bear the pain and, more particularly the long drawn out nature of the process, no more, and vented her anguish and frayed nerves in a howl of frustration.

When the last fugitive hairs from around her anus and in the crevice of her anal divide had been pulled acheingly out, leaving her crotch and crease hairless, red and inflamed, as sore as if she had had a kettle of boiling water poured over them, she had thought there was nothing more she could be made to endure in the way of 'processing. She was wrong. The final scene, the one that would nearly break her, the moment she was to look back on, when floggings and backbreaking labour had been forgotten, was about to begin.

With little time to rest, she was made to turn over, and kneel on all fours on the table, her long lovely hair now fallen loose and hanging about her face. Fingers moved through it, searching, selecting, then there was a small hideous crunching sound and scissors cut though the handful of hair, near her scalp, and a large luxuriant tress dropped onto the table beneath her eyes. She moaned in despair, horror and loss. Again the fingers roved, the scissors chomped through the glorious threads. Remorselessly the crude barbaring continued while she wept openly and bitterly, until the curtain that had hung around her face lay pitifully on the metal surface below her. When all had gone, the scissors were replaced by a buzzing clipper that completed the work, leaving her with a head as bald as an egg.

Through her tears she heard one guard remark to the attendant," Funny thing. They all blub when they lose their hair. Even the toughs from the criminal side break when the scissors get to work. Quietens them down wonderfully."

Subdued and tearful, Eve allowed herself to be led by the leash, walking a little stiffly from the soreness of her raped anus. She was deposited in a small bare cell, a mere stone box, with a plank bed screwed to the wall, an empty shelf and a covered bucket in the corner. Such light and air as she enjoyed came from a small barred window set high in the wall. She guessed she must be somewhere in the basement of the barracks.

"These solitary cells can get a bit lonely," one of the guards remarked," but never mind; there'll be a special welcome party for you later, when you can meet your new comrades."

Her companion seemed to think this very droll. Eve wasn't sure she found it reassuring.

An hour passed while she waited. The assault on her rectum had upset her bowels and her bladder, and she had crouched shamedly over the bucket out of necessity, not choice. Sitting lonely on the plank, her bottom aching from the hard surface, she had absently passed her cuffed hands over her head, bursting into fresh tears when, instead of comforting silk, she found only smooth scalp. The minutes passed slowly until the door opened with a clang, and she was ordered out.

"Time to meet your new friends," the guard said, and tugged on her leash to pull her from the cell. They walked down a long bleak corridor lined with similar cells, then up some stairs to ground level and a door out onto the square.

She blinked a moment in the sudden sunlight, then saw that dozens of women, all as naked and bald as herself, were drawn up round three sides of a low wooden platform. At first she only had eyes for the naked women, standing in well-drilled rows, totally silent and unmoving, caught in an iron discipline, then she lifted her gaze to the platform itself and gasped at the realisation of what her 'welcome' might be. She should have known, of course. Daphne and Gordon had both referred to it, but the reality was something else. Approached by half-a-dozen steps from the rear, the platform was about twenty feet square, plain planks with a crude guardrail. Set in its centre, black and menacing, was a pair of solid wooden posts, leaning in towards each other to form a sturdy triangle. If she hadn't already got the message, it was spelt out by the straps fastened to the bottom of each rail, and the short chain, with its butcher's hook, that hung from the apex

With set face, but chin held high, she marched across the intervening ground and mounted the steps to the scaffold. Made to stand to the post with her back to the women, she was ordered to spread her legs wide. A guard knelt to each ankle, buckling a strap tightly round it, fastening her firmly with parted thighs, then made her raise her cuffed wrists for the hook to be threaded through the connecting links. The chain was ratcheted up to leave her tensioned painfully at the triangle, every limb pulled taut, the muscles in her shoulders protesting already before the black hide whip hanging from the posts had even kissed them.

Another uniformed woman, later Eve found she was the Superintendent of the 'freezer', stepped to the edge of the scaffold and addressed the waiting women.

"Pay attention," she barked, "today we are joined by Number two-one-three Eve. She has applied for immigration. Please welcome her in the traditional manner."

While the woman had been speaking the taller of her two guards had unhooked the leather thong and moved behind Eve's drum taut figure, stretched helplessly against the triangle. The Super nodded to her, and the leather lifted. It made a peculiar thrumming noise as it flew, then cracked loudly across the stretched shoulders. Eve felt herself driven forward, despite her strained position, and fire leapt across her back. It was even worse than she had expected, and she'd not been kidding herself it could be easy. Her breath was knocked out of her by the blow, and she drew it back in with a strangled sound as the pain in her back flowered. As the whip fell away to hang at the guard's side, the parade cried as one woman, "One."

She could feel the skin tightening across her shoulders, where the thick welt lay from just under her left arm to run across and curl into her right armpit, where the tip left a searing blister of agony. The guard lifted the leather snake again, and the thrumming was repeated. This time she used the backhand but, like a true professional, she was equally strong on both. A matching welt ran from right to left, the other armpit bitten and bruised this time. Again Eve was driven forward as she gargled in agony and the watching women chorused, "Two."

Three matched One and four twinned Two, and the crowd continued to show proof of their mathematical skill. Eve hissed and gasped, her throat almost strangled by the sheer weight of the pain. It was far, far worse than a flogging on the buttocks. Maybe it could be shown scientifically that the neuron messages were no stronger, that the total of tissue damage reported to the brain was no worse than if a heavy penal was tearing into the buttock flesh, but there was a missing element. Even in the most dire beating of the buttocks, the female body and mind made a connection with the womb and clitoris, blurring the boundary between agony and eroticism in an evolutionary ploy the female had developed over thousands of generations to help her survive rape, mutilation and childbirth, and still function as an efficient reproductive system. Time and time again, Eve had found herself wet between the legs after a beating, or spotted the tell-tale glistening of erotic dew on a girl's sex fleece after she'd been caned. Somehow it didn't work for the back. The connection just was not there. It was pure pain, total torture, with not a crumb of erotic relief

Not even when the guard dropped her aim, let out her arm, and sent the wicked length seeking out her tender sides and vulnerable breasts. Five wrapped itself across her back below the shoulder blades and curled round hungrily to bite deep into the under-side of her right breast, lifting the heavy globe, so that it bounced on her chest as the leather released its grip, leaving her writhing helplessly as far as her stringent bonds would allow, punctuating the count with a strangled cry.

She howled and writhed again as Six tore just as bitterly into her left teat, leaving a searing welt three parts of the way around its base. She was hardly aware for some minutes, as she hung and squirmed on the hook, that the parade had been marched off into the barracks. By the time she had been released from the straps and chain, the parade ground was deserted again. Mercifully, for the first time since they had come for her at the reception, that afternoon, the cuffs were removed completely, and she stood, bowed over her wounded breasts, arms cradling their throbbing welts, hands cupping her anguished armpits, where livid lumps, like pickled walnuts, showed where the lash's tip had struck home.

"Can't hang around feeling sorry for yourself," a guard announced, not unkindly, "your room-mates will be able to do something for you I expect. Time you joined them."

Still clasping her wounds she followed on her leash, this time to an upper floor of the barracks, rather than the grim 'solitary' world of the basement.

"Welcome to your new home," the guard said, throwing open the door of a large bare cell, and unclipping her leash. As the door slammed shut behind her with a metallic clang, she looked about her and sized up the new surrounding.

Six plain plank bunks were arranged in pairs around three walls. Five were occupied by assorted females, as naked and hairless as herself. A big girl in her twenties, probably a blonde by her skin colouring, who seemed to be their leader, swung her legs to the ground, and came over to hold her gently by the arms.

"Hi, Eve. I'm Kath. Sorry about your back. It must be bad just now, but it'll pass. We all got the same welcome and as you can see, we survived."

"Jeez! I never want to go through that again," Eve groaned, "it's quite the worst thing I've ever come across."

"I know," the blonde sympathised, "it's got nothing to recommend it at all. At least if you get your arse whipped, you can wrap your cunt around the pain and use it to warm up your belly, but a flogging on the back is hell, plain and simple."

She seemed to hesitate a moment, before she said suddenly.

"Sorry to have to give you bad news, but it's best you know the worst and get used to it. That was your welcome to the freezer. We all got it, and we'll all get a similar farewell when our time is up."

"But that's at least a month away," she said in consolation, "you can forget about it for the moment. Come and meet the others and let's see what we can do about your back. Here, Jose. What've you done with the salve?"

A dark skinned girl, Hispanic Eve thought, jumped down from one of the top bunks with a tube of ointment in her hand. Between them they laid Eve out on her belly on Kath's bunk and began, with exquisite gentleness to work the soothing salve into the livid stripes that covered her back.

"Better?" Kath asked.

"Mmmm," Eve agreed, feeling the sharpest edge of the pain softening under their care, "though I never imagined for a moment that there'd be any such stuff available in this place. So far it's been uniformly grim and girl-unfriendly."

"And so it is," Kath assured her, "the only reason we've got this stuff is because the Doc knows her own hide could be on the line if we got scars or infections. They daren't risk sending us back marked for life. Damaged goods and all that. The men would never stand for it, and they'd have her trussed up tight, and a strong male arm skinning her back with a bullwhip if we got into serious trouble. So they slip us this stuff from time to time so we can take care of any damaged patches."

"Well, I for one am very grateful," Eve declared, "actually I feel a touch better already. When I first came in I thought I wanted to die. Now I think I might just bear to live, though my back still feels like a disaster area."

"Looks it too," Jose assured her, "but a good night's sleep and you'll find it merely sore by morning, though you'll be stiff for days."

In the event it was a correct forecast, exhausted by the gruelling events of the day, she fell asleep almost as soon as she curled up in the blanket of the spare bunk. She'd thought the rubbing of the coarse material on her lacerated back would drive away sleep, but she was fit and healthy and had been through a lot in a short time and nature took over to restore her well-being.

Not that the morning brought her any comfort. Besides

the throbbing in her back, various other parts of her anatomy were still actively protesting at the abuse they had suffered from the pressure hose or the Nordic medico's sadistic fingers. And when she tried to swing herself out of the bunk in response to Kathy's urgent shaking, and the clanging bell that had woken her in the first place, she groaned at the stiffness in her back and followed the others out of the cell half bent as is suffering from arthritis in old age.

The guards were opening the doors all along the corridor and groups of naked women were spilling out and making their way to the parade ground. When all had been formed up in lines, and the numbers checked, they were marched off in the chilly dawn to a dining hall for breakfast.

The food was simple but adequate, porridge, bread and margarine, even the choice of orange or apple to finish and, she was relieved to find, plenty of it. They were not intended to starve while they trained. She learnt in cautious whispers from Kathy and Jose that breakfast was the same every day, but they got a little variety in their other meals, which were also adequate.

"It's the same as with the salve," Kath explained, "they daren't risk returning us to our men in anything but prime condition."

After breakfast some numbers were called, 213 among them, and she had to leave her new friends and report to the office. She waited in line until called and stood in front of the Duty Officer's desk.

"213," the latter read out from the list in front of her, "I see you're applying for immigration. There are some special remarks regarding your treatment, and we'll deal with them later when we have assessed your progress. Meanwhile you'll go the standard course, like all the Eden born girls. You'll get light duties the first few days, then settle down to make your pair. When you've completed a respectable pair of drawers we'll see about the next phase."

'Light duties ' consisted of collecting, emptying and

cleaning the lidded pails that served for nightly needs in all the cells. Not actually very hard work, as befitted her healing back, but a humiliating task for a young woman used to commanding others and being provided luxury bathrooms wherever she went. Still she had been warned, and Daphne's fortnight of humiliation had inoculated her to some extent and she accepted it for what it was, a trial and a lesson in humility. To reinforce the point, she was set to fill in the rest of each day scrubbing the floors of the endless stone-flagged corridors, still naked and on her knees, with periodic visits from guards, who rewarded her efforts with cracking strokes of whip or cane on her bare bent buttocks. Nothing very much in themselves but, by the end of each day, she had collected the equivalent of a considerable thrashing

After a three day stint as latrine lady she joined the rest in their daily routine.

Kath, Jose and a third girl, Carla, had all been to the same college together and had come to serve their time immediately after graduation. The other two girls, Mary and Connie, were only just eighteen. They were friends, and had elected to be initiated as women after high school. Now that she was pronounced fit, Eve joined them on the parade ground after breakfast each morning for some strenuous exercise.

The drills were many and various, but all were calculated to take a woman to the edge of endurance. There was pack drill, with each girl carrying a backpack loaded to half her body weight. Hunched under the load, they were set to march steadily round the edge of the parade ground, until their legs felt like jelly, and their shoulders ached. To keep them moving when their tired muscles screamed for rest, the guards, positioned strategically round the tract, would lash out at legs or bums with their dog whips or the swagger canes they carried on parade, quickening the pace again and drawing short yelps of distress from the sweating, naked girls.

At least it seemed to have some sense to it, even if useless, but shot drill was designed to try the spirit by its totally futility. Each side of the square were piles of antique cannon balls, each weighing fifteen pounds, simple spheres of cast iron stacked up in pyramids, four balls in a row at the base, tapering to a single shot on top, a total of thirty lifeless lumps of iron. A girl given shot drill had to pick up a ball in her hands and run with it to the far side of the square to set it down on an empty base. One by one she had to carry the awkward heavy balls until she had built up a full pyramid on the far side. Then she repeated the useless labour by carrying each ball back to where it had come from, until all was just as it started.

A smooth fifteen pound round shot was an uncomfortable burden for a girl, requiring considerable effort merely to grip it safely, let alone run bare foot across a sandy parade ground under a quickly heating sun. One slip and tender finger tips would be pinched, one sign of slackening and a whip or cane would wrap itself round the sweating straining thighs or buttocks. and all this for nothing. And sometimes one run was not enough. Special category candidates, and Eve had that honour, might have to repeat the performance all over again, starting with already aching limbs and sore feet and fingers.

As she dragged herself back with the other girls, after her first morning's experience of hard physical exercise, her naked body streaked with sweat and dust she asked Kath when they could look forward to a shower.

"No showers here," Kath informed her, "Once a fortnight you go back into the waterwheel for a dowsing. That's the nearest thing to a shower around these parts."

She'd only been here a few days, and this was her first time in the rapidly rising morning heat. Seemed like Daphne had known what she'd been doing after all.

With the end of exercise came work, the traditional 'pair'. The girls were marched into the workrooms and sat at benches and looms. It was a very old regime, harking back to the days when women made all their own cloth and clothes. They started with a spinning wheel, learning to produce fine cotton thread from the heaps of raw cotton dumped in front of them. Learning was rapid under the whips and canes, and the hours long, and each girl had to produce enough material to make the cloth that would eventually be her 'pair'. When she'd completed her stint at the spinning wheel, she was transferred to the weaving shed, and worked a loom to weave a form of coarse cotton cloth. quality was controlled by the usual mechanism of stinging cane and bare female buttock, but even the most stringent application could not guarantee more than a very rough and uneven material.

From the weaving shed Eve progressed to the more congenial work of cutting out and sewing her 'pair', clumsy and humiliating drawers, their baggy legs coming almost to the knee and fastened at the waist by tapes.

And between the different work rooms there was the 'hook'!

The 'freezer' was meant to be self-supporting to a high degree. Much of the food came from the farm attached to the establishment and worked by the women. They even grew the cotton for their drawers, and the power for lighting, pumping water, etc., was largely produced in the mills. Eve had heard rumours of the mills, but women seemed to shy away from recalling them too vividly. It was soon apparent why. It was an amazing sight that greeted her the first morning she was sent to work her shift on the wheel. In a large stone built chamber, as bleak as any of the multitude of others she had visited already, but rather larger and higher than most, a long horizontal cylinder ran across one side. It was built like the wheel of a watermill, with long plank 'paddles' forming the outer surface, but arranged, not to be driven by a stream, but as a set of steps, for this was a treadmill, and some eight or ten girls were steadily climbing the endlessly descending staircase, holding onto a rail in front of them to keep their balance. That was bad enough but their sweating nudity and straining limbs were not the only thing that sent a shock of apprehension through her. Each straining naked female had a brutal iron hook thrust up her anus, from which a rope ran over a pulley above to be fastened to a cleat on the wall. It did not need much imagination to guess at the effect, if the girl slackened even for a moment in her upward climb, and her weight fell on the hook that penetrated her rear. The guards had no need to use whips or canes in here. The hook would work just as effectively as the lash.

One of the bored guards slackened a cleated rope and let down an unbaited hook.

"On your hands and knees girl," she ordered, and Eve dropped obediently into the required position. The guard came round to her head, carrying the hook. Eve's eyes opened wide at the sight close to. It was even larger than she had thought, a serious intruder for a tender female sphincter, as large as a man's prick, to which the business end had a distinct resemblance, no doubt intentional.

"Here, give it a good suck," the guard suggested, offering the pseudo penis, "you'll make it easier on yourself when it goes in."

This was no place for modesty or protest. The woman obviously meant it kindly, and Eve could see the sense in her suggestion. She gathered her saliva and put her mouth over the blunt helmet end, coating it as thickly and completely as she could. The guard gave her a minute or two to make the best job she could then took it out of her mouth and went behind her kneeling figure. She had been prepared for what followed and her conscientious lubrication certainly softened the blow but, even so, the penetration of her anus was torture. The thick solidity of the iron was definitely girl-unfriendly, and no amount of preparation could make it anything but a nightmare to have that unfeeling metal phallus stuffed rudely up her arse. She grunted and blew and tried to relax her sphincter as much as possible to aid its entry, but she was panting and sweating all over again, by the time it sank fully home.

"Up, girl," the guard ordered, and reinforced the command by jerking none too gently on the rope attached to the hook. Propelled by a shaft of agony that lanced her belly she sprang to her feet, her legs bowed to accommodate the intruder as comfortably as she could, and moved over to the wheel, where it rotated remorselessly, the steps descending in a never ending succession. Urged on by more tugs on the hook, she climbed the moving stair until she could grip the handrail, then went on climbing step after step, to maintain her position. The guard tied off her rope on a cleat. Now she was tethered firmly and obliged to keep walking if she wanted to avoid deeper impalement. For the moment she could cope, it was just like climbing the stairs to a higher floor, but the floor never came, only another flight of stairs. She was fresh for the moment, but the other girls had been on for some time already. Her neighbour was sweating profusely and groaning mournfully, as she desperately tried to keep up, and keep the hook from pulling on her sore anus or pushing into her tender bowel. Next to her an older woman seemed in dire trouble, her rope almost continuously taut and dragging exhausted howls from the suffering wheel walker. It seemed she was at the end of her shift, as well as her tether, and at that moment the guard slacked the rope and the dog-tired woman let herself drop with the wheel until she could collapse on the solid ground below.

Eve couldn't spare her more than a parting glance, she had troubles of her own to think about. The pace was beginning to make itself known in her unaccustomed legs. True she had been fit enough when she entered, and worked hard since, but this climbing made demands of its own on slightly different muscles, which were becoming tired now. Besides, the soreness in her bum was getting worse with the continuous motion, and had become a constant nagging pain, without even having the pressure of the rope on it. By the time her first break came round, she was more than ready.

They each walked for twenty minutes without a break, then were let down for five to recover, after which they were

223

sent back onto the unending climb for another stretch, keeping the wheel loaded with sufficient toiling females to drive the generators. It was the worst form of forced labour she could imagine, and Eve was no different from her sisters in this grim establishment, in physically cringing when it became her turn again to do a stint on the hook.

Life in the freezer seemed an interminable round of labour and pain. There was too the humiliation of the lack of hygiene provided for the sweat-soaked, dust coated, nakedness they lived in, a grimy filthiness only relieved by another visit to the 'waterwheel', where she spun in agony under the lash of the icy jet, coming away bruised and sore but, for the moment, clean. With the bruising bath went another crude barbaring to restore the polish of her scalp. Eventually though the month was up and her degrading drawers completed. Most of her friends had left one by one as their own terms were up; had stood to the triangle in the yard for a farewell flogging, and left the next morning, their welts still livid, clad only in their newly manufactured underpants. From what the others told her, she understood they would be received by their relatives at the gates and taken off for a 'coming-of-age' party, still dressed in no more than their drawers, and carrying their weals and polished skulls as badges of rank.

But when her own time came she found herself, not straining at the triangle, but standing in front of the superintendent's desk.

"You've done well, so far," that official admitted, "but I have to consider the comments and recommendations made by your sponsor, and agreed with by yourself. You do agree that your case required more than the standard treatment, as awarded to girls who have grown up under our customs?"

"Yes, Ma'am."

"And that you are by nature and experience a young woman of more than commonly strong will"

Again Eve agreed it was so.

The Superintendent seemed to consider for a moment,

then pronounced.

"Then you will do two weeks on a chain-gang, to help curb those unfeminine leanings. You'll be returned to us here in a fortnight."

The chain-gangs operated from an entirely separate establishment, being part of the criminal, rather than the social, system. Eve, still aching from a further bruising washdown in the 'waterwheel', found herself attached by one leg to a chain of half-a-dozen women of all ages, sentenced for theft, fraud or domestic disobedience. Each, as she had observed while still a free woman, had her prison number permanently burnt into her shaven mons. Her belly had quaked at the thought of the pain of such a marking, but also at the humiliation of having to carry the mark for the rest of her life. And it was with immense relief that she heard that, as a candidate for immigration, and not a criminal, she would be spared this ordeal.

She was spared nothing else. The first week her gang was assigned to refuse duties in town, hitched to a heavy wagon to tow it from street to street, encouraged by whistling cuts of cane or whip to bare buttocks and backs, then made to collect the garbage from the houses, under the scornful eyes of passers-by and householders. Eve found herself watched by several women she had known socially, and blushed to be seen so, toiling naked at this humiliating task with the chain linking her to the rest of the gang, more and more disgustingly soiled as the days passed under the unrelenting sun.

The second week the gang was sent out into the country to mend roads. With only primitive shovels and barrows, they dug gravel, filled pot-holes, heaved heavy kerbs into position, spread the hot steaming tarmac over the road bed under the mocking laughter and lustful gazes of the men who drove the machines. At least, Eve consoled herself, the guards make sure they can only rape us with their eyes.

Dog tired, she would drop into sleep alongside her companions, lying like sardines along a hard plank bed, too weary even to notice how the days were passing. It was with surprise she received the news that her time was up, and her leg iron was opened to allow her to leave the gang, and ride the truck back to the freezer.

And then two thoughts hit her at once. To night she would be flogged in farewell at the triangle, in front of the paraded inmates, tomorrow she would be sent out into the world, naked save for her drawers, to meet an unknown sponsor.

She'd plucked up courage to ask the Superintendent if she knew who the man was but other than confirming that someone had been appointed, she could enlighten her no further.

"I shouldn't worry," the officer said, "someone will be meeting you tomorrow."

Once more she found herself, dripping from her punishing bath, her head freshly clipped, strung up tight on the merciless timbers. While her sisters watched and counted, the ritual six stripes were laid across her flinching back, and she screamed as the lash lifted each breast in turn, leaving a searing brand under each full firm globe. Jose was long gone now, but other, newer fingers helped soften her wounds with the clandestine salve and she fell into exhausted sleep, still wondering what kind of man might be waiting for her. "Daphne, Daphne," she thought, "I hope you've picked the right one for me."

Standing on the steps of the grim gateway to the 'freezer', naked but for the drab cotton knickers, her back still sore and aching, her breasts bare and rocky nippled, she looked about her in distress. Had she been forgotten? Was no one coming for her? Before she could experience real concern a chauffeur driven limousine swept up to the gates. She started. She'd seen that car before. Right at the beginning of the adventure. It had been bearing away the patronising Scot she'd met at the airport.

Now Angus was getting out and walking towards her.

"What are YOU doing here?" was all she could think to ask.

"Come to collect you, lassie," he said. "Didn't they tell you I'm to be your sponsor? Come along. We have an appointment." and he took her arm to guide her to the waiting car.

"Where are we going?"

"To a wedding."

"Whose?"

"Yours if you like. You have a choice. You can marry me or you can accept me as just your titular sponsor, a kind of Godfather figure and go back to live with Gordon and Daphne and young Daisy."

Feminine-like she could only reply idiotically, "But I haven't a thing to wear."

"This is the Eden equivalent of the old Scots custom of marrying in your shift," Angus reassured her. "The woman leaves all her past behind her, and her new husband is not responsible for her debts or past misdemeanours, so will you marry me?"

She thought of Gordon with the two sisters and how she would be an intruder at a sensitive time for them, she thought of Angus's firm but sensitive treatment of her in the stables, Above all she recognised that he truly wanted her, even in her present degraded condition. It occurred to her with a sudden jolt of perception that he was actually a strong and very handsome man, who would complete her life.

"Yes please Angus, if you'll have me," she answered softly.

And now for the opening of next months title EVE IN EDEN by *Stephen Rawlings*

PROLOGUE
IN ANOTHER PLACE..

"Gillian's ready now, Mr Platt," Alison said, putting her head round the door of Platt's office.

George Platt looked up from the account book he was working on and smiled at the bright, helpful face of his kennelmaid. "Thank you, Alison."

Platt took a medium weight cane from the selection hanging from a row of hooks on the wall and swished it experimentally through the air. Pocketing a couple of other items he followed Alison out into the yard.

The yard was a brick-cobbled square some twenty yards across enclosed by Platt's office and lodging, the stores and work rooms and the kennel block itself. Iron rings had been set at waist height in the sections of blank wall between the overlooking doors and windows, while from under the eaves above them projected heavy wrought iron angle brackets.

It was from one of these brackets that the only other occupant of the yard was suspended.

She was a woman in her early twenties, very slim and pale-skinned and, apart from a broad black studded collar fastened about her neck, completely naked. Her taut body hung from her upstretched arms so that her toes dangled two feet from the ground. Thick leather cuffs secured her wrists to a few links of chain and the ring that hung over the hook on the end of the bracket. A leather strap had been buckled about her knees, while another set of cuffs with a trailing chain bound her ankles. These constraints shaped her body into a slender arrowhead, twisting slightly from side to side as far as the chain that held her allowed. The stretching of her pectoral muscles exposed the pale hollows of her armpits and pulled her small high breasts into pointed pink-topped lozenges.

Nervous breathing caused a rapid swell and contraction of the shallow double-dome of flesh under her navel that perfectly complimented her lean waist. Her head, crowed by a mane of blonde hair tied in a simple pony-tail, hung forward between her upstretched arms as though in shame. Her eyes stared sightlessly down at the ground.

A flick of Platt's cane across her midriff jerked her back to her senses. Blue eyes wide with apprehension met his own stern gaze.

"Now then, Gillian," he said. "You know why you're here."

"Yes, Mr Platt," she whimpered. "To be punished. I'm so sorry. I'll never do it again, I promise!"

"No you won't girl," Platt said assuredly. "This session will make certain of that. Alison: lift her feet."

Alison grasped the chain trailing from Gillian's ankle cuffs and climbed the small stepladder placed beside the unfortunate girl, drawing the chain after her. Gillian bent in the middle like a jack-knife, the strap about her knees forcing her legs to remain straight, until her feet were almost level with her bound hands. Alison hooked the ankle chain over the bracket and then reached between Gillian's legs and chest. A snap ring dangled from her collar, and this Alison fastened to the strap about her knees so that Gillian's face was pressed against her shins.

Alison stepped down.

Now Gillian hung like the gourd of some exotic fruit ripe for picking, her hips almost at shoulder height, leaving her genitalia completely exposed. Her tightly bound knees squeezed her thighs together and forced her mounded cunt lips, from which the golden curls of her belly hair had been trimmed back, into an unwilling pout.

But it was the orifice below this that held Platt's attention. He poked the dark pucker of Gillian's anus with a stiff forefinger, making the girl jerk helplessly within her bonds.

"Now, girl," Platt said, "what's this?"

"My... my bottom hole, sir," Gillian said despairingly.

"And what's it for?"

"To void my excrement, sir."

"And what else?"

"To... to give pleasure to anybody I'm serving, sir."

"Good," Platt said. He took up a stance to one side of Gillian and rested his cane across her tight buttocks. "Now we're going to drive that message home so you'll never forget it."

The cane swished through the air and smacked into her flesh.

Gillian yelped, twisting on her chain like a plum bob. A thin red weal burned across her bottom cheeks and the split peach of her cunt that rose between them. Platt let her come to rest, then asked:

"What can be put up your bottom hole, girl?"

"Cocks, fingers, dildos.. bum plugs... anything! sir," Gillian gasped.

Smack!

"And how often can these things be put up there?"

"As many times as my user wishes..."

Smack!

"And do you have any say in the matter?"

"No, sir... not my place, sir..."

Smack!

"What if it hurts you a little?"

"I'm... here to suffer, sir."

Smack!

"So will you ever refuse your bottom hole to anyone again?"

"No, sir... they can cram it full with whatever they want, sir..."

Smack!

"What are you?"

"A bondslave... a pack bitch..."

Smack!

"And don't you ever forget it," Platt said, lowering the cane.

As the girl hung sobbing and trembling he examined the results of his handiwork. Her bottom was criss-crossed with weals and scarlet with heat, but the skin had not been broken. Long experience had taught him just how much force to use on such occasions. Now there was one final detail and the punishment would be complete.

"You'll stay up here until lunch, girl," he told Gillian, "then back to work. I'll see you later to make sure you've learnt your lesson. Understand?"

Gillian nodded as far as her bonds allowed and said faintly: "Yes, Mr Platt... thank you."

Platt took out of his pocket one of the items he had brought from his office. It was a hook set in the end of a length of inch- thick wooden dowel with a shallow screw thread carved into its surface. "Now, I need a place to hang a hook. Do you know of one, girl?"

Tremulously Gillian replied: "If it's convenient, sir... please use my bottom hole."

With the tapering wooden thread forcing her anal ring open, Platt screwed the dowel into the yielding tunnel of her rectum until only the hook end was visible. Then from another pocket he took an old tinplate alarm clock, checked it was wound, set the alarm and hung it on the hook protruding from its fleshy mount.

"That'll remind us when you're ready to come down, girl."

He turned to Alison, who had been watching the whole procedure in attentive and fascinated silence.

"Gag her. I don't want to hear a peep until the alarm goes."

"Yes Mr Platt," Alison said dutifully.

Platt returned to his office. Through the window he could see Gillian's pale, slender form dangling in the sun. He noticed she shivered occasionally, probably having a cry to herself now the worst was over, he thought.

Still he knew it had been necessary, and in the long run it would make her term of service easier. George wanted the girls under his care to be the very best, so sometimes he had

236

to be cruel to be kind.

To be continued............

The cover photograph for this book and many others are available as limited edition prints.
Write to:-

Viewfinders Photography
PO Box 200,
Reepham
Norfolk
NR10 4SY

for details, or see,

www.viewfinders.org.uk